Somebody's Home

"*Somebody's Home* kept me riveted from the first page to the last. A gripping psychological thriller you don't want to miss!"
— Lucinda Berry, bestselling author of *The Perfect Child*

"*Somebody's Home* starts like a hurricane out at sea: some wind, some waves, a sense of approaching danger. But the story moves fast, gains velocity, and suddenly you are turning the pages, unable to stop, heart in your throat, knowing that something terrible is going to happen and nothing will stop it. The threats come from all sides, and it's so hard to know who to trust. The characters are wonderful and complex; the setting feels like the house next door, which makes it all the more terrifying; and the ending nearly killed me. Kaira Rouda has written a terrific, gripping thriller."
—Luanne Rice, bestselling author of *The Shadow Box*

"Taut with foreboding from the first page, Kaira Rouda's *Somebody's Home* is an unsettling portrait of an antisocial man, a master of the universe, and the women caught between them. The rotating points of view and incisive, clear writing are sure to keep you flipping the pages until you reach the shocking conclusion!"
—Katherine St. John, author of *The Siren*

"Trust your instincts and grab a copy of Kaira Rouda's *Somebody's Home*. In Rouda's latest thriller, a mother trusts *her* instincts when she knows the person on her property is threatening her family. But what if the threat is coming at her from all sides and more than one person is hiding a dark secret? A compulsive, fast read, *Somebody's Home* reveals what people will do to protect not only their homes but the families within those four walls. A captivating read."

— Georgina Cross, bestselling author of *The Stepdaughter*

The Next Wife

"Rouda hits the ground running and never stops . . . [*The Next Wife*] is so much fun that you'll be sorry to see it end with a final pair of zingers. The guiltiest of guilty pleasures."

—*Kirkus Reviews*

"This gripping psychological thriller from Rouda (*The Favorite Daughter*) offers a refreshing setup . . . Rouda keeps the reader guessing as the plot takes plenty of twists and turns. Suspense fans will get their money's worth."

—*Publishers Weekly*

"In *The Next Wife*, two women go ruthlessly head-to-head. Kaira Rouda knows how to create the perfect diabolical characters that we love to hate. Equally smart and savage, this is a lightning-fast read."

—Mary Kubica, *New York Times* bestselling author of *The Other Mrs.*

"Rouda's talent for making readers question everything and everyone shines through on every page of her propulsive new thriller, *The Next Wife*. Her narrators are sharp and unpredictable, each one with a tangle of secrets to unravel. *The Next Wife* will leave you tense and gasping, with a chilling twist you won't see coming."

—Julie Clark, *New York Times* bestselling author of *The Last Flight*

"One of the most insidious, compulsive books I've read recently. Kaira Rouda has a way of drawing you in with great characters, fast-paced writing, and a story that won't let you go. Brilliant, dark, and dazzling."

—Samantha Downing, *USA Today* bestselling author of *My Lovely Wife* and *He Started It*

"One man. Two wives. Kaira Rouda has masterfully created cunning twists and sharp narration that take you on an unexpected and delicious journey and will leave you with a gasp. Devious and fun, *The Next Wife* should be the next book you read!"

—Wendy Walker, bestselling author of *Don't Look for Me*

"I absolutely inhaled *The Next Wife*. Nail-biting suspense, dark humor, and family intrigue. I savored every page and now have the worst book hangover. Loved it!"

—Michele Campbell, internationally bestselling author of *The Wife Who Knew Too Much*

"No one writes deliciously devious narcissists like Kaira Rouda. *The Next Wife* showcases her remarkable talent for making unlikable characters alluring. With twisted egos, lavish wealth, and three women vying for power, this compelling, compulsive thriller is sharp, fun, and shocking. I was riveted by every word."

—Samantha M. Bailey, *USA Today* and #1 national bestselling author of *Woman on the Edge*

"Kaira Rouda has a gift for writing characters we love . . . to hate. Dark and devious, *The Next Wife* is a fast-paced, twisty thriller that will have you laughing, shaking your head, and gasping out loud right until the end. A perfect one-sitting read."

—Hannah Mary McKinnon, bestselling author of *Sister Dear* and *You Will Remember Me*

The Favorite Daughter

"Kaira Rouda's husband, Harley, may have recently been elected to Congress, but she isn't looking to make a name for herself just as a politician's wife . . . The *Gone Girl*–style domestic-suspense novel follows Jane, a narcissistic perfectionist dealing with the death of her daughter."

—*Washington Post*

"[An] exceptional psychological thriller . . . Suspense fans will be amply rewarded."

—*Publishers Weekly* (starred review)

"Will hit you right in the heart."

—Bustle

"Rouda delivers a wickedly perfect thriller with *The Favorite Daughter*."
—*Good Life Family Magazine*

"Delightfully wicked fun!"

—*Kirkus Reviews*

"Involving psychological suspense that reveals the cracks in what seems like a perfect life."

—*Booklist*

SOMEBODY'S
HOME

OTHER TITLES BY KAIRA ROUDA

Suspense

All the Difference

Best Day Ever

The Favorite Daughter

The Next Wife

Women's Fiction

Here, Home, Hope

A Mother's Day: A Short Story

In the Mirror

The Goodbye Year

Romance

The Indigo Island Series

Weekend with the Tycoon

Her Forbidden Love

The Trouble with Christmas

The Billionaire's Bid

Nonfiction

Real You Incorporated: 8 Essentials for Women
Entrepreneurs

SOMEBODY'S HOME

KAIRA ROUDA

THOMAS & MERCER

Text copyright © 2022 by Kaira Sturdivant Rouda
All rights reserved.

No part of this book may be reproduced, or stored in a retrieval system, or transmitted in any form or by any means, electronic, mechanical, photocopying, recording, or otherwise, without express written permission of the publisher.

Published by Thomas & Mercer, Seattle

www.apub.com

Amazon, the Amazon logo, and Thomas & Mercer are trademarks of Amazon.com, Inc., or its affiliates.

ISBN-13: 9781542026116
ISBN-10: 1542026113

Cover design by Damon Freeman

Printed in the United States of America

To Andrea Peskind Katz, with love
Thank you for your insights, encouragement, and
friendship

CHAPTER 1

Somebody is in my home.

I don't know what to do.

As I watch from the street, I see activity, movement in the kitchen—only for an instant, and the next second the house is as still as before.

I pull out my phone. Do I call her, or 911?

The car parked out front is familiar, but nothing else makes sense. Something is wrong. I know it.

He's in there.

I must do something. There's no time to wait for the police.

I swallow and push the car door open, stepping quietly onto the empty street.

I know the truth before I see the lanky shadow move across the kitchen window.

Somebody's home, and he isn't supposed to be there.

I crouch down as I run up to the front door of my house. I left it unlocked on purpose, in case she came home and didn't have her keys.

I know now that was a big mistake.

All this is my fault.

I clamp my hand over my own mouth to muffle my scream as I turn the handle and step inside.

FRIDAY

TWO DAYS BEFORE

CHAPTER 2

TOM

A bolt of lightning illuminates the sky, and raindrops the size of river rocks pelt my windshield. Today is unusual. It never rains in Southern California. Not in October. October is for fires and destruction, for Santa Ana winds and red-flag warnings. The rain doesn't make sense. Nothing about my life makes sense.

I've just spent a week in the desert with my buddies, shooting guns, drinking beer, partying. I loved it, every minute of it, but now it's over. I have no choice. I'm back home, but it's not my home anymore. I'm parked across the street, contemplating my options. Staying dry and practicing controlling my anger all at the same time. I have anger issues. Just ask my folks. I came this way. But it was one of the things my friends and I talked about as we each imagined the target of our anger on the beer can as we shot. Anger causes mistakes. When you're angry, the guy who owns the land told us, your actions are sharper, you sweat, your heart races. You're jumpy. Like now. I wipe my hands on my jeans and take a deep breath to calm down. He taught us that, too, out there in the desert. Meditation, or whatever they call it. It's harder to do now that I'm back. It's always been hard for me to relax, to breathe.

I look out the window again as the windshield wipers smack the rain away. That's my house, the only place I've ever lived. I know every floorboard squeak, especially on the stairs. But I won't climb them any-more. My so-called parents and the new owners have made certain of it. Sure, I knew my dad was moving to take another job. And I guess I knew they'd need to buy a house out in Timbuktu.

But why do I have to leave?

No one gave me a chance to have a say. Two weeks ago I received what was basically a verbal eviction notice from my own parents. A "Dear Tom, we're moving. Sorry. The new owners need the carriage house for themselves" talk from my lovely stepmom. I didn't even know the house was on the market. They never put a For Sale sign up in the front yard. Sandi told me it was a private transaction—the perfect buyer had simply appeared. God's will, she said. Is that God's will or yours, Sandi? Just bam, we're out of here and you are, too. Too bad, Tom.

Sure, because she felt bad, my lame stepmother said, "You, of course, are welcome to move in with us in our new home in Temecula, just until you can find a place of your own." Oh, thanks, Sandi. Your new place is just for the four of you—you and Dad and your real boys. Three bedrooms. That's it. Got it. She didn't say that part, but she should have. Since then, I've been to their new place, with and without them, scoping it out. There is no room for me.

Actions are louder than words. We talked about that in the desert this week, too. Actually, I suppose I learned that when I watched my real mom drive away all those years ago. People say you can't remember things from when you're six years old. But that's a lie. When you look out the window and watch your mom back out of the driveway, when you watch your dad spit at her car window, when you see the fear in her eyes, the hate in his—well, you remember. No matter how young you are.

I push away the memories of seventeen years ago and stare through the pouring rain at the same driveway. I suppose it's good I went to the desert this week. I made friends, real friends, guys who think the way I do, guys who know how the world works and what's wrong with it these days. I got out of my rut. But I'm back from the desert now, and sitting in my car in a freak rainstorm staring at a house that's no longer mine starting on Sunday, two days from now. Sandi said it was a gracious concession by the new owner to give me time to pack up since I was gone all week.

Two days to try to get a new place to live just doesn't seem very *gracious*, if you ask me. But they didn't. They think I'll just go along with the plan, do what they expect, move out.

That's what they all think. I pound my hands on the steering wheel, release a bunch of tension, and stare out the car window again.

I don't want them here. This is my house. Mine.

Sandi said, "The new owners are lovely." Bullshit. She doesn't know if they are lovely, she doesn't know anything about them. In the desert, hanging out by our campsite at night, we talked about how to profile people, how to watch them, figure them out without them even knowing it. I'll use that new skill to figure out who these owners are, what they are. Whoever they are, they move in today, in this pouring rain. Serves them right.

I can't believe this all happened behind my back. *A private transaction.* I was in the dark until one of the boys let it slip that they were going to have horses at the new house. We were hanging out, the little kids and I, two weeks ago before Sunday dinner, and Davis let it slip.

Their new house was a done deal. I wasn't invited.

I did think it was odd that Sandi'd had some people over to the house. She's a loner usually, just fiddling around in her garden, cooking in the kitchen. I should have figured out the lady with the big jewelry and G-wagen Mercedes was a real estate agent. I blame myself for that miss. I never did see the "lovely" buyers. I must have been at work at the bar or something.

I had simmered with the information of their new house all the rest of the day. That night, at Sunday dinner, after prayer, I told my dad and stepmom that I knew about the new house. The little boys' eyes were huge, like I was getting them in big trouble. I hoped I would. I felt my dad's rage then, directed toward them for once.

My stepmom—Simple Sandi, as I think of her—blinked, her big brown eyes full of water about to overflow. "Of course there's room for you there, son. Always. We love you."

"Stop being so dramatic, Tom. It's time for you to grow up, get a real job, your own apartment. Take care of yourself," Dad said, his blue eyes alight with self-righteousness, his anger focused on his favorite target. Me.

I needed Sandi to stop crying, tears dropping onto her meal. It was gross. And an act. She wasn't sad for me. She was just embarrassed she got caught.

My parents are so self-centered. They should have given this house to me, or at least let me rent from them, pay them monthly until I could buy it outright. My birthright, sort of. I grew up here. This town is all I know. I told them I'd work hard, handle the upkeep. Why the rush to leave anyway? Dad says his new job came with a pay bump, and part of the deal is he must live in the community. But I'm not sure I believe him. Who leaves a big coastal megachurch for an inland congregation? No one. Ever.

I'm not proud to say I begged him to let me stay, to let me keep my home.

It didn't work. Dad said, "You're twenty-three years old, son, without a college degree or a job."

"I work at Cody's," I said. The bar is a dive, but my shifts there keep me afloat. Barely.

"A bar? You think you can afford this house, or any house for that matter, working part time at a bar? I love you, but you need to get yourself together. The Lord provides for those who take care of themselves, and it's time, son, that you do just that. You're vacating the carriage house. We paid off your car. We've done all we can for you, son. We'll be praying for you."

I'd stormed out of the house after dinner that night and headed straight to Cody's, despite the fact that I wasn't scheduled to work. I was fired up, ready to fight someone, anyone. Instead I met some guys, my real family. When they invited me to go hang out with them in the desert, I jumped at the chance. Screw my dad's moving-out timeline. Screw them all. Sandi's fake love, the "little boys," and their new house.

And as for dear old Dad? Doug the Dick, as I call him in my head. He can take his fake love of God, his superior righteousness, and shove it. I know who he really is, what he's really done. I've watched him all my life: smiling at a Black family walking into his church and then rolling his eyes. Or shaking a lesbian couple's hands and then quickly wiping the germs away on his holy robe. I mean, it is depravity, I get it, but why not just kick them out? Why not be an up-front dick like he is to me?

"Let us pray for the weak, the needy," my father preaches from the pulpit every Sunday. But the truth is, when he walks past a homeless person sitting in squalor on the street, his eyes fill with hate. "Get a job!" is my dad's refrain in the face of an open hand, as long as no one else is around. I know, I've been around. When a homeless man shuffled into a service and sat in the back pew a few years ago, dear old Dad had the ushers escort him out.

"Get him out of here, please. We'll pray for his soul, to ease his suffering, that he gets back on his feet," Dad told the congregation as the man begged to stay. It was raining that Sunday, just like today.

I squeeze the steering wheel tighter. I want to kick something but remember what my friends told me this week: hold on to the anger, unleash it when it's time. These guys made sense to me, right away. From the moment I met Vic at the bar, he talked my talk. He understood where I was coming from. He knows how hard it is to be a man in this world, how hard it is to compete. They all do.

"Man, let me show you the truth. The way. You don't need them, you'll have a new family," Vic said that night at the bar. I'd run out of the house without my wallet, taking just my keys, and driven to the bar. Vic could tell I was pissed. He bought me three beers before he asked me what was what. I liked that. Quiet companionship. No demands. Just understanding. When he asked about a girlfriend, if that was my problem, I'd laughed.

"What's a girlfriend? Dude, they all suck. They all want money and who knows what," I'd said.

"True that." Vic clinked my glass. He was lanky, dressed all in black. His eyes were bright black, like a crow's. He'd been to the bar before, but we'd never said more than hello.

"You don't have a girl, either?" I'd asked. That amazed me. He has everything. A sick Harley even.

"No. Don't need one. Don't trust them. So what's wrong?" he'd asked finally.

"My family sold my home out from under me. I live in the carriage house. I have no place to go." I'd tried to mask the emotion in my voice, the pain, but I knew it was there.

Vic put his hand on my shoulder. "Sit tight."

He stood up, paid our tab, and walked to the back of the bar, where his friends were hanging out. The next thing I knew, I had a group of guys who understood me. After this past week in the desert, I have focus. And something I haven't had in a long time: confidence. There's nothing wrong with me. It's all of them. Especially good old Dad.

But I still need a place to live. My new friends can't really help me with that.

A white moving van turns the corner and starts down my street. It's a huge one, and as it lumbers toward me and my house, I realize these people must think they're staying here for good.

They're wrong. I'm going to get my house back. They won't feel comfortable here. I'll help them understand that, one way or another.

The van stops in front of my home, bright hazard lights flashing in the storm. From where I sit in my lame Toyota, the house is gone, obscured by the huge white truck and the relentless rain.

Maybe that would be easier. Just get rid of the place so no one can own it. In my mind I see myself pouring gasoline down the stairs, striking a match, igniting the place like a pyre.

Maybe I should do it. I mean, what do I have to lose?

I stare at my reflection in the rearview mirror. Nah. I couldn't do that. It's my home. I need to save it, not destroy it. It's the last place I saw my mom, my real mom. Someday, just maybe, she'll come back looking for me. I need to be here when she does.

I hear my dad's voice in my head. "Don't be a baby, son. She is never coming back. She is a sinner, and we are better off without her."

I know better. I do. That's why when it comes to 123 Cherry Hill Lane, I'll get it back, one way or another.

It's my home. The only one I've ever known.

CHAPTER 3

JULIE

Despite the churning in my stomach that tells me I'm a fool, I urge myself to believe this is the new start we need.

My daughter, Jess, drives my Tesla SUV too close behind the moving van, and the rain and road spray make the windshield impossible to see through.

"Jess. Windshield wipers on high. Now."

"Mom. It's automatic. This is what the car thinks we need, so we're fine. It knows best. So do I."

At age seventeen, Jess is convinced she is right about everything. That she knows all. It's my fault that her world has been so insular, so bubbled. Her self-confidence is based on lies.

When I was growing up, I had zero confidence. Not in myself, not in my future. My days were spent hiding from the spotlight, quietly avoiding eye contact. My mom told me I was beautiful; the kids at school told me the truth.

"Julie, why don't you have a playdate?" my mom would ask at the start of every school year. "Invite a friend over?" But I never would, never did. I was embarrassed by my mom and her round shape, by Dad's absence, by our small home and the cloud of gray that seemed to surround us. My life was different from the other kids' in the neighborhood.

When I was growing up, my mom's ugly car spit dark exhaust in our wake. I could smell her coming in the pickup line at school. The wipers were frayed and lacking rubber, just two metal sticks shifting water around. In Florida that was a problem almost daily.

I stare through the unseasonal, unforecasted rainstorm and hope this isn't some kind of sign about this move.

This is our new start—at least it's supposed to be. I'm going to learn how to take care of myself and my daughter. I'm going to have the career I never pursued. I'm going to have a life of freedom and respect. I'm going to be in charge of my choices, in control of my life. I'm no longer going to be on Roger's time, on his schedule. I'm not his prop for social events, and I won't be monitored for every expenditure like I'm a thief in my own home. I will relax, finally, and find my roots again. And it all begins today.

I squish my forehead between my palms, forcing my eyes off the road. We aren't driving fast, maybe twenty miles an hour in this mess.

Nothing too terrible could happen at this speed, even if my daughter drives us into a tree.

My eyes fly open again. Jess stops the car. Water races past us in the gutters like a river.

"I'm not loving this," she says, pointing at the house through the rain-coated side window.

"Honey, it's perfect. Just wait. And you're still in the school district, so really, we couldn't have asked for a better start to our new life." I pat her shoulder. I purchased 123 Cherry Hill Lane using cash I'd saved up in my ironically-named-at-the-moment rainy-day account and a savings account Roger set up for me. It all happened so fast, like it was meant to be. I'd been at the gym, jogging on the treadmill, when Judy Thomas, the know-it-all real estate agent in Oceanside, jumped onto the machine beside mine.

"Don't kill the messenger, but I hear there's trouble in paradise. Can I help?" Judy smiled, her perfect white teeth glistening in the morning light.

I'd told only one friend about my plan to leave Roger and begged her not to say anything. Thanks, Sheila. That's the other reason I left my life. I didn't have any real friends. No one does, not here in this pressure cooker of coastal privilege.

I had tried to hide my surprise. "I don't know what you're talking about, Judy." I pushed the button to increase my jogging speed as she leaned over and pulled my emergency shutoff cord.

"I have a pocket listing. Motivated sellers. They need to get out of town quietly, and quickly. Roger is a beast. We all know that. My listing has beautiful potential for a fresh start." Judy handed me a towel.

I wiped my forehead and nodded.

"Let's go have a look, shall we?" Judy led the way through the club to her huge Mercedes.

She was right. I loved the home. The sellers accepted my cash offer, and two weeks later, I closed on the home we're parked in front of now.

Beside me, Jess bites her lip. I know she's thinking of a better outcome, the one where her mom and dad stay together under one roof, no matter how miserable, and she proceeds through senior year without the upheaval.

If there had been a choice, any other way to handle Roger, I would have done it. But he wasn't going to change. He controls everything in my life, and I cannot take it anymore. Control plus lack of any attention left me heartbroken and depressed. But I'm moving on. The truth is, I stuck around too long for Jess, and that's why we're sitting in my electric too-smart car, on a street I'd never visited let alone thought I'd live on, hoping for the best. The rain will stop. These showers never last for long in Southern California.

Turns out a lot of things don't last long, and nothing is what it seems here. Not really. And I went along with it, all the way. I'm a walking ad for plastic surgery, for example. Literally. Nothing is real. As soon as Jess graduates, I might move somewhere else. Maybe a place like where my mom lives, a simple community where people actually care about their neighbors. I want block parties and Fourth of July picnics where I don't have to dress up. I hope, maybe, on this end of Oceanside things can be different. But if not, I'll move on. This house is a resting place. Somewhere to hide and get away from the isolated joke my life has become. If it feels right, I'll stay. I do love its bones, its early 1900s history. It has a warm presence on the street, and a backyard big enough for a dog. I wanted a dog, but Roger would not allow animals inside the home. Period.

Cherry Hill Lane will be the opposite of Roger's house. It will feel like a home.

My phone rings.

"Ma'am, we're gonna try to wait out this rain. It'll cost extra, but everything will be ruined if we start unloading now." The moving guy sounds emphatic, and I suppose he's right. As my grandmother would say, man plans and God laughs.

I haven't moved since before Jess was born, and back then I didn't have any belongings worth worrying about. In retrospect, that little house I grew up in, the one I was always so embarrassed by, held a lot more love than our oceanfront mansion ever did. I wish it hadn't taken me so long to see the truth.

I turn my attention back to the movers.

"We're parked behind you. It's fine to wait. It can't keep raining like this." I know I sound less than certain, but that's how everything feels right now. For too long I've allowed Roger to call all the shots. For too long I was afraid to stand up for the life I deserve. But I have now. As I hang up, I glance behind me. No one has followed us here, at least not yet.

Jess is on her phone texting someone, likely her father. I'm not naive. As much as I tried to keep this move a secret, this house purchase out of the press, I know the fact that Roger Jones's wife has left him will be news. Roger is a big deal in Orange County, and he doesn't like dissension in the ranks, not in the company he fought so hard to build from scratch, and not from his family. I appreciate the iron-fisted approach to business; it has made him wildly successful. When applied to his personal life—his wife—it feels like a slow strangulation. I take a deep breath and calm myself.

I need to enjoy this storm before the real one arrives. He won't let go of me without a fight and a lot of bluster, we both know that.

"Mom, can I have some people over tonight?" Jess squints her blue eyes and smiles. She is so self-absorbed she actually thinks this will be a good idea.

"Absolutely not." I shake my head. "We won't be even close to ready for guests."

"My friends want to see the new place," she whines, saying "new" with air quotes.

"You haven't even seen the place." I sigh. I know she hates it when I sigh. I didn't want to worry Jess with all the details or rock her world with the news of the separation until it was in motion. Roger left for his latest business trip on Wednesday, and the movers showed up on Thursday. I'd hired a big crew. By the time Jess came home from her friend Bonnie's house Thursday evening, our things were packed up. Jess had yelled, told me I was a fool to leave our beautiful home, to leave our life. "What is wrong with you?" she'd screamed before stomping off and slamming her bedroom door.

I'd given her a few minutes to calm down, to text Bonnie, to tell everyone I was ruining her life. And then I'd knocked on her door.

"We're leaving in the morning. Nine a.m. I've called you out sick from school. You're going to love our new home, maybe even more than here. You'll be back at school on Monday. Perfect, right? Love you. And you can always come home, visit your dad here. Think of this as an adventure."

She didn't respond that evening, but I didn't expect her to, not really. I hoped to show her a new way of life, a more solid and thoughtful way of being in the world. With less stuff and more hugs. I'd grown up with it. I knew I could show it to my daughter. Make her feel it, too. But I was running out of time.

"Give me a couple of days to get us organized, unpacked, OK? I want your friends over here all the time. We'll have lots of sleepovers." I jump as the windshield wipers snap to life and violently attack the rain.

"Mom, you need to relax. You're going to give yourself a heart attack or something. I think I'm a little old for sleepovers, don't you?"

"It's a metaphor, honey. I want you and your friends to feel at home here. I know they will." My heart pounds. We're so close to being free. I just want to go inside my new house and hide. I'm afraid Roger will appear any minute. I'm afraid of his anger, of what happens when he thinks he has lost control of someone. I reach over and pat Jess's hand. "I'm OK. We're going to be fine."

"Well, I know I will be. I'm going to college soon. So I'll be out of this mess." She smiles, full of confidence. She's reading her phone. "Oh cool. Bonnie is having people over. I'll go there tonight. Spend the night."

"I thought we'd have dinner together, celebrate our new home?"

"No, thanks. You can have this creepy old place to yourself."

We both look out my side window at the white colonial. It's not creepy—it's classic, with symmetry and stature, peeling white paint and all. It just needs a little work, and that is something I love. As soon as Jess and I are settled here on Cherry Hill Lane, I'll start my interior design business with a home office where I can entertain clients while Jess is at school. I'm so excited.

Jess sees rain-soaked creepiness, while I see nothing but natural charm.

It's easy to fake things these days. But this house, my new home, is genuine and traditional. Unlike me. Cosmetic changes upped my marketability. Too bad almost everything Roger fell in love with—my perfect breasts, my oval face, even the fullness of my hair—was fake. I thought changing myself would make me popular, but once I'd fallen in love with Roger, I became isolated, insulated by money. I found myself in a gilded cage of Roger's design. I had been a willing participant in the process: the clothes and jewelry, the bubble of wealth and entitlement—the entire charade our life together became. Of course I was. It has taken me years to see the real harm of this artificial facade. My mom saw it happening in real time, even before I met Roger. She begged me to stop after the first few surgeries. But I was addicted. I loved the attention. She had no idea what it was like out here in Southern California. What it took to compete. To win. And then, when I met Roger, I thought I had won the grand prize.

I glance beside me and see Jess's profile. My daughter doesn't look anything like me. Sure, she does have the same size feet and, unfortunately, Roger's same stubby fingers. But otherwise, she looks like me before. The me from Clinton, Florida. The girl who thought she was ugly and lacked the self-confidence to make friends. Nobody knows that me out here. I arrived with a full scholarship to UCLA and never looked back. I tell people I'm a third-generation Californian, and it works. Nobody here knows my real roots, my real story. They know only the new and improved and highly valued Julie. The one who strides confidently into $500-a-plate dinners, who shakes hands with the captains of industry. The Julie with a gaggle of untrue friends.

I've never been back to my hometown. I feel like I would look like an exotic creature, something they have never seen down there before. I'm anxious for my lips to deflate, my face to fall, the filler to wear off. I can't go back home until I look more like myself. Until I look like the little girl they bullied, one who now, finally, has the confidence to follow her dreams.

And to think, I tried to do this to Jess. I'm embarrassed by the number of times in the past that I've offered to give Jess a tune-up. I even pressed Roger to let me fix her big forehead when she was a toddler, but he thought I was ridiculous. He was right. I was being ridiculous, and shallow. And I'm ashamed by the memory.

We stood in our palatial kitchen, me holding a one-year-old Jess on my hip.

"Please, she won't remember the surgery, and it will help her in the future, I promise," I'd begged. Because even though we were married and had a child together, Roger controlled the money. All of it. Well, Roger controlled everything.

"I forbid it." Roger's tone was sharp, and Jess whimpered. "People don't do cosmetic surgery on babies."

Roger smiled and kissed me on the head. His voice softened as he touched Jess's nose. "I don't know where that forehead came from, but she'll grow into it, honey. She'll end up looking just like you." His finger touched the tip of my perfect nose. He somehow thought that her forehead—my real forehead—would shorten, shrink, become perfect on its own. "She'll grow into a beautiful young woman just like her mom. You'll see."

"No, she won't," I had mumbled. I don't know if Roger suspected all the plastic surgery I'd had, but I don't think so. He likely didn't care as long as I was a good reflection, a prize he'd won. I played my role.

But Jess refuses to do likewise, thank goodness. Sure, she's plain and flat-chested. She has my original nose. Her hair is thin, a washed-out dishwater blonde. Her blue eyes are set a little too far apart, and her forehead—well, if she had a brow lift, let's just say it would make a world of difference. What she does have is innate confidence, belief in her own power in the world, and the knowledge she belongs. My daughter is so much stronger than I'll ever be.

"Say, Mom, do you think I should have a little work done before I go off to college? I mean, sorority rush is brutal," Jess says. As if she is reading my thoughts, she smiles and looks at me. She is bringing this up for the first time.

"Oh, no, actually I think you have been right all along. You are perfect, just the way you are," I say.

She looks at me with a smile, as if I finally get what she's been trying to teach me. "Are you sure? No nose job, boob job, brow lift? Nothing else?" She shakes her head and drops her phone in her lap. At least I have her attention. "I guess I'll be fine during rush. I already know a bunch of Kappas from Oceanside. Don't worry, I'll pledge even looking pathetic like this."

I'm the worst mother. The worst.

"Honey, you're gorgeous. Natural. I'm so sorry I ever suggested any surgery. I was just, well, I got caught up in it. I'm so sorry." I fight back tears as I realize what I have done, the seeds of doubt I've planted in my own daughter about her looks.

"I know you come from a place of love, Mom. I mean, you just want me to look like you. To fit in at school. But I'm popular. I'm a Jones. I'm rich, and smart, and I host great parties at my huge home. So I'm fine."

I hate that popularity is tied to money, to your parents' status. I guess it's as hollow as looks.

"You're more than fine."

"I can't wait to go to college. I wish I'd picked that school in Maine, actually. Far, far away from this crap."

I want to ask what crap, but it's likely me, leaving her dad. I think I'd better pivot.

"Oh look, the rain is letting up." I turn away to look out the passenger-side window and wipe an errant tear. I understand Jess's anger and confusion, and that she is directing her feelings at me. I take a deep breath, turn back toward her, and touch her shoulder. "It's all going to turn out great, honey. Trust me."

I watch Jess's face soften a little, her frown dissipating. Who knows? I suppose, when you get right down to it, our differences may be more about age and entitlement rather than a substantial difference in value systems. I mean, because of my choices, this is the only life my daughter has ever known.

"Let's go check out the creepy house." Jess opens the car door, and I follow suit.

The gutters flow with water like a river, but the rain has turned to a fine mist. I hop over the runoff, and I'm standing on my front lawn. It's real. I look down at my bright red rain boots contrasting with the vivid green grass. I feel like Dorothy in *The Wizard of Oz*. I click my heels together.

"Oh my god! Stop that!" Jess says.

I'm an embarrassment as usual.

Jess isn't a fan of *The Wizard of Oz*. Or me, I suppose. I don't know if she's ever watched it. Did one of her nannies play it for her? I wish I could go back in time, focus more on mother-daughter activities that didn't involve spending a lot of money. I'd say no to the luncheons and yes to the park. If I could, I'd take my little girl's hand, and we'd run out onto the deck and head to the beach to build a sandcastle. Did we ever build a sandcastle together? We must have.

"Ma'am, we can get started." The mover climbs out of the cab of the truck, and the two passengers hop onto the street and begin wrestling with the cargo hold gate. My treasures are all in there, everything that matters to me.

"Yes, please do." I wave to them as I head up the front walkway of my new home. My first actual home of my own. When I graduated from UCLA, I dreamed of a time when I'd walk across the threshold of my first house. But it never happened. Life took me to Orange County, and almost immediately to Roger. I had apartments of my own, but that's not the same. This is a new beginning. My first home.

Everything is in slow motion as I pull the key out of my purse.

Only one thought runs through my mind: I hope I haven't made a huge mistake.

CHAPTER 4

JESS

My mom has clearly lost it. She's a mixed-up Barbie doll. The timing doesn't make any sense.

She's leaving my dad. I mean, why would my parents split up now? They've been miserable together for years—just ask yours truly, who has become adept at racing to my room or a friend's house when things get loud and mean. But it has worked for them. They always seemed to make up. Dad would go back to being a workaholic with control issues, and Mom would return to shopping and Botox cocktail parties and working out. I'd get a new toy purchased by a nanny, left outside my bedroom door in the morning. The value increased with age, of course. All's good in love and war, right?

Status quo worked for seventeen years and now this? We're going to get real, discuss feelings, and hold hands now? This is just as fake as her boobs and his shallow attempts to pay attention to what's going on in my life.

Come on.

I mean, I am gone in the fall. I worked hard to get into a good school, and I did it. Couldn't they just pull this nonsense when I go to college? And look at this place. I mean, really? We're barely inside the front door and I feel like running. Maybe I'll ask Bonnie if I can live with her family, just for senior year. People do it all the time. I'd be like an exchange student, only I'm just from across the tracks.

I don't know anyone who lives over here, and I don't want to. I have a manageable life. At home. My home. Mom says she's filing for custody of me, until I turn eighteen. But really? I'm a grown-up. I need my dad for tuition and spending money next year. I need my mom for what? I'm not sure. I was curious to see what she was up to—that's why I agreed to come along this morning. But I've seen it. I'm good.

"Look at this hand-carved railing on the steps. Exquisite." My mom is trying to get me excited, but it won't work. "They just don't make houses like this anymore. This is old-world craftsmanship, Jess. Look at the baseboards, the crown molding. Swoon."

Is there a hotline you can call when your mom loses it? I need one. We could call it Real Talk. You know, how they're always worried about teen suicide rates and, like, guns in schools—and sure that's a problem, but what about the parents? The ones who leave a perfectly good house and husband—OK, Dad is a little controlling but still—and move here to nowheresville in a haunted house.

I need a lifeline here. Someone? Anyone.

My mom pops into the entry hall. Her eyes are all shiny, like she's stoned. She's high on this house. Crap.

"Jess, let me show you your room."

I'd rather die. "Mom, I don't like this house. Do you remember the movie *Paranormal Activity*?"

"Oh stop. You will love it here. Come on."

She starts up the stairs, and every other step emits some weird creaking sound. I'm not living here. I follow her upstairs to humor her. She's so darn excited.

"You know Dad is going to find you—us. He probably already has." I reach the top of the stairs and she turns; some of the shine is gone.

I know how to rattle her. It's my superpower.

"It's fine. He will move on, just like you and I are." Mom turns and opens a door. "Here's your new room!"

The floor is crooked. That's the first impression. Second, it's old and smelly in here. On the plus side someone left a phone charger in the corner, plugged in under the window. I slip the power cord into my phone and stare down at the street. All the other houses on the street are old like this one, but they seem to be standing up straight. This one, our "new" house, feels like it is slouching, slanted. I'm used to new, sprawling, California cool. Instead, this house is two stories. Old-fashioned instead of contemporary. I walk to the other side of the room and look out over the puny backyard. I'm used to seeing the ocean out my back windows. This—well, this isn't right. I don't belong here. I want to be at home, the way things were. Is that too much to ask? I graduate in the spring. Just give me a stable home with parents I can ignore and coexist with until then.

Not this, not a whole new life.

The rain has stopped. The windows are still streaked, like the house had a good cry. I touch the pane, cool on my fingertips.

"Those are the original leaded windows. Gorgeous, right? What do you think, honey?" Mom really wants me to like it here. She's hoping it so much it makes me feel bad. "I have so many ideas. Your room is going to look amazing."

"I like my room. At home. With Dad. Let's go back home. You guys have fights all the time. You can work this out." I am begging my mom. I'm surprised when tears pop into my eyes. I wipe them away. "Please."

"Oh, honey." Mom tries to pull me in for a hug, but I'm not falling for that. "Your dad and I need to live apart. I need a fresh start. Someday I hope you'll understand. We have irreconcilable differences. It doesn't mean we love you any less."

Could she sound more like a divorce textbook? It's not your fault, blah, blah, blah. I get it. Their house of cards has tumbled down. The only thing left for me to do is get away from them a little sooner than I'd planned. It's not like either of them actually misses me when I'm gone. They never did. When I was at camp, or away at a friend's house for the night, they didn't have to keep up the facade of caring. The struggle of hanging out with a kid, even one of their own creation, was a drain. I get it. They had more important things to do.

"Maybe I can stay with Bonnie, you know, until you finish the renovation?" I smile. This could be a win-win. Bonnie is my best friend. She's smart, and she has a great house. We're almost like sisters because both of us are only kids. Unlike my mom, she gets me.

"Absolutely not. This is the fun part, the before and after. All the furnishings will make this our home. You'll love it. And once I set up my home office, I'll be Oceanside's designer to hire."

Oh my god. Now I've heard everything. "You are going to work? Really?"

"You know, you're being very condescending. Think of this as a mother-daughter adventure, something you and I are sharing together. You used to care about that. I want to spend quality time together, like we used to when you were young." Mom huffs. I don't have any real memories of quality playtime, aside from the command school performances where she'd play the role of the hovering, doting mom. I mean, don't get me wrong. She loves me, just in her own superficial way.

And she loves to play the victim, and for sure, she's had great experience with that over the years. My dad's a dick a lot of the time. "Look, honey, I'm getting a divorce. I bought my first house, and I'm going to make it fabulous. Can you please cheer me on? Just a little?"

"Are you trying for *Real Housewives* again?" I ask. Dad kept her from doing the reality TV show last time; now there's nothing to stop her. He told her one famous person in the house was enough. Dad is high profile in town, owns almost everything that is cool, real estate wise: the mall, the five-star hotel at the beach, the five best restaurants. He's Mr. Oceanside.

"We'll see. I'm sure they're still interested, but I don't think I am anymore. Dreams change, you know. It's exciting. The future is filled with unlimited possibilities!" And with that she's out the door, merrily losing her mind.

For a moment, I consider calling an Uber and heading back to my dad's house. No way. Not an option. My mom's high on the house, but my dad's . . . well, he's tough. A lot of work. You have to keep him happy. He's in charge. He's always right. I've found it's best to keep my distance because he doesn't really vibe with my friends. He's a big believer in one-sided discussions, lectures about his way of doing things.

"I'm a self-made man, Jess. School only gets you so far. You need hard work, discipline," Dad said once. We'd been sitting in his home office, and I'd just brought my first middle school report card to him. I was beaming with accomplishment: all As. He glanced at the piece of paper and pushed it across the desk to me.

"Grades are meaningless. It's how you apply yourself in the real world. I'm worried about you in the real world, actually." He'd scared me just then, with his candor, his focus on me.

"I'll be great in the real world." I smiled and held my report card in my lap.

Dad started to say something but stopped. "We created this, so it's likely not your fault in the end. You'll have a trust fund."

"I'll have a big career. I'm going to be like you," I'd said, standing up, wounded by his words. I ran out of his office, hoping to avoid hearing him chuckle. But I still heard it. His laugh boomed down the hall, chasing me to my room.

Since then, I mostly coexist with him. The artifice that surrounds our family in our home—the grand chandeliers in every room, the obnoxious library stuffed with books no one has read, the huge pool and even bigger private beach, the scurrying and uniformed staff—all of it is too much for three people. But I don't say anything about them being phony, greedy, and the rest. I keep quiet.

That way he can imagine I agree with everything he does and says. Interactions are breezy, superficial, and rare. My allowance hits my account every week, like clockwork. So would I move back to my dad's house without my mom there as a buffer? Never. My dad's a little bit ruthless. He's a lot of a know-it-all. And he's too busy to really listen, to anyone.

I still cannot believe my parents are splitting up. This is ridiculous. I need space. College can't come a minute too soon. All I want is to be free from all this—both of them. This house.

I'm staring out the window when I see a guy, kinda cute, walking down the gravel driveway of our house. He's carrying a beige duffel bag. He's not part of the moving crew, that's for sure. He's too skinny for that. He has dark hair and an ambling, carefree gait.

Who is he? He has to be older than me, or go to another school. I know everyone at Oceanside High School. And why is he here, at our new, creepy house? I walk across my bedroom and look out at the backyard. There he is.

I watch as he opens the door and disappears into the little shedlike structure across the grass from our house. Weird, and sort of wonderful, I suppose. This could be fun.

I wonder whether my mom saw the cute boy in our backyard. Maybe I'll keep that little secret to myself, at least until I find out what his deal is.

I hurry across the room and grab my phone. I need to text Bonnie. She's not going to believe any of this.

CHAPTER 5

TOM

I toss my stuff onto the couch and pace back and forth. I smile as the brown dust from the desert puffs out of my duffel. The stars at night made me think anything was possible. I remind myself I was happy there. But now, I'm home.

I need an answer, a solution. Maybe I should walk across the backyard and explain the situation to them. I'll go on over and knock on the back door of the house, my house, and explain to the new owners what has happened, tell them it's a mistake. Maybe they'll listen. Maybe they don't really like it, don't really need it. Maybe they've already realized this was all a big mistake. Maybe they'll let me stay.

I kick the wall, and my boot sticks. Yanking it out creates a huge hole in the drywall. Cheap, of course. Guess it's not real solid, like my stepmom claimed.

"It's a wonderful family home. Great bones," she'd say of the house. The funny thing is, she wasn't the original woman of the house. No. That was my real mom. But she is long gone. Sometimes when I remember my dreams, I see her in them. Sometimes she's trying to hug me, and I turn away. Sometimes I ask her how she could leave me. I was just a boy.

My dad has always said she ran off with the choir director, a woman, but I doubt it. He said she was a sinner, a disgrace. But I don't believe that at all. Something else happened, something bad, or she would have come back for me. I've tried to find her over the years, googling her name, but I've found nobody. It's like she vanished in a puff of smoke. In my dreams she'll still be back for me.

And then, along came Sandi. My real mom hadn't been gone for more than six months when Dad fell in love with my Sunday school teacher. Miss Sandi, as I called her then, was smiles and light. Crafts and Jesus. She wrapped me in hugs that felt like sunshine and safety. I think the only reason she agreed to date Doug, my dad, was because I was his son. A motherless six-year-old.

"He's just the sweetest little boy," Miss Sandi said when Dad came to pick me up after service. Doug was assistant pastor at the time. He hadn't ascended the throne yet. Sandi's dad was one of the true believers, a deacon in the church. Now I realize how young she was when she started dating my dad, younger than I am now. Back then, though, I just missed my mom's embrace. Sandi tried to replace those hugs. I know she did her best.

"You're so good with him, Sandi." My dad poured on the pastoral charm. "Say, how would you like to join Tommy and me for supper?"

It's not really a date if you're chaperoned by a six-year-old boy, am I right?

Sandi had blushed, squeezed my hand, and said, "Is that OK with you, Tommy?"

I'd nodded. Sealing her fate, I suppose. But screw her, she sold my house out from under me.

I kick the cheap wall again, satisfied with the feeling of pain in my right toe, the crunch of the drywall caving in. The carriage house was an add-on. Built decades after the main house. And my dad paid for it, so you know it's not the finest craftsmanship. No way. He's so cheap. This place is actually more like a shed than a carriage house. Two small rooms: a kitchenette and a living room with my bed, a coffee table and a couch, and a small bathroom. Sure it works for me, but it's built cheap. See? I kick the wall again for good measure and make the hole bigger, the size of my boot.

My dad and Simple Sandi built the shed ten years ago as a rental so they could make some extra cash. They thought this spot, this shed, this accessory dwelling unit, would be a hot Airbnb rental, if you can imagine. But then Oceanside City Council changed the rules on short-term rentals, and their moneymaking scheme went up in smoke. Until I moved out here four years ago, they just filled the place with junk.

It's depressing in here, I must admit. But still, it's mine. I walk to the only window I have, the one in the kitchenette that looks toward the backyard and the house beyond. I still think I'll see Doug walking out the back door or Sandi fussing with her garden, and that's stupid and weak. They're gone. Have been, since before I went to the desert a week ago.

I'm the only member of the Dean family left here.

I turn away from the window. I should be grateful for the shed, and I am—I was. It's tough here in Orange County. It's like a case study for the haves and the have-nots, and the haves like it that way. Meanwhile, some people are working two, three jobs but can't move up, can't even afford an apartment of their own. That's my problem. I work at the bar and in construction, but I'm chronically poor. I'm not alone. It started when these foreigners moved here, all these Mexicans taking the jobs, taking the apartments. They can't even speak English, yet we're flooded with them.

I should have been born in the 1950s. That's when Orange County came into its own. People could find the perfect wife, get married, have the perfect life. People had a chance to own land, to have some space of their own. I've researched it. Everything that's wrong with this place happened in the last fifty years. My new friend says Vietnam changed everything, that it changed him.

He's helping me see where I belong. We sat for hours, side by side, staring at the stars last week. His name is Block, which is what he looks like—short with graying hair and bright blue eyes—but he can take down a man twice his size in a second. I've seen him in action, in the desert.

The first day I arrived, I was nervous. I only knew Vic from the bar. Turns out I fit right in with these guys. You wouldn't know us if you saw us all out together; you wouldn't know what we are, that we have a special bond. There are so many more of us than you think.

Someone is knocking on my door. If those fucking people are asking to borrow a cup of sugar, I'm going to lose it.

I yank the door open and can't help myself. I smile. All my anger just ran out. I'm staring at a beautiful girl. "Well, hello."

"Hi. Um, do you live here?" She's looking past me, into the carriage house. She wants to come inside.

Shit. I just kicked a hole in the wall, and that's another reason, one of many, why I can't invite her in. "Um, yeah. It's my place." I step out onto the front stoop and close the door. "I'm Tom. Who are you?"

"I'm Jess. My mom just bought the house. Does she know about you?"

The way she says "the house" is dripping with disdain. She'd better love my house. She *should* love my house.

"Tom?" She's staring at me.

"Oh, I guess the agreement is I have to move out after this weekend." I shrug. "That's all I know. No one told me anything, well, except that someone was moving in today. And that I'd be moving out."

"That would be us." Her cheeks flush. Is she flirting with me? No way. I'm an incel, celibate but not by choice, just because girls around here all think they're better than me. Sure, they'll start a conversation with me out at the bars in Newport where all the fancy girls go, but then they ask their first question: What do you do? They want to know how much money you make, right away. Don't even give you a chance. Once I lied, said I was in investment banking, but that backfired when the bitch expected me to pay for all the drinks. I told her I had to hit the head and escaped out the back door. Pay for your own drinks, bitch. Another night, I asked for a girl's phone number after we'd danced, close, for most of the night. She typed it into my phone as I watched, my body tingling with lust.

"Call me tomorrow. Let's do something," she'd said, kissing me before walking away to join her friends.

I really thought she was the one. The next morning, I called to ask her out—maybe we'd walk the beach or rent kayaks or something and cruise the Back Bay. In my head, we were a perfect fit. I dialed the number, and it was answered by a used-car dealer somewhere in Chino. She'd given me the wrong number on purpose. Now I knew why her friends were all laughing when they left the bar.

So now I don't really go out, not there at least. The crowd at Cody's is old, mostly guys. I've given up, actually. Vic says it's better to be celibate anyway, that most of the guys have made a pledge against women. They're distractions, good for only one thing.

But this girl, she's new, and not from here. She might actually be flirting. I touch the side of the door and lean closer to her. She smells like oranges. My brain is on fire. This never happens to me. I'm the loser, the loner. Girls run the other way when they see me. But not this one. I need to say something. I cough and force words out of my mouth.

"Well, welcome to the neighborhood. Are you from out of town?" I'm out of practice talking to women. I hope I don't sound stupid.

"No, we're from across town. Other side of the tracks, literally." She laughs as she says this, as if this is all funny for her. "We lived in the Cove, at the beach."

Why would anyone go from the ocean to this? From the magical land of the haves to here, the cheapest part of Oceanside? "What happened?"

She blinks. I probably messed up. I always do.

"My parents are splitting up. My mom needed out. She picked this crappy house. Ah, there she is now."

I look behind her and see her mom. They look nothing alike. "You don't look like her."

"She doesn't look like her." Jess turns and walks toward her mom. "Better go. See you."

"Hey, can I get your number?" I can't believe I just asked a girl that. I'm an idiot. My brain screams: YOU ARE AN IDIOT. You know you can't trust a woman. Remember that stupid girl in college? She laughed in your face when you asked her out. You have important plans this weekend. Ignore her. This is temptation. Stay strong. But then I see her smile, and my resolve melts.

"Sure." Jess grabs my phone and adds herself as a contact. I watch as she sends herself a text from my phone. "There. I've got your number, too."

I hope it's really her number. I hope she can't hear my heart thudding in my chest. When she gives it back, our hands touch and a bolt runs through me.

"Thanks," I manage to say.

I watch her walk across the grass, admiring the way she looks in her skinny jeans, the way her hair swings across her back. Her mom gives me a quick dismissive nod. She doesn't like us talking, that much is clear.

For her part, Jess turns and waves. "See you around."

Was she blowing me off or just saying goodbye until later? Ugh. I shouldn't trust her as far as I can throw her. I'm supposed to swear off all women. Block says they're all trouble. But I don't want to. She's gorgeous. She's different. And she lives across my backyard. Maybe this is the universe's way of helping me, of getting me out of my rut? Maybe Jess is an offering, an apology for everything I've suffered through? For my parents double-crossing me. For my mom leaving me. For every girl who laughingly rejected me. For the shit show my life has become.

"See you around, Jess!" I call as they walk inside the back door of my house.

Jess stops at the back door, turns, and smiles. And then she disappears into the house.

I can't believe how cute she is. And also, she is right. The house doesn't suit them, so there's hope. And her mom is hot, but she's also jumpy, nervous, and clearly unhappy. She'll figure out she made a mistake soon. In the meantime, we'll spend a little quality time together. Like maybe right now would be a good time for the sprinklers to come on. After that huge downpour. That could be a mess, right? She'll need my help to fix the sprinkler system.

This is working out just fine. *God works in mysterious ways,* Doug the Dick always tells his flock. I take a moment to duck behind the back hedge and flip on the sprinkler system. I'm back in my shed admiring my decorating before they pop up. I hear them hiss and spring to life. Perfect.

My place looks as good as it can get, I have to say. I've added a lot to the walls to prepare for hosting my friends this afternoon. I'd panicked when it was time to leave the desert and hastily invited them over. Who knows if they'll actually show up.

My phone lights up. It's Jess. She texts: Hey, do you know how to work the sprinklers? They're on for some reason!

I text: Sure do. Meet me on my porch. I'll show you.

She texts: Ok.

The next thing I know, Jess is walking toward me, down the gravel driveway. My plan worked.

I walk outside. "Hey. Long time no see." I am a blubbering idiot.

"Hey." She steps up on the porch, and it takes every ounce of willpower I have not to touch her hair, her arm.

"What's your story, Tom? I mean, why are you living out here by yourself? Do you like it?" Jess asks, her blue eyes bright and shining. "Seems like I'd be bored. And kind of lonely."

I allow myself to think she might actually care about the answer.

I take a breath. "It's all I have. Had. I guess it's your mom's now. I don't know, it's just frustrating. Have you ever felt like no matter how hard you try to get ahead, you just can't? I'm not bothering anyone out here. Why can't we all just live and let live? Leave each other alone."

Jess touches my shoulder, and my body ignites. "I feel like that. Out of control right now. I mean, my parents are getting a divorce, and I'm not sure what I'm supposed to do between now and college. I don't get why they couldn't just keep faking it at least until I was gone."

"Well, maybe we can help each other out? Hang out?" I shrug. "I mean, I'm not here for long, but you know, live in the moment."

Jess grins. "Yeah, live in the moment. And maybe we should turn the sprinklers off. The grass is getting soaked."

I try to care about the lawn, which is becoming a lake, but I only want to stare at Jess. I force myself to focus. "Ready?"

"For what?" Jess asks.

I want to say "I'm ready for you to help me figure all this out, before it's too late." But instead I say, "We have to sprint through the sprinklers to get to the control panel. Come on."

I grab Jess's hand and pull her into the yard. We're both soaked immediately. And she's more gorgeous than ever. She's laughing, and mud and water and grass dance in the air like a dream. I reach into the bushes and turn off the system. The sprinklers hiss to a stop.

Jess's white T-shirt clings to her chest, and she's laughing as she wraps her hair into a ponytail. "That was fun. I never do stuff like this. I'm always, like, always trying to impress somebody. My so-called friends usually. We don't do spontaneous."

I bite my lip. I have so much to say to her. But I need to take my time. "I'm all about spontaneous. I've got nothing to prove, nobody to impress." I've got nobody, truth be told.

Jess starts walking back to the driveway, stomping in the muddy grass like a little girl.

I see her mom come out on the back porch. She isn't amused. "You're ruining the lawn!"

"Mom, Tom and I saved your stupid lawn. The sprinklers turned on," Jess yells.

Jess's mom's hands are on her hips. "You need to come help unpack." She's talking to Jess, but I feel her watching me. "And Tom, you need to pack up. Remember? It's part of the arrangement."

She says that and my anger ignites. Pack up and go where, exactly?

Jess says, "I'll text you later. Sorry about my mom."

I shrug and force a smile. "It's OK. I guess she cares about you, you know. You're lucky. I get that I'm the bad boy out back."

Jess's eyes twinkle. "I like bad boys. See you around."

As I watch Jess walk to the back door, I wonder whether things would be different if I had a mom standing on the back porch, watching my every move. I know Sandi tried, especially at first. But then she had her replacement boys, her real boys.

And that's when she stopped watching. But I never did. And now, in the worst joke in the universe, a gorgeous girl moves into my house and I'm kicked out. Or, rather, I'm supposed to be kicked out.

But that's not going to happen. The desert opened my eyes, for real. I'm not a loser. I have options. I'm not going to let anything or anyone push me around anymore. No one's going to get in the way of me being me.

Who am I kidding? I'd let Jess get in the way of it. In a heartbeat. We could get rid of her mom. Her mom is rich. She could leave, go somewhere else, anywhere else, and then it would be just me and Jess. We'd both get what we want. I wave at her mom and head back to my shed. I've got things to do, but none of it involves packing.

This is my house. End of story.

CHAPTER 6

ROGER

Life got interesting quickly this week. I go away for a typical business trip and enjoy a little stopover in the Big Apple two nights ago. I love seeing the latest on Broadway. I love that I can afford the best seats in the house. I hate it that Julie won't come with me, that she says she has to be there for Jess in her last year of high school. *Be there doing what exactly?* I'd asked over and over. Our daughter ignores us. She's barely home. My wife just doesn't want to travel with me anymore.

And now, she doesn't want to live with me anymore. I came home to a half-empty house this morning. Of all things. She's being completely impulsive. It's unacceptable, and mildly embarrassing if anyone finds out. I'm used to fixing things, to taking charge. I'll do it again. Right now.

As I turn onto Cherry Hill Lane—a street without a single cherry or hill to be seen—I glance in my rearview mirror. Someone is following me. What the hell?

I pull over to the curb a few houses down from where I'm going and wait to see what the guys in the blue car do. They have to be with the government. The car is old, and they are both overweight, from what I can see. Why the hell would they be following me?

They pass by me slowly. The guy in the passenger seat meets my eye and smiles.

I push the button, and my window drops like a bullet. German engineering.

I stick my head through the window as they drive by. "What? What do you want?" The car doesn't stop until it reaches the end of the block. I could just turn around, head back home, and confront Julie another day. I don't really want any witnesses, especially ones who look like cops.

But why would the cops be following me? I roll up my window and call the office.

My assistant du jour answers.

"Get Smith on the phone."

"Yes, sir."

"Hello, Roger!" Smith's perpetually cheerful. He's the opposite of me. That's why he's my COO. I imagine him in his office. He has a stand-up desk, which is ridiculous but totally him. His suit is crisp, navy blue or black. He is drinking a protein drink with whatever the latest fad diet tells him will make him live longer and look younger. Collagen? Bone broth? Both? Who knows? On his stand-up desk he has placed a single photo of his wife, Rose. She is, he tells me, very demanding but worth it. I suppose I'm a little like his wife.

Smith asks, "What's up?"

"I'm not sure," I admit, although I'm loath to say so. I'm not good at being wrong, or unsure. I'm not good at anything but certainty and winning. I pull down the visor and slide the mirror open. Too many scotches last night on the red-eye flight home, that is clear from my complexion. It's likely why I didn't notice half my home was packed up. A miscalculation. I'll detox later. Maybe this weekend.

Maybe not.

"I think I'm being followed. By cops. Oh, and Julie moved out for real this time. Bought a hovel of a house across town."

"Oh man, I'm sorry. I'm sure you can convince her to come back. You always do." Smith is right about that. She pulled this same charade five years ago, albeit without the addition of a new place to live. That time, she was frustrated with my lack of attention—presents instead of presence, she'd said. So I bought her a second home in Maui and took a month off work to be with her there. Sure, it's lovely on the islands, aloha and all that, but that was the longest month of my life. I love to work. I need to work. But I did it, and she stayed with me.

This time feels different, though.

I realize Smith is still on the phone. "Let's table the Julie issue. I'll handle it. The bigger question is, Why would someone be tailing me?" I flip the visor up and stare down the street. There they are. The sun is coming out, and the road is drying with a mist of steam. I'm on the wrong side of town. And I'm being followed.

"No idea, boss. There's nothing to look at here. The company is doing better than ever. The Phoenix deal is about to close. We broke ground in the inland empire. Things are humming. Jones Real Estate Development is on a roll." Smith's cheerful business facts reassure me. I love to know my real estate empire is booming, still growing. So if I'm not being followed on behalf of disgruntled business clients—something that has happened in the past—who would be having me tailed? I try to think what I've done lately that could leave me exposed.

Maybe my wife is having me followed?

"OK, Smith, thanks for the updates. I'll likely be in later today. Or not. Can't tell how this situation is going to unfold."

"Do you want me to send our security guy? I can get him to you in half an hour."

I think of the guy who sits behind the front desk. He's a retired cop. Good guy. But not a guy who scares away undercover cops. I'm sure they're sleazeball, off-duty dudes hired by Julie. That's what they are. I'm convinced.

"I'm fine. I'll deal with them." I hang up on Smith. It's too early for all this shit. I imagine he's slumping against his desk about now. He should have a desk chair. Everyone has a stupid desk chair. My watch tells me my blood pressure is high. I push the button to dismiss the warning. Of course it's high. Stupid watch. I pull it off my wrist and stick it on the dashboard. Jess got it for me. Sometimes she notices if I'm wearing it. Sometimes, she says, she's worried about me. Mostly she's a typical teenager, though. She really only cares about herself and her generous allowance. That's probably all my fault. Long hours at the office don't lead to much bonding. We dance around each other like acquaintances, exchanging pleasantries, trying not to get in each other's way. I mean, consider the alternative. My childhood was chaos; my parents moved every two years or so. Nothing was solid, nothing dependable, not even dinner.

My family, the three of us, are calm elegance. No drama. Just luxury. That's all I need. Maybe Julie has decided that isn't enough, even though it always has been. And does Jess agree? Does she still worry about me enough to notice the watch on my wrist? I guess she's not that worried, is she? She left me, along with her mother. And that's not good for my heart. In fact, I'm feeling very used. After all I've done for both of them? It's ridiculous.

Despite the stupid tail, I pull away from the curb and park behind a Toyota Camry across the street from my wife's new home. This is a street for Camrys and Civics. Why the hell is Julie living here?

One thing I do know is that my daughter never goes anywhere without her phone. I know her location at all times, along with my wife's. My security guy insisted on installing the trackers in case of kidnapping. I went along with it. If I need to find my women, I can. Today is no exception. And so when I track my daughter, I see that she is inside the house across the street. And so is my wife. The ugly old white house with the white moving van in front. The van filled with my stuff, at least some of it. I wasn't surprised when I flew in from New York last night to find Julie asleep in our bed, in the master bedroom, and as usual, I knew I wasn't welcome. I lumbered off to one of the guest bedrooms I've claimed as my own. It's a pattern we've gotten into recently, a pattern that has become the norm. I didn't even check on Jess, just assumed she was asleep in her room. If I had, though, I would have discovered their plot, their lies. Jess's room was empty this morning. I'd been cleaned out except for the furniture in the master and my guest room. Julie left just enough furniture to fool me and my drunk brain when I arrived home.

This morning I found myself alone in a half-empty home, yelling for my wife and my daughter. I know I must have looked unhinged as I raced through each room, calling their names. The staff was just coming to work.

"Where are Julie and Jess?" I'd demanded, finding Hilda in the kitchen unloading a dishwasher as if nothing were wrong.

"I don't know, sir," she'd answered, eyes wide, knife in hand as if she needed protection.

"They're gone. Jess's things and furniture are all gone from her room. Julie's clothes, too, and so much more. You must know something."

"No, sir. I know nothing, sir." Hilda was white as a ghost, backing up toward the door before running outside. "Mrs. Julie gave me the day off yesterday. I know nothing."

She didn't have any answers, or at least none she would divulge. I don't know how long Julie has planned this, but it is unacceptable. I must calm down. Use my brain. Fortunately, I know where they both are, right now. And knowledge is power.

I squeeze the steering wheel. I realize I cannot confront Julie in front of Jess. That would be the worst form of parenting, even for me. Plus, I can't handle the drama of both of them together. Jess will pretend not to care, while Julie will act hysterical. No matter how nonchalant my daughter is at times, I know she shouldn't be a pawn in her parents' relationship. But this is all Julie's fault. Instead of getting roped into helping her sneaky mother move into a new house, my daughter belongs at school on a Friday of her senior year. Sure, she's already been accepted at USC, a great school. I'm excited about the network of connections for all of us to make. It's good for the whole family. It means you've arrived in Southern California, that you're somebody. We're all somebody now.

For a moment, my brain flashes on the encounter with Angel, just before I left for New York. Maybe that's my future, maybe I can make something of her like I've done for Julie, for Jess. If need be, I could. But I'm not giving up on this family. I push Angel's gorgeous face out of my mind and stare at the ugly white house where my wife and daughter are hiding.

I guess it's OK to use the move as an excuse to miss school. This has to be a bit unnerving for Jess, as well. But she's messing up my plans by being inside that run-down house. I am reluctant to confront Julie about her unwise decision in front of my daughter and the moving men.

Someone is watching me. I look down the street, and the car is still there. But it's not their eyes I feel on me.

My wife is standing on the sidewalk next to the moving van. She's wearing ridiculous shiny red rain boots, and she is staring at me.

I roll down my window. I yell, "Julie. This is not acceptable."

One of the moving guys appears from the other side of the van and steps beside her. He points at me. I can't hear what he says to Julie.

The big guy yells, "Get away from here! She doesn't want you around, asshole!"

How dare he talk to me that way? The moving man seems pretty sure of himself. He must not know who I am. What I'm capable of doing. I can ruin him and his entire moving company if I want to. And I suddenly want to.

I grab my phone and take a photo. Of Julie and her silly protector. Of his moving van's hideous logo splashed on the side of the truck. And of course, of the ugly house.

"Just happened to be in the neighborhood. I'll catch up with you later, sweetie." I'm not smiling. I roll up the window and enjoy watching her reaction.

Julie looks upset. The sweaty moving guy's arm is around her shoulder. I imagine that is a small comfort to her, despite his size.

She knows power lies in money, not muscle.

She knows she's outmatched, always has been. That's the deal you make when you marry someone like me. When you make a commitment, I expect you to keep it. For better or worse. For richer, and richer. Because I know richer is my most attractive feature. Look at her, look at me. Look what beauty and perfection money can buy. My kid looks more like me, poor girl. Julie warned me, of course. Funny thing is my daughter likes herself just fine. Go figure.

I pull away from the pathetic scene and focus on the blue car at the end of the block. They aren't a security detail for Julie, or they would be parked in front of her house. They would have rushed to her defense when I stopped in front of her new ugly house.

They are something else. I wish I knew what. I pull up to the stop sign and stare at the driver. He stares back.

Screw them. I'm going home. I need a shower, and then I need a plan. I'll go into the office, get my lawyer to meet me there. There is more than one way to compel a wayward spouse to come back home. Because, despite the fact that she's upset with me right now, I need her. Julie and I are good together, we're compatible. And that's all I need. I want to come home to peace, and beauty, and luxury. I don't need high-brow conversation or wild sex—there are other people to fill those needs. At home, I need stability. Routine.

I need my wife and daughter at home. And I am a man who gets what he wants.

The rush of confusion I felt this morning when I woke up to a half-empty house has given way to clarity. I know where she is. She knows I know where she is. It's checkmate. I just need to decide when to make my move. I pull into the intersection and watch as the cops do likewise.

They can follow me all day if they want to. There's nothing to see here. In fact, I'm one of Orange County's most prominent real estate developers. Maybe I'll give the sheriff a call? He's a friend, a good guy. He can get these idiots off my tail.

I punch my assistant's number. "Get my lawyer to meet me at the office in an hour. Tell him it's important."

"Yes. Sir. Um, sir?" Her voice is quavering. "There are people here, asking for you."

"Tell them I'll be in this afternoon." I hang up. I hate weakness. It's as aggravating as the relentless drip of a leaking faucet.

But the thing I hate more than weakness is being abandoned. By my wife. When I'm on a business trip. It's unacceptable.

Period.

And this charade of a new home is not going to last. She'll be back where she belongs again soon, with Jess trailing along behind.

She just doesn't know it yet.

CHAPTER 7

JULIE

I need to shake this off. My hands still tremble from the encounter outside. I will not let Roger ruin this. I will not. He's trying to scare me, but he is the one who got nervous and drove away. Maybe he is beginning to accept the new reality. This is my new life, or at least the start of it. I resist the temptation to watch the front yard, to make sure Roger doesn't come back. I need to move on. He needs to move on.

With the movers still here, I know I'm safe. I turn back to the unpacking task at hand. It feels good to rip open the packing tape, to break a fingernail in the process. This is life, real life. The life Jess has always deserved, the life I need to live. I know, it's a bit late, and she's already seventeen, but I have to try. I've already visited the synagogue down the street and will try to attend Shabbat service tonight if I'm up to it. I need to find a connection to God again and, through Him, a way back to myself. I lost her years ago. I ran from her years ago, but it turns out, deep down, she was with me all along.

Roger's world was never real. This time, I won't go back to him. Not for money. Not for a second home in Hawaii. Not again. Of course, it helped having the moving guy standing next to me. His arm around me felt comforting, real. I miss that type of connection, that type of real emotion. I felt protected, cared for. I wish I could keep him around for a bit, until the dust settles and Roger moves on without me. Because he's going to have to.

I turn my attention to the box of cookbooks on the kitchen counter. I love this kitchen. It's white and bright, with huge windows and stainless-steel appliances. It's the room that drew me to this home. I pull off the packing tape and unwrap the first book. It's one of my favorites. The Barefoot Contessa showing me how to entertain elegantly and with ease. Her husband is always in the photos scattered throughout her cookbooks. She even called one *Cooking for Jeffrey.*

I wish that had been my dream. I wish I had decided to find that kind of love, that sort of long-term relationship that got better, not worse, through the years. I told myself we were meant to be. Turns out it's easy to fool yourself. Turns out it's not that hard to turn off your heart and plop down the black American Express. I imagine Roger's hand reaching out and taking the card back, trying to take everything back. He is ruthless in business. I don't expect him to be otherwise with me.

I place the cookbook on the counter and walk to the front door, scanning the street.

"He hasn't come back, ma'am, we're watching," the man who protected me earlier tells me as he walks in with a lamp.

"Thank you," I say. "What's your name?"

"Max," he says.

"I'm Julie," I say.

"Your ex seems like a complete ass," the guy says. "I know some guys who do private security. Let me know. Excuse me."

A chill tingles my neck as I watch Max carry the lamp into the next room. I remind myself I'm in control. I am not afraid of Roger. He would never physically hurt me, right?

But maybe my faith in Roger's ultimate humanity is wishful thinking.

I was always good at seeing the bright side, fooling myself, I suppose. When I moved here, down to Orange County, I thought I had it made. I was working at a medical spa in LA, and I'd already become the poster child for before and after, literally—my photos hung on the office wall to inspire our clients to do more, be prettier. Surgery or fillers, lasers or Botox, we had it all. I had it all. I couldn't stop, didn't want to stop. It was my first compulsion, an impulse that culminated in changing everything about my appearance. Roger, I suppose, would become my second.

One afternoon at work, my boss at the medical spa—the doctor who made all of me possible—called me into his office. His name was Dr. Profit, of all things.

"Julie, you've been an outstanding staff member. Our very own real-life before and after. I think our growth is in large part due to you. Please sit." He motioned to an all-white leather chair in his all-white leather and chrome office.

At first I thought he was firing me. "Glad to be here. I mean, you're the one who does the surgery, I'm just a willing model. I love the way I've turned out, as you know." I was singing his praises, but then I noticed his unwrinkleable brow was trying to look serious. "Is something wrong?"

Dr. Profit smiled, his lids smooth and taut, blue eyes shining with excitement. "I'm opening a second location, in Orange County; you know the demand we have from down there. I mean, once the Housewives discovered us."

What a relief. I'd been in awe each and every time one of the Real Housewives from anywhere slipped into our offices in disguise. Someday, I wanted to be one of them. "I know. They all love you."

"Well, I'm glad I make them happy." He glanced at his hands, held them up, and then flexed them. "Here's the magic."

His refrain. He loves his hands.

"I want you to manage the Newport Beach office. I'll give you a bump in salary to replace any loss in your aesthetician book of business. I bet your clients will drive down for you. You're that good." I wondered if I should flex my hands but decided not to.

"Thank you. I've always wanted to move down there," I said, and it was true. I needed more space, a fresh start. Though I'd always dreamed of being an interior decorator, this college part-time job had become a career. After graduation from college, while my girlfriends all went to work at corporate jobs, I got my aesthetician's license. I'd found the world of beauty very enticing, and personally rewarding with the free surgeries Dr. Profit performed. Maybe someday I could do both—interior design and manage the beauty spa—in Orange County. Maybe someday I could be a star on *The Real Housewives of Orange County*.

"I'll be down there two days a week. Otherwise, you're in charge. Can you start next week?" Dr. Profit asked.

We shook hands, gently, and the deal was made. It was the best decision I'd ever made. At least I thought so. I found a tiny apartment above a garage in Laguna Beach, a block from the ocean. The office in Newport Beach was even sleeker than the one in LA. My smiling face greeted me from the wall in every exam room. After work, I'd head to the bar at Fig & Olive. It wasn't a pickup scene like some of the other hot restaurants on Coast Highway, but there were plenty of single guys at the bar.

Including Roger Jones. At first I didn't know if he was my type. I never fell for any of the frat guys at college, never dated guys my own age. I'd had some nights out with older men I'd met around town and even the ex-husband of one of my beauty clients. But Roger was different. More confident. He had a big smile and a strong handshake, a full head of silver-gray hair, and an impeccably fitting business suit. He sat down at the bar beside me and introduced himself.

I didn't feel anything, not right away, but Roger always told people he knew I was the one. I guess, actually, the second one. When I told him my dream was to be an interior designer, he hired me to decorate the oceanfront mansion he was building in Oceanside. On the spot. I told him I wasn't qualified, didn't even have my license, but he told me not to worry, that we'd do it together. He had all the contacts I needed. And that was true.

In one night, that night, I landed the biggest and only interior design project of my career and met my husband. I didn't know I would be designing a home I'd live in one day. Fate is funny that way.

You find what you think is your dream, and eventually it becomes your nightmare.

I remember the first day we met at the construction site. Roger's dream home would rest on two acres of oceanfront land. I'd never seen a lot like this. The house, when I first saw it that day, consisted of a foundation and a few steel beams. But I could imagine it all. I thought back to the days when my mom would find me drawing floor plans on big white sheets of paper, cutting up her *Southern Living* magazines and making design boards. This was a bigger scale, but I knew I could do it.

"So this is where the kitchen will be," Roger explained, taking my hand to pull me up to the foundation level. "Would love your ideas for the space."

I know, seems silly I wore heels to a construction site, but I love heels. I felt sexy, and competent. Roger hung on every word. "I'd love to see this entire kitchen in automotive white, all of it. It will read like a sleek cloud, a white space that gives all attention to the ocean. But of course, all the state-of-the-art appliances. Can you see it?"

Roger had grinned. "All of it. Very clearly."

By the end of the tour, we had a handshake agreement. By the end of the week, we were a couple. On our first official date, Roger slid a blue velvet box across the table during dessert.

"What's this?" I'd asked. My cheeks were flushed because of the expensive red wine we were drinking. Now they felt even hotter. My heart pounded in my chest. It had been only a week.

"Just a little something. I like to spoil my women," Roger said.

Inside the box was an emerald-cut ruby, set on a thin platinum band. I'd never held anything so spectacular in my hand before. "Oh my goodness."

As I slipped it onto my right ring finger and looked at my hand in wonder, Roger said, "This is just the beginning of a wonderful relationship. I know it."

And right then, sitting across the table from him, I knew it, too. I'd never known anyone as confident, charismatic, intense—and rich—as Roger. It was a whole new level. And it was what I deserved, what I thought I wanted.

I was too young, too impressed to see the truth. Roger was the opposite of my mom, the opposite of everything I grew up with in small-town Florida. He was self-confident, sophisticated, sleek.

Roger loved me because I looked good by his side. At first, he treasured me, opened doors for me, and purchased extravagant jewelry for me. No boyfriend had ever bought me so much as a flower bouquet before. I made him feel younger. And I loved him because he represented the stability and luxury my single mom and I never could have imagined. I know the old adage about finding a guy like my dad. That's not it, not really. I never knew my dad. He died in an accident before I was born, killed by a drunk driver while coming home from the night shift at the factory in town.

I walk into the kitchen, my head filled with memories instead of fear for the moment. My mom never recovered from losing my dad. He was her high school boyfriend. She'd never been with anyone else. After he died, food was her only comfort. Food, and telling me stories about the father I'd never know. Stories that I realized when I grew older were all lies.

My mom would say her silent Kaddish prayer for my dad's soul as I climbed into bed, and I'd fall into a dreamy sleep, feeling the love of two people through my mom. Much as she tried, though, can that ever be enough? As I grew older, I asked my mom if she'd remarry. I asked my mom if she wanted more in life. All I remember is her being at home all the time when she wasn't working at the bottling plant. She never had a hobby, unless you count coming up with a new romanticized adventure for my deceased father. By the time I was in high school, she was virtually a shut-in. An obese, hovering shut-in. I was suffocating.

"No, you are all I need." She'd smile.

The feeling wasn't mutual. I was ashamed of her, embarrassed by our poverty. I'd been a natural at school with plenty of time to study due to a nonexistent social life. With a full scholarship to a California college, I found my escape. I would re-create myself, literally, and leave my smothered, suffocating childhood far behind. When I found the part-time receptionist job at Dr. Profit's medical spa in Beverly Hills, I jumped at the chance. I didn't know he hired me because I would be a good guinea pig, but when I found out, I was a happy coconspirator.

I glance at the mirror on the kitchen wall and think about all the surgeries I underwent with Dr. Profit. When I first started working for him, my sophomore year in college, it was the basics: Botox and some filler. But when he pulled me aside and explained how he could open up my eyes with a brow lift and sculpt my nose, chisel it, I agreed. After those surgeries came the boob job, fat implants at my temple and my cheeks, and lip fillers—whatever latest and greatest new products Dr. Profit wanted to try, I was the model. His most stunning before and after. I was turning into the cover model on my mom's favorite magazines. I was *Vogue*, *Glamour*, and *Vanity Fair* worthy. The little girl with the big nose and forehead was becoming beautiful. Valuable. Men actually began to ask me out by senior year in college. And my shyness was slowly replaced by a confidence I'd never felt; a self-esteem that had never taken hold began to bloom. That's what a new face and body can do for you. At least for a while.

By the time Roger came along, I was an entirely different-looking person from the girl who had moved to California. And I was ready for love. I finally believed I deserved to be loved. Roger represented a life full of possibilities and wide-open spaces. And love. I thought we were in love.

But he just wanted a companion, the notion of a wife. The routine of a beautiful young wife, waiting at home, sparkling and comforting. Roger always would be too busy with work to care about me deeply. I'm still not certain he knows what love is. I didn't know that about him when we met. He hid his childhood stories from me as much as I hid my upbringing from him.

I wipe away another errant tear and focus on unpacking. I unwrap another cookbook. This one is vegan, always more aspirational than useful. It looked good on the shelf. It wasn't realistic to plan meatless meals with Roger around. He'd scoffed at my one attempt, said it was ridiculous. Maybe now I can try it.

Max sticks his head in the kitchen. "Julie, we're just about finished."

I swallow. It's fine. I'll be fine. Jess and I will be OK alone.

"You guys have been great," I tell him. "And thanks for the extra protection."

"You want my friend's help, he's at this number." Max hands me a note. "Didn't like the look on that old guy's face."

"Thank you," I say. I take the note from his hand, tuck it into my back pocket. "I'll be fine. I have an alarm system."

Max shakes his head. "Those don't do anything if someone is determined to get in, just saying. But suit yourself."

The hair on the back of my neck tingles as I watch him walk out the door. I squeeze my eyes together. I am determined to start over without fear.

Jess and I will find a real connection cooking together in this wonderful, bright kitchen. I can see it now. As I'm picturing the mother-daughter scene, I realize I haven't heard a peep from Jess. I tell myself she's up in her new bedroom, likely unpacking her stuff. Making this house her home.

I tell myself this, but I know my daughter. I'd better go check on her, just to be sure.

CHAPTER 8

SANDI

It's odd ringing the doorbell here, at the place I've called home since Doug and I were married sixteen years ago. The home I put my all into. I fell in love with this house during our first date, the three of us after Sunday school: Tommy, Doug, and I. We'd gone to the diner around the corner. Tommy had a grilled cheese and french fries. He had a big grin on his face the entire meal, and so did his dad.

I felt the connection between Doug and me during lunch, and I knew it was more than a common love of his son.

We'd finished lunch and were walking through the parking lot when Tommy said, "Do you want to come to my house?"

Doug said, "Son, I'm sure Miss Sandi has a lot to do this fine Sunday afternoon."

"Please!" Tommy squeezed my hand, and I looked down into his sweet blue eyes. "I want to show you my climbing tree!"

How could I not go see his climbing tree? "I'd love to, if it's all right with your dad?"

"Of course," Doug said. "Why don't you ride over with us, and I'll run you back to the church for service tonight. Sound good?"

I slid into the front seat of Doug's car, Tommy in the back, and thought, *Yes, this sounds good.* "Very good."

The rest of the afternoon was full of laughter and iced tea. Tommy showed me his big climbing tree—one we'd eventually remove to build the carriage house—and then took me on a tour of the house. Doug followed behind, unusually quiet.

"This was my mommy and daddy's room, but then she left us, and now we're alone," Tommy said, pointing to a closed door. "This is my room."

Doug had dropped his head at his son's candor. "Sorry, it just doesn't get any easier on us. He needs a mom and a dad, he does." My heart had flipped over in a somersault when Doug touched my shoulder. "A woman of God. A caring, beautiful soul like you."

Our courtship moved quickly from that day forward. My parents were thrilled that the assistant pastor of our church had plucked me from the flock. I had the attention of the ultimate man of God. And I gained a bonus child in Tom. I'd already fallen in love with him in Sunday school. I knew I could be the mom he never had. I knew we could become a real family, the three of us, with God's help.

I look up at the house now and remember all the hope and promise. I remember slipping into my mom's wedding dress, the simple wedding ceremony we had here, in the backyard, under Tom's climbing tree. This is my home. I know every creak in the stairs, every divot in the grass in the backyard. I know the names of each flower I've planted in the garden. I know when the hummingbird feeders need to be filled. They're empty now. I should tell the new woman of the house.

I swallow and force a smile onto my face.

Don't get me wrong. I'm happy to be in our new house, even if it does feel a bit like living in the country. I guess it is living in the country. On the plus side, we're blessed because the children have a real yard to play in, a creek at the edge of our property to make a mess in. They're glad about that. So all in all, everything is as it should be. Once I get to know some people at the new church, I'll have friends again. I tell myself to be thankful for my blessings, remind myself of everything I have. I say a prayer and ask for forgiveness.

I wipe the tears from my eyes and slip on my glasses. I see the new owner of my home through the diamond of glass in the front door. She's smiling, carrying a cookbook. I didn't peg her as a cook, but I'm glad to see she'll put my kitchen to good use. I love the gas stove. It was the fanciest appliance I'd ever seen, ever cooked on. The stovetop at the new house is electric. It's just not the same.

The door flies open, and the new woman of the house shakes my hand.

"Hey! Sorry for the mess. As you know, we're just moving in today. Did you forget something?" Julie asks. She's so warm and likable. And even though I know she left her husband, and her life couldn't be perfect, she makes it look like it is, like it could be.

Sometimes I wish I could be as brave as she is, and God knows I've made plans that I failed to implement. Maybe someday I will. But I know I could never be as beautiful as she is. There is no "someday" about that.

"Oh, no, I'm just here to drop off these keys I found after our move. Apologies for not giving them to you sooner. I've never done a move like this before, and well, my checklist got lost during our move. Apologies. Here." I hold up the key chain. It's ugly, I see that now, with a pink cross made by one of the girls in my fourth grade Sunday school class. It's not the kind of key chain a woman like Julie would ever use.

"I understand. It's been a busy time for me, too. Would you like to come in?" She takes the key chain and slides it into her pocket. The plastic cross dangles from her designer jeans.

Before I can answer, I hear Julie catch her breath. She's looking past me, out to the street.

"He can't do this," Julie says with hands on her hips. Her face is angry.

I turn around but don't notice anyone on the street except the team of movers and the huge white van. It's twice the size of the one we had when the four of us left town for our "fresh start."

"Are you OK?" I ask.

Julie blinks and meets my stare. "Yes. Fine. I just need to make a phone call. Can you excuse me, please?"

"Of course," I say as she walks back into the house and leaves me standing on the front porch alone. Memories flood my heart. Of bringing my first baby home from the hospital, climbing these steps while carefully holding him in my arms. Tom's face when he opened the front door, stared down at his new baby brother. And then, two years later, another baby boy and the same wary welcome from Tom.

The red plastic feeders are empty and beside me, somewhere in the bushes, a hungry hummingbird clicks with dismay. I want to call after her, to Julie, to tell her to feed the hummingbirds, but I don't. It's not my place. Literally. Not anymore.

I take my time walking down the porch stairs. The hydrangeas I planted years ago are in full bloom, lilac, the promise of redemption, the hope of the next life, where everything will be perfect for me and all who believe. I believe that. I duck my head and say a prayer: "Lord, please give me the strength to carry on. To be the wife and mother my family needs. To make our new house a home. And watch over Tom. Help him to become a good man, help him see the light and feel the love I have for him still. Forgive Doug, oh Father, for his sins at our last congregation. Help him walk the narrow, righteous path for his sake, and for his sons'. Help him to be the pastor his new church expects. That his family deserves. I ask all of this in Jesus's name. Amen."

My phone buzzes in my pocket. It's Doug. He asks, "Where the hell are you?"

My shoulders dart to my ears. "I told you, I had to drop off the keys. I forgot to give the new owner the keys."

"Of course you did," he says. His voice is a growl, an angry dog. "You need to get back home. My car won't start. I need yours."

"I'm heading back now. What happened to it?" I ask.

"Tow-truck driver said someone flooded my gas tank," Doug says. "Shithead kids."

"I don't understand," I say. "Why would kids do that?"

"Because we're new, that's why. Fried my engine. I'll need to get a loaner." Doug exhales. "Just get back home."

Ever since we moved to the house in Temecula, strange things have been happening. The flowers I planted in the front garden were trampled, the circuit breaker overloaded, and now this. It's a new subdivision. Everyone there is new. A chill runs down my spine. It must be someone from the church who hates Doug and wants revenge. What else will they do?

"I'm coming. It's Friday. It will take a bit, what with the beach traffic," I say. Doug hangs up on me without another word.

I straighten my back and roll my shoulders down. I think of my boys, home with a furious father. There is much to do still, for my family. Much prayer needed in this life. One day, once the kids are raised, there will be plenty of time for me. There will be an eternity in Heaven. I was raised in the church, and I believe what the scriptures tell us. Literally. A mother's role is to show love and discipline, to guide gently, to comfort. A wife's role is to be the helpmate. And to forgive. But only up to a certain point. I was raised to believe divorce is a sin. I think of Julie.

Sometimes you must sin and ask for forgiveness later. Sometimes you don't have any other choice.

I reach the sidewalk and look back at the front door, at the flowers, at my past. I think about Tom in the carriage house and the hairs on the back of my neck tingle with fear. I imagine him punching a wall. I think about the crowd he's hanging out with, the lost men in black, drinking and smoking and looking angry. I saw him one night when I stopped by Cody's, the seedy bar where he works. It was a month or so ago. I was there to ask him to dinner, to try to get him to talk to me, to open up. He'd laughed at me and told me to go home. That I wasn't welcome in his life. Not anymore.

"Tom, what did I do to lose you? I love you," I'd said as he walked me out into the night.

"You had your real boys, remember?" I hate that he uses the words Doug uses to describe our younger sons. I hate that Doug makes Tom think he's less than them, that somehow it's Tom's fault his mother left them. I've spent my time as his mom trying to overcome that feeling. To stop the need that Tom has to put others down because he feels poorly about himself. It's a hole in his heart, and I'm afraid it's getting bigger and darker every day.

"You made your choice, Sandi. You'll do best to stick to it."

"What did you say?" a man asks as I stare blankly at the house.

"Nothing. Sorry." I must have spoken out loud. My heart thumps in my chest. The man is just one of Julie's fancy movers, that's all, not one of Tom's new friends, thank God.

"OK then. We're out of here." He gives me a look before he hurries up the ramp inside the huge truck.

I need to get back to help Doug with his car, but I know I should visit Tom. Truth is, I don't want to visit Tom, but I should. What sort of mother would I be if I didn't check on him? I think of his small hand in mine during Sunday school. I think of his smile when I'd make him his favorite grilled cheese. I remember his constant struggle between the dark and light. He always wanted to believe my love, I know he did, but his birth mom's abandonment was always there, too, casting a shadow of doubt and desertion he couldn't escape.

I think of the man Tom has become. This is his last weekend staying in the carriage house. I don't know where he'll go from here. He has a part-time job at a bar, and no college degree. He can't afford to take care of himself. When he dropped out of community college, I begged him to reconsider. But Tom is stubborn, like his dad.

And when I tried to convince Doug to let him live with us now, in our new place in Temecula, he wouldn't have it. I asked Doug if there was a job, any job, at the new congregation for Tom.

Doug laughed in my face. "We don't want or need him here, Sandi. Focus on Davis and Danny. Let's raise them right. Tom's a lost cause."

Maybe. But I was raised to believe in the goodness of people, and I didn't want to give up. Even though I know it's not good for the younger boys to be exposed to Tom's anger, to his hatred for other people, to his hints of violence. No, the boys don't need his type around them. But it's still hard to leave him behind. Even knowing all he is, all he's become.

"The boy is a man. He's twenty-three years old, and he needs to make his own way. Period," Doug said the last time I asked. "I've prayed on this and made my decision. Don't push me on this, Sandi. He's not even your son. End of discussion."

He knows how that hurts me. He knows I did my best to raise Tom right, but he was already damaged when I came along. He'd already learned too many things I never would've taught him about making fun of those less fortunate, about feeling superior, about hate. He'd already begun teaching those things to my boys, teaching them how to play violent video games, showing them things online that should never be seen. Telling them that immigrants were the reason he couldn't get a job, that stupid girls got all the breaks in community college. That women like me should be seen, in the kitchen, and not heard.

I'd caught them, the last time, before we moved. Tom had both of them over to the carriage house, and they were playing some horrible video game. I knocked and walked in without an invitation. Yanked the console from the wall and ordered the little boys to the main house.

Tom had stood up and rushed me, coming face-to-face with me as I held the power cord. "Don't do that again, Sandi. Don't."

I hadn't backed down. "I love you, but this is wrong. You know it."

Tom smirked, flexed his muscles, making his tattoos bulge, and said, "Sandi, get back in the kitchen where you belong." He yanked the cord from my hand and started laughing.

I'd left in tears, hurrying to discipline my sons, to tell them again about the dangers lurking in those games, in that carriage house.

But I love Tom, I do. I must. I'm his mother. It is my duty. It's what God wants, what He demands.

I look up at my house, her house, and realize I shouldn't disturb Julie again, but I don't think she'll mind if I visit Tom. I hope not. I walk quietly down the driveway to the back, careful not to make too much noise on the gravel. I find Tom standing in the backyard, arms crossed in front of him, staring at me. I swallow.

"Hey, how's it going?" The smile on my face stretches from ear to ear, but it doesn't reach my heart. Or his.

"Guess how it's going. I have exactly two days before I'm homeless." Tom kicks the ground with the toe of his black boot. He wears a black T-shirt, ripped black jeans, and a scowl. Everything about him is dark, cloudy, fitting of the rainstorm earlier today. But now that it's sunny, he looks out of place like a bruise.

I step closer, but before I can give him a hug, he steps back. My mind flashes to when we first met, how he craved my attention, my hugs, my cooking. But I wasn't enough, never could be enough.

"Tom? Please? Can we talk?" I look behind him to my favorite maple tree, a small ornamental one I planted five years ago. Beneath, a bird lies on its back, wings at awkward angles, dead. I take a deep breath. My God, poor creature.

"Look, I know you did your best. OK? So thanks. But I don't need you trying to mother me right now, I don't."

"Can we pray together?"

"No. I need you to go. I have some friends coming over. You know, the guys I went to the desert with. They're great guys, really great."

Tom kicks the toe of his boot on the front step of the carriage house. He knows how I feel about these so-called friends. He's egging me on.

I saw them at the bar, and I noticed a few of them hanging around before we moved. The men are tattooed, and their eyes see you as a challenge, a threat. When I had stepped out on the back porch of the main house, Tom had told me to go back inside. "Now, Sandi!" he'd yelled, trying to impress them. None of them smiled. All of them smelled of danger and sin.

I will plead with him one last time. "Come on, Tom. They look like they're up to no good, I can feel it. They're all filled with anger. You're better than them, you are." I feel my hands come together in prayer. It's a reflex.

"You know what? I'm not better than them. I'm one of them. They know the way the world should be, and they have a plan to set it straight. It's good for you, too, if you could open your stupid mind to it. Anger fuels change. It's powerful when used correctly. They're teaching me how to use mine," Tom says. His eyes shine with righteousness; his words darken the world.

"You're wrong, son. They're wrong. The world is good. People are good. Love fuels the world, not hate," I manage.

"You're pathetic. And I said no prayers." Tom pushes my hands apart with a level of violence I have never felt from him. I step back. I hold my hands up in surrender. What have they done to him? What has he become?

"OK, I'm going. I don't want to fight with you, I'm just trying to help you. You need to be out of here by Sunday at noon, do you understand? I'm so sorry. Please, if I can help you, call me. I'll be praying for you, son."

"Right, sure thing. That's going to help a lot. You folks have been great, all of you. So glad I don't need you anymore. And *Mom*?" Tom says in a voice filled with anger and disgust. "Tell *Dad* thanks again. For leaving me homeless. I really appreciate it. I'll look forward to turning my anger into something more tangible soon."

He's terrifying me. What is he threatening? "You understand we had to sell this house. Do you think I wanted this to happen? Do you?" I say with water spilling from my eyes. "I loved this home. And I love you. But things have changed. Your dad changed jobs. We had to move. It wasn't a choice."

"Such a sad story, Sandi. Boo-hoo. You're weak. Go home to your little boys, your real boys. But be careful. Because when they grow up, they're going to be just like me. The pastor will make sure of it." Tom turns, walks inside the carriage house, and slams the door.

I'm alone on the lawn shaking. I feel dampness soaking through my shoes. The grass has been overwatered, especially after the rain. I should tell Julie to have the sprinklers checked.

I should tell Julie I don't think Tom is going to leave. But it's not my place. I really shouldn't be here. My father, the deacon of our church and a former head pastor, would not appreciate my behavior. I am to listen to my husband. His word is the rule. Doug would never have allowed me to come here, to talk to Tom. As far as he's concerned, his oldest son is a lost cause. Dead to him. This visit was a mistake. I look up toward Tom's old bedroom, the big room that Davis inherited when Tom moved to the carriage house. I see a young woman's face. We meet eyes. That would be Julie's daughter. I lift my hand to wave, but she disappears.

She's probably wondering who the pathetic woman standing in the backyard is. I hurry down the driveway, and I'm about to cross the street when I hear someone call my name. I turn and see Julie on the front porch.

She yells, "I'm sorry I couldn't visit. Maybe some other time?"

We both know there won't be another time. Look at us. We aren't friends. We have nothing in common except the house.

"Sure." I wave and force a smile. She ducks back inside before I even start to walk across the street.

That's the thing with rich people, I've noticed. They act all nice and seem normal when they need something from you. But really, we're discardable, forgettable once they get what they want. And she got it. She has my home.

Stop coveting what others have, my dad's voice booms in my head.

Maybe Julie will love every room of the home like you did, I tell myself, not quite believing it but hoping it is so. Doug told me to stop thinking about the old house, that we're in the country with fresh air now and I should be grateful. He told me we'd work all the bugs out in our new place, but bugs aren't the problem. Something else is going on out there, I told him. The morning after our power went out, the electrician agreed. He told us someone had cut the main power line to the house. That's not a bug—it's purposeful.

"For God's sake, let the past go, Sandi, and stop bringing it up. Are you trying to make me mad? This is a fine place. A couple of bored teenagers are messing with us because we're new to the street," Doug yelled on the morning I discovered my hydrangeas had been stomped to death. "It is what it is. Do you think I wanted this?"

As if he were the victim. As if he is the only one who has suffered because of his choices.

I'd dropped my head and wiped my eyes, lifting another decapitated flower from the destroyed garden bed and dropping it into the trash bag. "No. I have never tried to make you mad." And that was the truth.

Now I take one last look at my home on Cherry Hill Lane. It is perfect in my eyes. I hand painted every cabinet in the kitchen. I retiled the powder room just a month ago. I slide into the driver's seat and take one more look at my front garden. Does she even know how to take care of my plants? Has she ever even gotten her hands dirty in God's green earth? What about the hummingbirds?

She's going to change everything. I know she is.

I say a quick prayer to apologize for my sins before driving away. I decide I will stop in at our old church just to ground myself, to help me let go. Doug doesn't need to go anywhere right now. He can wait for me for once. This tiny act of defiance brings a small smile to my face as I pull into the mostly empty parking lot, amazed as always by the size of the church. Five thousand worshippers fill the sanctuary every Sunday morning. It's magnificent. When I met Doug, he was assistant pastor of this place. Two years after we married, he was appointed pastor. It was everything I'd dreamed of, being first lady of the largest Christian church in the county. It was an honor. It was all grace. When the rumors first started about Doug and the divorcées, I didn't pay much attention. It was only after an entire group of them complained to the diocese that I had to get my head out of the sand. I had to face the disgrace, to fall with him.

My faith in God never wavered, of course, even as everything I believed Doug to be crumbled in the wake of the scandal. But it's over. He has been punished, sent to the country congregation. Despite Doug's fall from grace, I have always been welcomed here with open arms. I am a victim, too, they say, although I am not sure what to call myself. A survivor? A fool?

Since today is a Friday, I walk into the small prayer chapel and find myself alone. I hurry to the first pew and take a seat.

"God, please grant me the serenity to accept the things I cannot change, courage to change the things I can. And the wisdom to see the difference. Help me as I try to build a new life in the country for my boys. Help me protect them from the evil that has swept Tom away. Please save him from the darkness in their ways. Help him to turn his life around before it is too late. Amen."

I stand and walk out slowly. I miss this chapel. I miss this congregation.

"Mrs. Dean, is that you?" It's the new head pastor, the man who has taken Doug's place here.

"Hello, Pastor Lovett," I say, smiling at the man. It isn't his fault what happened here. Not one part of it. It's all on Doug. It's all because he couldn't resist the temptation sitting in front of him in his life-af-ter-divorce ministry. Charlene Melon was his downfall. Or was he hers? Still, my face is the one bright red with shame.

"It's so good to see you here. Is there anything I can be of help with? The women's leadership team has missed your voice and your gentle leadership. We all miss you." Pastor Lovett has kind blue eyes, a wrinkled brow, and several chins. I believe he is the perfect fit for the congregation: the unattractive anti-Doug. It's just what they needed. While Doug is smooth and charismatic, handsome and slick, Pastor Lovett is soft-spoken and meticulous. I've spent years watching Doug's energy ping through the crowd, his sermons creating a frenzy of faith and devotion almost as if he were a king or a rock star. Pastor Lovett is a shepherd. No one will ever accuse him of being a false idol, of having the spotlight on himself and not the church. And I have no doubt he treats everyone equally—men, women, white, Black, brown, gay.

"Oh, I was just in the neighborhood and thought I'd drop in for some spiritual uplifting. I love this chapel." I take a moment to breathe, to take in the stained-glass windows, the sun pouring in, the red carpet, Jesus on the cross. The main sanctuary is modern, state of the art, gigan-tic. This room feels like church. It feels like God is here.

"I love it, too," Pastor Lovett says. "How's the new congregation?"

We walk toward the door. I don't want to talk about where we are now, the narrowness of my husband's views that will infect his new flock like a disease. I want to focus on my fond memories of here. "Please tell the women's group hello from me. I miss my friends."

"There is nothing but love for you here, Mrs. Dean. You are wel-come anytime. And the boys, too." Pastor Lovett holds open the door to the parking lot, and I step through.

He doesn't need to add that Doug is not welcome here ever again. We both know that, and we both know why.

And because everyone else knows of his multiple infidelities—of the shame he has brought on our family, to our marriage—because of that, because of my husband, I will not be back to this church again. The weight of it hurts my heart. It's as if the disgrace he should feel has transferred to me, sticking to me like superglue. I can't clean it off.

"Bless you, Mrs. Dean. The Lord knows your pious heart and will send His peace," the pastor says as we walk outside into the parking lot.

I nod goodbye to the new pastor of Oceanside Christian and open the door to my car. All I can do is hope He sends peace soon. And get home to my boys. They are my only chance for a brighter future. But given the way Tom and Doug have turned out, it may be a false hope.

That's why I have a plan. I don't have any other choice. I just hope I can survive long enough to implement it. Dread forces tears from my eyes, clouding my vision like fog, making it hard to drive. I pull over into a gas station, knowing every minute I am not home I'm testing Doug's patience and fueling his temper.

CHAPTER 9

JESS

This house is weirder than I thought.

I mean, first there's a lady standing on the grass out back looking like she's from the olden days wearing a long flowery dress and a cardigan sweater? I mean, really? Who dresses like that? Likely by now her shoes are soaking wet. The whole backyard is like a big puddle of water. I hope she has more than one pair of shoes. She really looks like she belongs on a covered wagon straight out of the pioneer days.

But she's not on a wagon; she's awkwardly lurking in our backyard. And then just a few minutes ago Tom comes out and the two of them stand there like oil and water. He's all dark and edgy and sexy, and she's just not. He even hit something out of her hands. I'm not sure what she was holding, but he could have hurt her. She looks so thin, like a saltine cracker. I thought he might have crumbled her a little, but she seemed fine when she walked away. She even glanced up to my window and tried to wave to me, but I didn't want any part of that. Weird stuff happens here. I'm sure it's haunted. One hundred percent.

I look around my lame new bedroom. I've hung almost all my posters and stuff from my old room. I mean, they have carried up my furniture, including my bed. I guess it feels OK in here. It's fine. It's not like I'm staying, but I need Mom to think I am. She's in this whole rah-rah-girls team spirit. Julie and Jess against the world—as if. She's so excited to bond, and make food together. It's weird. I don't want to hurt her feelings too much, so I'm playing along a little bit. Hanging up posters was the least I could do. And now, I'm done.

The good news is Bonnie wants me to move in with her and her family. Just until the school year is over. I think it makes perfect sense, but I bet Mom won't like it. I just need to tell her how I'm unsettled here, how my life is in Oceanside, not here. I know she'll say we're still in Oceanside, but come on. This is not at all like my Oceanside.

I will tell Mom how she's ruining everything with this stupid house. Why couldn't she have done what all other divorced people do and get a condo at The Point? I mean, that's where everybody's dads go when they get the new girlfriend. Is that what my dad has done? I really can't see him having time for that, what with me, my mom, and work. In the opposite order. Truth be told, he really just likes work the best.

Still, I know usually it is the dad who leaves, not the mom. The moms keep the house and the kids, and the dads keep the cars, most of the money, and their mistresses. Then they marry their mistresses and make more kids to leave. That's how it usually works. But not with my mom. No. She has to uproot both of us and leave Roger with the big house and all our friends in the real Oceanside. How did she even find this part of town?

I don't really blame her. Dad's super intense, super workaholic. Super untrustworthy. He always says he's going to change, but then he'll miss Mom's birthday party for a business meeting. Or he'll say he'll be at my stupid year-end volleyball tournament, but he forgets. I get it, I guess, that she wants to have a "real relationship," as she calls it. She's tired of "being alone and married."

"It's all been fake. My whole life with your dad. Look at me. Look at all this. We're running out of time, Jess. I need you to understand the real world. I need to be in it again to find myself," she said when she told me we were leaving. I don't get it, but what I do know is I'm her kid. And since there is more than just herself to consider, couldn't she have waited until the end of my senior year? I'll be away at school in the fall, and she could move to any fixer-upper she wanted in the whole city—heck, the whole state. But no, she picks today to make a stand. It's so frustrating. So selfish.

So she made her choice. I hope she'll honor my choice, because I'm out of here.

My phone lights up. It's a text from Bonnie: Get over here. I need help setting up.

Bonnie's party tonight will be epic. They always are. She pulls them together quickly, so only the cool kids know about it, and the parents don't. Classic Bonnie. Everybody who is anybody is coming. Bonnie promises even Seth will be there. He's already at USC, a freshman now, like I will be next fall. He's so hot. I don't know why he'd come back for a high school party, but if he does, oh my gosh. I must admit I stalk his socials, and he just keeps looking better and better. He's way above my dating grade, but a girl can dream. I'm pretty sure most all my hook-ups to date have been because I have the biggest house in Oceanside, a private beach, and permissive, nonpresent parents. I'm cute, but I'm no Bonnie. Bonnie has the looks, an American Express platinum card, and the house situation. She's a triple threat, and my bestie.

I text: K. Need to talk to mom.

She texts: OMG you were doing that hours ago.

I text: Sigh. She's going to be mad.

She texts: But if you don't get back here you're going to die.

I text: True. I hate it here.

She texts: Go tell her now and get over here.

I text: You sure it's ok with your parents?

She texts: Yes. They love you. They don't care at all.

I don't really believe that. I think they love Bonnie so much they'd do anything for her, including, it seems, taking in a refugee from Cherry Hill Lane, wherever the heck we are.

I text: Sweet!

There's a knock on my door. "Come in."

It's Mom. I take a deep breath and smile.

"How is the favorite daughter doing?" she asks. My mom and dad always say I'm their favorite, obviously since I'm the only. I don't answer. I'm not in the mood for this. "I love what you've done to the place," she says, looking at all my crap on the walls. She's lying. She is a firm believer in no crap on the walls, in simple elegance. I don't agree.

"Thanks." I bite my lip. "So, Mom, I'm going to a party at Bonnie's tonight."

"Yes, you mentioned that. Take an Uber, the black kind." Mom doesn't trust regular Uber drivers. She thinks they will all abduct me and drive me to a remote field and kill me. Or worse.

"I will. But, Mom, I want to stay there. At Bonnie's."

"Sure, you can have a sleepover, but be back early in the morning; we have so much to unpack. This is going to be great, don't you think? Just the girls, hanging out, setting up our home. Do you remember when we used to do the weekly sleepovers in the orchid room?" She walks to my window and takes in my backyard view. I wonder if the wagon lady is still lurking around. I wonder if Mom thinks that lady is "great," the perfect addition to our new life.

We only did a sleepover once in the orchid room, as far as I can remember. My mom romanticizes our times together now because she didn't prioritize them then. I get it. She was busy lunching. But still, my mom is really nice. I just don't want to live here, even with her new laser-like focus on our relationship. Maybe especially because of the new focus. She's freaking me out.

I say, "I don't have that much to do around here. I mean, I'm almost unpacked. Well, at least the room stuff. I'm keeping my clothes boxed up until I get them to Bonnie's." I need to just spit it out. "I'm going to live at Bonnie's, just for the year. And then I'll be off to college. This way you can enjoy your new home, get going on all of those hobbies you've been neglecting. We can still hang out, but you won't have to worry about me!"

Mom turns from the window. "No. You will not live like an orphan at Bonnie's. You will live here, at your home. This is the whole point. I am worried about you, about who you've become."

I exhale. She's so dramatic. "What are you even talking about? Who I've become is a high school senior who can't wait to get to college, a good college that I studied my butt off to get into. You should be proud of me, not doing whatever this is."

"It's an intervention. I think we need to reconnect, to get grounded," Mom says. She's truly losing it.

"Mom, my home is in Oceanside, the real part. Not wherever this is. I am miserable here, and I always will be. It's nothing personal. It's for my sanity. You made your choice to leave Dad. Let me make mine."

"To leave me?" Her voice cracks with emotion, and tears flow down her cheeks.

Damn it. I knew this wouldn't be good. Bonnie's confidence rings in my head. "Besides, you need your space. Dad's put you through a lot. Remember, you need to find yourself again?"

Mom walks to me and wraps me in a hug. "This is a new beginning. A new home that I'm going to fill with love. This is our last year together before you do leave me for college. I can't wait to spend as much time as possible with you. Have fun tonight. I'll see you in the morning."

She's acting like that's it. Like she's won. She hasn't. I'm old enough to take control of my life. "I'm moving to Bonnie's house."

She drops her arms to her sides and takes a step away from me. "No, you aren't." She walks out of my bedroom and turns at the door. "Don't bring it up again."

"Or what?" I raise my voice. I wonder if sexy Tom out back can hear me.

"Just don't. Or you'll be sorry." She yanks the door closed behind her and leaves me in shock. She's never told me no, not that I can remember. Ever. Whatever I wanted I got, and more. It's too late to start acting like she's in charge, like she cares this much. I mean, come on.

My mom just threatened me. She's never done that before. I'm not certain what she's threatening, but I don't care. I'm going to move to Bonnie's, tonight. I am.

If she tries to get in my way, I'll get Dad involved. I'm sure he would be happy to team up with me against her. Dad's busy, but I know how to sweet-talk him. And he's always trying to get me on his side when they fight like this. I remember the last time she tried to leave, how he showed me the pictures of the Maui house first before he whisked Mom away for their "long-deserved" month vacation to reconnect. The nanny and I found it amusing that I hadn't been invited. Amusing, but typical.

I walk into my lame bathroom and stare into the mirror, trying not to let the hurt back in from those days. I'm like a pawn in their weird relationship game. They pull me out when I'm needed, but most of the time, I'm left to my own devices. I touch the tip of my nose with my finger. My mom's real nose, it has to be. I like the way I look. I'm unique. It's cool. I wonder if someday my mom will regret all the surgeries she's had, all the toxins she's put into her body for the sake of some weird idea of beauty. Who knows? It's not my path, that's for sure.

From my bedroom I hear a man laughing, and it's coming from the backyard. I walk to the window overlooking the yard and see a handful of guys, all dressed in black, milling around. Tom's in the center of the group, laughing, patting people on the back, welcoming them. My mom isn't going to like this, not one bit. They're tearing up the grass with their boots, for one thing. And I don't think Tom is supposed to be hosting parties. I think he's supposed to be getting out of here. Interesting, Tom. Bold and interesting.

Who are they? I wonder. As I stare down at the small crowd, Tom steps out of the center of the group and looks up. Our eyes meet. He waves. I return the gesture and watch as all the men below start high-fiving Tom. My stomach flips.

Who do they think I am? What's he telling them? This is creepy. And, I have to admit, a little exciting. Still, I need to get out of here.

I pull out my phone and request an Uber. Black car. I look around the mess of my room and decide I'll just take enough for the weekend at Bonnie's. I can always come back and get the rest of my things later once Mom has calmed down. I find one of the empty packing boxes and toss my clothes and makeup into it. I grab my backpack, my computer, and I'm set. Really, I can live quite simply. Or I can just buy all new things. If I tell Dad I'm on his side, I'll have unlimited resources. Maybe I'll play that card, maybe not. Maybe I'll just move back in with him. Who knows? The world is full of choices, all of them better than here. Except for Tom. He's a good part of here. I think about going out back and flirting with him in front of his friends. The thought makes my heart race. But I'm late. For now, I just need to get to Bonnie's house. I'll see Tom later.

I want to get back to a normal street, in the normal part of the suburbs, where I belong. The Oceanside I know has an *ocean* out the window, not rows of houses as far as you can see. I mean, this house has neighbors everywhere. I could throw a rock and hit the house next door. It's claustrophobic. I can't see any neighbors from my real house. We don't really have any. I like it that way. I didn't know how much space we had until now. All I can see from the bedroom window out of my real house are trees and grass and the ocean. I've got to get out of here.

I hurry down the stairs, ignoring the squeaks and groans of each step. I hope my mom isn't lurking around trying to stop me. I don't see her. Before I go out the front door, I glance down the hall toward the backyard. All the guys are filing into Tom's tiny cottage. I don't know how they'll all fit in there, but I don't care. Maybe all the people here are used to being squished together. Maybe they like it.

Even if he is cute, that's weird. People should want space, distance. This is all strange.

I dash out the front door without looking back.

"Jessica?" the driver says as I yank open the door to the black SUV.

"Jess," I mumble. I hate my full name. I glance at the driver ID taped to the front dash and have no idea how to say his full name. I should have checked the license plate number. I push my box inside and sit beside it in the back seat. I pull the car door shut and hope he isn't a serial killer. He must be legit here for me. Right? He knew my name. I don't really like how his dark eyes are staring at me in the rearview mirror, but I'll be fine. Nothing bad ever happens to kids from Oceanside. We're the blessed, the perfect.

I look at the house one last time. Poor Mom. I know she's excited about her fresh start, but I can't be. Everything she's running away from is my real life. And I like it there, very much.

"Um, you can drive any minute, sir," I say. I've got places to be, doesn't he realize that?

A little voice inside my head is sorry, though. Sorry I can't buy into Mom's new life plan. Sorry I can't see myself living in a strange house on the wrong side of the tracks.

I am sorry she doesn't feel like we're really connected, but she should remember I'm out of here soon. Off to college, off to the real world.

Sorry, Mom. You do you, and I'll keep being me. I like my life just fine the way it is. A tiny part of me worries about leaving my Barbie doll–looking mom all alone in a house with a bunch of Tom's friends in the backyard, but I'm sure she can handle things. I mean, she's the one who asked for all this.

"We have a problem," the Uber driver says.

You can say that again.

CHAPTER 10

ROGER

I stand in the foyer of my home and stare out the window at the idiots on a stakeout or whatever they call this. I'll tell you what this is: it's harassment, pure and simple, and I hate it.

Here's what needs to happen. My girls need to come home. Julie will apologize for the disruption this has caused, and we will all get back to normal. Jess will be fine moving back in here as soon as possible. I know my girl, what she's used to, how she's been raised. There's just something restless with Julie, something I can't put my finger on. I don't think another home is going to fix it this time, although I have been looking at a killer ski-in, ski-out in Aspen.

Would Julie like Aspen? Would she be happy with me there? Would she be happy with me anywhere? Damn it. I gave her everything. I walk to the window and stare at the car again.

I see them, but I'm disguised behind tempered bulletproof glass. My home is a fortress, and they're fools to try to mess with me here. They're parked across the street, absorbed in some sort of conversation between the two of them, but I know they're watching me. And how the hell did they get into my gated community? They must have a pass, but who put them on the guard gate list?

I wonder again if Julie sent them, if she's paying a couple of jerks to keep track of me. That's it. I can go out there and pay them more, set up a double cross perhaps. Julie looked nervous the second time I drove by her ugly new house, but she didn't run into the arms of the movers. She'd been talking to some sort of weirdo neighbor and I just waved, and that's all it took. She dashed inside like she'd seen a ghost.

I'm not a ghost. I'm her husband. And that should be scarier. I have all the power here. All the resources. Without me, she is nothing. I need to make a plan. She likes it when I tell her what to do, how things will change. She is used to me being in control.

And I'll do better. I got all caught up at work again, and with my side hustles, but I can modify. I need my girls, my life the way I like it. The smell of Julie's perfume that lingers through the house, the sound of Jess running down the hall about to meet her friends at our pool. I will not die alone like my dad. I will not.

Here's what I'll do. I'll let her keep that hovel as a project. She'll move back home, with Jess, but she can go redecorate that house during the day. She's bored, that's what it is. Plus with Jess off to college next year, she's going to be lonely. She's already lonely. I told her I'd joined all the parent clubs and groups on campus that money can get us into so we'll be able to go up, take our girl to football games, and have access to all the best tailgates. It's supposed to be a who's who of Hollywood celebrities and captains of industry like me. That's why I was pushing so hard for USC even when Jess wasn't that interested. Julie was on my side, with dreams of USC versus UCLA games in her head. Sure, she went to UCLA, but she was a scholarship girl. This time, with Jess, we'll be the big rollers, the top donors. We have arrived.

Jess will love it there, she will. I know I would have.

My parents didn't have the money for a school like that, and I didn't have the inclination to be the poor kid at pressure-cooker college. No, I had to become one of them. I was *driven* to become one of them. And I did it. I put myself through community college and worked in real estate the whole time. I outsmarted and outworked everyone in my path. And I've arrived. Too bad my mom and dad aren't around to see everything I have, everything I built. I think about my dad, working long hours at the factory. My mom's shoulders permanently rounded from the weight of the world. Their lives were about surviving. Mine has been all about thriving. Cancer got her first, as my dad watched. Then it was his turn to fade away, alone.

As for Julie, she should be glad the kid isn't flying off to school somewhere in Boston or New York like Jess wanted. No way was I letting that happen. I need to keep my ladies close, I need to know what they're doing. It's important for me to have their energy around. It's part of the plan. So we'll check in on Jess often, drive up for special things. We'll see her, I promised Julie, but it won't be like now, living together under one roof. I predict she'll boomerang after her undergrad years, so there's that to look forward to. I need to tell Julie that. That will give her hope for the future. We'll all be together. All kids boomerang these days. Who wouldn't boomerang back to this house, this lifestyle?

But for now, I just want them back. Like it was, I should say, because I hate being alone in this mansion right now. I walk through the living room to the wall of glass framing the ocean view. We have it all here, doesn't she get that?

I check the time and wonder where the hell my attorney is. People don't keep me waiting. Ever. Not my employees. Not my staff.

And never my family. It was my vow, to myself, to never be kept waiting, to never be without support. I work as hard as I do so I can have everything—everyone—I want.

My phone rings and I answer.

"My apologies, Mr. Jones." It's my attorney.

This had better be good. I put the phone on speaker and bellow, "Where the hell are you?"

"I've been in a car crash, an accident. They're taking me to the hospital for some tests. I'm sorry." There is a lot of background noise and sirens. Sounds plausible. I may even believe him, but this is the worst timing.

"Look, thanks for calling. Can you send another partner over here?" I will take whoever I can get on a Friday afternoon. But they better be good. "And I hope you're going to be OK."

I hang up before he can answer. He needs to focus on himself, and finding me another attorney. I turn back to the ocean, to the view that screams I've arrived. Front row, baby. When you grow up poor, you don't even know places like this exist. I never even saw the ocean until I was in my early twenties. And then I found out there are entire communities filled with luxurious homes, cars, people. Each family a precious work of art, a treasure insulated from most of the unpleasant things in life. Like evictions. Like the power being turned off. Like being hungry. This country is turning into the haves and the have-nots, and I guarantee you I'm going to have as much as I can get. No matter the cost. For my daughter, of course. This is America. The place where you can make your dreams come true if you work hard enough, if you're smart enough. Nobody helped me get here. And nobody is going to take anything or anyone away from me.

I remember back when I was a kid cutting the grass for rich people, my dad would drop me off in the wealthiest neighborhood we knew of, nothing like this place of course, and I'd go door-to-door offering to work, to do whatever they needed done. I was fourteen and handsome. On one particular evening I had worked all day, and my last job was mowing an expansive lawn. I told the owner of the huge house that the yard cost twenty dollars. She laughed at me, said she would only pay ten. She tossed the bill at my face and slammed the door. I don't know if she'd always had money, too much of it, or if she worked her way into it like me.

But it didn't matter. I learned a lesson that day: when you're rich, you do whatever you want.

I look out at my beautiful backyard, the saltwater swimming pool, the expansive deck, the ocean sparkling in the distance. The pool makes me miss my daughter. She loves getting a tan. It's a beautiful day. She should be sitting out by the pool with her friends, right here, right now.

I'll call Jess. I know deep down she's a daddy's girl, even though she's a bit skittish around me. I can be, well, "intense" would be a good word. But we're good together. She calls me Daddy-O sometimes and asks me to check my blood pressure on my watch. Sometimes, when I least expect it, she'll come up and hug me when I'm sitting watching TV. Sometimes she's not even asking for anything in return.

My attorney is calling again.

"What? Did you find someone to come over here?"

"Not yet. But don't worry. I will. I'm so sorry about this. I hope it doesn't affect our relationship going forward." I hear the beep of machines in the background. I know he's not lying, but I also know he doesn't sound competent. I need competent.

I wish I could remember his name just now. "Look, you've made your calls. I'm sure when one of the guys at the firm finds out what happens, they'll jump at the chance to take over my business." I smile. That was fun.

"No, I'll be back on my feet by Monday. They're keeping me for a couple of days, observation, that's all." He sounds desperate. "You wouldn't make a change, not after all we've been through?" And he adds in a whisper, "I know everything."

I hang up on him again. He shouldn't sound so desperate. And he shouldn't be threatening me. Sure, you cut some corners on your way to the top, and I'm no exception. I had to make a few deals with the devil, a few agreements only the good old guy in the hospital knows about. But it's all confidential attorney-client privilege. If he dies tonight of his injuries, my secrets go to the grave with him. If he lives, he better keep his mouth shut. I know he will.

Nobody, I mean nobody, is going to threaten what I've built. I created a real estate empire and fortune by working harder than anybody else, by outmaneuvering the competition.

Nobody's going to bite off a chunk. Not even a nibble.

Not some scumbag lawyer.

And certainly not my wayward wife.

Julie should know better than to pull a stunt like this.

This is a ridiculous idea. She'll get over it. Quickly.

I'll see to that. First step is getting Jess back home. That will be easy. I push the button and call my daughter. She's always been easy to manipulate: it's all about money to her.

I walk out to the foyer to place the call. The jerks are still out there, watching me.

CHAPTER 11

TOM

I wonder what Jess thought of my friends. I saw her up there in my old bedroom, watching us down here. Did she want to join us? It's ridiculous because we just met, but suddenly I want to hold her hand, introduce her to the guys. I want to show her off. We connect on some weird level.

She can't come down, though. Men only. But I wouldn't mind if she joined me later. Maybe I'll invite her over, see what her reaction is? I really can't stop thinking about her even though I should be figuring out how to evict them from my house. I don't know why I feel so attached to this stupid place. I mean, psychobabble snowflake shit would say that I don't want to leave because if I do, my real mom won't be able to find me. Because no matter how much Sandi says she's my mom, we both know she isn't, and can't be because she gave birth to two replacements. So I'm screwed. But this house holds me like a vise. I can't let go. I won't.

I kick the gravel driveway and tell myself to focus on the guys, on welcoming my friends. I tell myself to concentrate on the task at hand, but then I imagine kissing those perfect soft lips, touching her smooth skin, wrapping her in my arms. *Stop it.* I'm hosting my friends, the only guys who really understand me. This is important. I push Jess's perfect body out of my mind and clap my hands.

"Hey, everybody, come on inside. Beer is in the fridge." I push open the door to the shed, aware it's going to be tight inside, but we need our privacy. Jess's mom is in the house, within earshot of anything we talk about out in the open in the backyard.

This will be the last time I'll be hosting anybody for a while. I cannot believe I'm homeless. My dad sucks. I'm not listening to him, not ever again. He acts so pious, but he's the worst human being in the world. Preachers are. They can spout holy shit and then treat their family like dirt. Hypocritical shit.

He sold my home out from under me, but he can't make me leave. He doesn't have the balls.

"Hey, can I talk to you for a minute, XL?" Vic grabs my arm. He looks different outside the bar where I usually see him. He seems bigger, stronger. Powerful. I want to be just like him, and I'm working on it. When he says jump, we all ask how high. "Out here."

"Of course, Vic, whatever you'd like." I glance at the house and will Jess's mom to stay out of sight. "What can I do for you?"

"Besides getting me the number for your lady friend up there." Vic points to my bedroom window.

"Uh, don't know it. She just moved in there." I just lied to my best friend. I had to. For Jess, and me. Vic told me he swore off women and told me to, too. I guess one look at Jess will do that to anyone.

Vic gives me a sideways look, rubs his chin with his hand. "Work on getting it, why don't you? Her mom's number, too."

I nod and swallow. I can't let Vic down. He's the de facto popular guy of the group. I think back to our week in the desert, how happy I was to be included. Vic said he was proud I learned how to shoot the AK-47 so well, so fast. I hadn't made people proud in a long time. Certainly not my dear old dad. I wipe the sweat from my forehead, hoping Vic doesn't notice.

I give him a quick smile.

"You OK, XL? I mean, if you can't do it, tell me." Vic laughs. Vic has beady black eyes. Eyes that make you realize he sees everything you're thinking, everything you're not saying. He's not just referring to getting Jess's phone number. He's talking about my plan, and I know he can see my fear like a big hazy cloud. I need to push through my fear like they said during our week in the desert. I need to step into my destiny and stop letting life shit on me. When you are under attack like I am, the only thing you can do is fight back. At least I'm clear about who my enemy is.

"I can do it, no problem." I meet his eyes and shove my hands in my pockets.

"Great. Grab me a beer, would you?" Vic leans toward me and flashes our symbol, two stacked OK signs. It's the way you know you're part of the friend group. If everything goes right, I'll be a hero to these guys. We'll keep hanging out at the bar, we'll go to the desert for target practice. Hell, we even have a basketball team, and I'm pretty good. I have finally found the place I belong. The thought makes me smile. "I'll follow you inside."

As we stand in my cramped kitchen, Vic looks out my only window and up at the second floor of my house, my old house. Shit.

"Really, who is she? The girl in the window? Are you hiding something from me?"

"Um, well, no, she and her mom just moved into the main house. My house. My old house." I know I'm stuttering, and I only do that when I'm nervous. But why am I nervous? I don't owe Jess or her mom anything. They're interlopers; they should leave. "They don't belong here. This is my house."

"I'd keep 'em around if I were you." Vic chuckles. "Think you can introduce us?"

"You're too old for Jess." Crap. I bite my fist. "I mean, of course, but the mom is hotter." That's true. I'm sweating, and he's glaring. I'm dead. I've seen what he did to Bucky, a guy who didn't do what he said one night at the bar. Vic told him to buy a round and serve us. Bucky said he didn't have any money. Vic punched him in the face, hard, and he went down like a domino. I bought the round, on the house, while Bucky lay bleeding and unconscious on the ground.

I've only seen Vic with one girl before. They came into the bar together, on some sort of date. I was working and they sat at the bar, but neither of them were smiling. The girl had stringy blonde hair and a busted lip. Her eyes were as dark as his.

"Tom, old boy, do you have a girl?" Vic had asked. His voice was deep, sinister sounding. I wouldn't want to be that girl—not at all, I'd decided.

"Uh, no," I'd answered, suddenly finding a spot to mop up on the bar. "I'm alone. Women are a waste of time."

"Good man. They are good for absolutely shit, isn't that right, Tammy?" Vic grabbed her wrist and pulled her close to his side. "You can't trust 'em as far as you can throw them."

"You're hurting my wrist, Vic. And you're an ass," Tammy said as she slid off the barstool. "Go play with your lost boys. You're a loser, you know it?"

"Fuck you," Vic had yelled, letting go of her wrist. "You're a whore."

Tammy ran out of the bar as Vic turned to me and said, "Don't date anyone. Understand? That's my last try. I'm done with them. I don't have any patience for them and their demands. We have more important things to do."

Back then I'd wanted to tell him that actually, I had nothing more important to do. But suddenly, he leaned forward and said, "We want you to join us, Tom. We want you to come to the desert with us."

"Yes, of course, I'd love that," I'd said, trying to keep cool, trying not to show how stoked I was to be included.

And then he'd moved away from the bar, joining his usual group in the back corner booth.

And I was in—in for what, I wasn't sure. But man was I happy. Now I'm a nervous wreck, and I can't let him near Jess. I won't.

After what seems like eternity, Vic pats my shoulder. He says, "After our little party here, you'll introduce me to both of them. I'll decide who's hotter. Understand?"

I swallow. I'll get him to like Jess's mom. Vic is forty. Jess's mom looks like she is in her thirties, but she has a daughter in high school, so she's gotta be older. That's what I'll do. Only Jess's mom can meet him. "Sure. Yes, of course."

"Good, let's get back to the meeting. After you." He pushes me back into my sitting area, where the rest of the guys are. As we take our seats again, I fight the urge to break away from him, run across the backyard, and tell Jess and her mom to get out. And this time it's not just because of me. You don't want to get the attention of guys like Vic. Guys like me. We take what we want, that's what the guys told me in the desert. And I've seen Vic in action. He has a problem with women. It's dangerous for women to be around him.

Why did my stupid dad cause this to happen? This is all his fault. All of it.

Vic says, "Take a seat, everybody. Make yourselves at home. Tom. Up here, next to me."

I'm surprised, but I hurry through the group of guys and take a seat right next to him. He pats my knee. "Thanks for having us over. And for the beers. Doing OK?"

"Yes, sure, of course. Just excited." I hope I sound convincing, but I think it is hard to slip things past Vic. Does he sense my hesitation? Have I worried him? I mean, it's normal to feel nervous, right? I know what's coming. Anybody would be a little on edge. I will stay on track, and not allow anything to deter me. I take a deep breath and try to calm my racing heart.

And then I realize what's changed. My heart is the problem. The only thing new in my life is Jess. If she gives me a chance, she could change my life. My path. If she feels the way I do, it could change everything. I want to run out the door. I want to talk to Jess, to laugh with her.

But for now, I'm trapped.

CHAPTER 12

JULIE

Jess's ride still hasn't pulled away. I watch from the kitchen window as the passenger door opens and Jess climbs out of the black Escalade. I wonder if she's changed her mind. Maybe she'll stay here, with me, instead of going over to Bonnie's house. My heart beats wildly despite the fact that I took a deep breath and keep telling myself to calm down. I tell myself not to get too excited. She probably forgot something. I'm certain she still plans on going to Bonnie's. She does it every weekend. Tonight is different, though, and maybe she realizes it? It's our first night in our new home. I had imagined sitting down to a meal we cooked together. Talking, really talking. I want to tell her how to avoid the traps I fell into.

I want to tell her to not be like me. But it may be too late, for everything.

The door opens. "Mom, the Uber guy won't drive. He says my credit card was fine when he accepted the ride but now it's declined, like the card deactivated on his way over here or something. He told me to get another and gave me a five-minute deadline. What am I supposed to do?"

I wish we were having that talk right now as I listen to my daughter, who has been given too much—way too much—money, freedom, and power in our family. Now here she is, standing with her hands on her hips, having a fit because her Platinum American Express has been declined. She was trying to leave without even saying goodbye. My heart hurts. But at least she needs me for a moment.

"Calm down, honey," I say, walking toward my daughter. "Your father likely cut us off, you know, to prove a point or something."

"What actual point does that prove? I'm not the one who left him. You did." Jess's eyes are fiery, her hands still on her hips. "I can't believe we didn't drive my car over here this morning when we had the chance."

"It was pouring, remember? We will pick up your car, don't worry. Maybe Bonnie can take you to it in the morning? Your dad is just messing with us. It's a control thing. Money is power. How about I drive you to Bonnie's?"

"OMG, Mom. You need to unpack." Jess huffs out the door, and I follow in her wake. At the car she asks the driver, "Can you switch the billing to another card?"

"No, you'll need to do it on the app," he says, obviously not pleased with either of us. I wonder if he hears the entitlement dripping from her words, her manner. I'm sure he can.

"I'm late, Mom. Bonnie expected me half an hour ago. Do you have a card that will work? I'm sure Dad cut off my Mastercard, too," Jess whines. I'm both saddened and embarrassed by her. It's my fault, so I bite my tongue. Roger and I made Jess into this.

"Honey, use this." I hand her my new credit card. A normal, lowly Visa. I smile when I see my maiden name on it.

"Whatever." It takes a couple of minutes for Jess to enter the credit card and reset her ride. I put out my hand for the card when she's finished.

"You're welcome." I take the Visa and slide it into my wallet.

"Thanks. But, um, what do I do for money?" Jess is used to plastic, to paying for whatever she wants, whenever she wants it. Instantly, no matter the cost. This, too, will change. I've talked to a friend who owns a yoga studio, and she needs part-time help. I know if Jess gets a job, it will help her appreciate the cost of everything, how hard most people must work to live the life she has. At least, I hope so. It's part of my plan for my daughter.

"Ready to go?" the driver barks from the front seat. Friday nights are busy, and he needs to get rid of Jess.

"Come home in the morning and we'll talk about it," I say as I push the door closed. I blow her a kiss, but she's already texting someone on her phone. Bonnie can cover her for the night. And now she has another reason to come home tomorrow.

Roger's little plan to cut off the credit cards won't affect me, or Jess. I've set up my new life. I have bank accounts of a respectable size, created by skimming a little from here and a bit from there over the course of the last year. It's easy to find money when you live a life this grand. Buy two dresses for the upcoming event in cash. Return one and credit my new Visa. Repeat. And then there are the savings accounts Roger suggested I have, which he funded for a rainy day, in case everything goes to hell, as he'd say. Those accounts, under my name only, are how I bought this home. Thank you, Roger, for your doomsday thinking.

I walk back to the porch and admire the beautiful purple flowers in the beds on either side. I'm going to learn what they're called, and take care of them. Just like I'm going to take care of Jess and myself. I take a deep breath and tell myself to relax. I have a plan for the rest of my life, I have a home and a fresh start. My attorney will serve Roger with the divorce papers on Monday. I remind myself this is everything I wanted when I made the plan.

Christmas was the last straw. Roger has always missed the big milestones in Jess's life, and truth be told, I wasn't the model mom. But when it came to Christmas, one day of the year, I put my foot down. We would spend that day together, and Roger had agreed. Over the years, he'd missed most of my birthdays, and Jess's, but he'd made a sacrifice of sorts when it came to Christmas, suffering through the day and pretending to connect.

Until this Christmas. Roger had announced he would be out of town, working a big deal somewhere in Europe. He knew I'd understand, he explained, because it's just a day like any other.

For some reason, this was it. My awakening.

"It's our only tradition. Please. For me and Jess, stay home." I felt tears rolling down my cheeks, and I was as surprised as Roger.

"You know, you're not even a Christian, Julie. It really shouldn't matter," he'd scoffed, shaking his head. "Crying doesn't look good on you."

His disdain, his callousness, pushed me over the edge. I was finished. I stood in our grand entry hall, tears soaking my shirt, mascara streaking down my cheeks, and Roger simply walked away. And true to his word, he was gone on Christmas Day.

I deserve more than an occasional dinner when Roger's assistant calls and tells me he can fit me in. I deserve to have a partner who is interested in me, who talks to me. And yes, it's my fault that I was seduced by the power, money, and lifestyle Roger could provide. I picked Roger's way of life over a true connection. I know that now. I remind myself that Roger cares only about himself, and about making money. He's climbing the ladder of success, and he's so far up there toward the top that he has room for nothing else. I remember how he said he loved his first wife, that he would find it hard to love anyone else.

I never believed him, not back then. But now I know his warning was the truth.

I walk up the steps to the porch. A chill runs down my spine, and I shake it off. My first night in my new house, and despite the fact that I'm alone, everything will be fine.

I step inside, flip on the front porch light, and slide the dead bolt into place. Sure, it would be great if Jess were here, too, but I need to learn to stand on my own. I walk to the back door and look out over the green, grassy yard. Earlier, Tom had a gathering of what could be described only as a biker club in the carriage house. Tattoos, black leather, shaved heads, all men. They all gave me the creeps. I almost felt like I should call the police on them, but what would I say? I don't like the looks of them? That would be prejudiced of me, judgmental. Not all guys with tattoos and black leather jackets are bad news, I know. Regardless, Tom is not a problem I'm going to solve. He will be gone Sunday. I can manage until then. Just to be safe, I slide the dead bolt into the back door and consider turning on the alarm, although it does seem a bit early.

All I know is I wouldn't want to meet any of those guys in a dark alley, or my darkening backyard. I heard them leave half an hour ago, thankfully before Jess did. As I stand at the back door, the carriage house door opens. It's Tom.

He's already seen me, so I give him a brief wave and pull the curtains over the window. The sheers don't do a good job of shielding me. As I turn away another chill runs through me. It'll be nice when he moves out on Sunday.

Very nice.

I head to the kitchen and pull the half curtains over the sink. Even though there are tall hedges shielding the property from other houses on the block, I feel exposed. And I know I'm being ridiculous. I don't know if it's Tom's friends, the settling sounds of a new house, or the stress of moving day, but I'm on edge. I'm not good at being alone.

I yank open the box labeled "bar" and find the vodka I packed. The refrigerator is old, but the ice is cold and that's all I need. I toss some cubes into the plastic cup, pour some vodka, and take a big sip.

I need to call my mom. I'm forty-five years old, and all I want to do is talk to my mom.

Esther picks up in one ring. "Are you OK? What's happened?"

"I'm fine, Mom. I left Roger. I moved out. Today." I take a sip of vodka and wait for what comes next.

"Well it's about time. He's a horrible man. Music to my ears. How is my granddaughter?" Mom's words warm my heart. She's on my side. I smile.

"She's good. Fine. She's not so keen on my new house, but she'll adjust." I slide into the kitchen chair and look around. It's got good bones, it does.

"Julie, honey, are you sure you're doing all right?" Mom's voice is worried.

"I'm fine. Jess and I will come see you at Thanksgiving. As always."

"Still can't believe that ridiculous husband of yours never came for Thanksgiving. Not once. You need to meet a nice Jewish man. Go to a Shabbat service."

"I know, Mom." I wipe the tears and finish my vodka.

"Roger always was a schmuck."

"Mom, I've got to go."

I hang up as something catches my eye on the driveway. There's a shape moving slowly, visible through the sheers covering the bottom half of the kitchen window.

It's a man, his boots crunching on the gravel, carrying a phone that lights his face up eerily, headed toward the street. It must be Tom, I tell myself. He's probably going out for the night. But then I remember: Tom already left.

I peer over the curtains and look down at the man. It's not Tom. It's a man with a full head of black hair. He stops, looks up at me as if he expected to see me, knew I was here all along. His eyes are dark and menacing.

He smiles, slowly licks his lips, and keeps walking away. I clamp my hand over my mouth to keep from screaming. I need to stay calm.

Tom moves out Sunday, and that solves the problem of the creepy men in black.

Jess will come home tomorrow morning and love this house, love this new life.

As I sit in the kitchen, drinking alone, I realize I might be wrong—about everything, and everyone.

CHAPTER 13

JESS

This is where I'm meant to be. I feel my shoulders drop, and my heart swells as I look at the street lined with gorgeous homes, just a short walk from the private beach. I see the Dolfert twins' stately palace—a grand display of wealth perched on the side of the cliff—and realize I don't want to see them. Not in my frazzled state. I don't know for sure what's going on with my mom. And I haven't even talked to my dad, but he cut my credit card off. Which sucks. I don't want my friends to know any of this, not until I work things out. And I will.

But right now, my family is a topic of gossip, and not in a good way. I mean, the gossip about my new over-the-top BMW for my Sweet Sixteen was good, despite the fact that it is now trapped in my dad's garage. This gossip is not. I realize they all must know by now. I need to get in front of it. And I will. I will talk my mom out of the ridiculous house on the wrong side of the tracks. We'll move back in with my dad. They'll make up like they always do, even though my dad is a jerk. I push the negative thoughts of my dad out of my head. I know I might need him on my side. I might need his cash to help me fund the life I have. But first things first: I must convince Bonnie to let me stay. That's priority number one. And it's Friday night, and I deserve to party.

"It's right there, just drive through the gate." I point to Bonnie's ginormous Mediterranean-style megamansion.

"Wowza. I've always wanted to see in here. These homes are for real, big as hotels."

I smile. Smug satisfaction. "Yep, but it's all just for one family. And they only have one daughter."

"Must be nice, honey," he says.

It's fun to have him think I'm someone special, someone who lives in this house. Not the one where he picked me up. Never the one where he picked me up.

"It is nice. Being me. Thanks for the lift." I hop out and toss the guy a quick wave. I feel his eyes watching me. He should be pulling away, but he wants a glimpse inside. He wants a story to share with the guys back wherever he lives. I turn around and stare at him. "Goodbye!"

He yanks the car into gear, shakes his head, and drives slowly out of the driveway. I wait until he's out of sight before texting Bonnie: I'm here! You never can be too careful. I learned that from my dad. Other people always want to take you down, hurt you, take your money away. They're jealous. You just have to be careful, that's all.

Dad would sometimes be home in time to tuck me into bed when I was a kid. He liked to read "The Three Little Pigs" to me and tell me there are wolves everywhere, waiting to steal from you. "You can't let strangers in too close, honey. Don't trust anyone but family." That's what my dad would tell five-year-old me, ten-year-old me, and whenever he could since I became a teenager. And I listened. "We have so much," he'd say, "and I've worked hard to get it all. They will do anything to take it all away. Be alert. Be careful. Never let them know how much you have." I never knew who *they* were, not really.

"Jess Bess! So happy you've escaped! Where the hell did your mom take you anyway?" Bonnie flings her too-skinny arms around me and pulls me into a pointy embrace. I know it's not possible, but I think she's thinner than when we were together yesterday in class. Thursday seems like months ago. I can't believe my mom has messed everything up.

"I can't discuss it. It's too ridiculous. Let's just say it is a part of town you've never seen, and never will." I hug her back. "I hate it there. Thank you for saving me."

"Of course. My parents love you. You know that. They'll love having another daughter for senior year." Bonnie grabs my box and leads me into the familiar grand foyer. The Pacific Ocean shimmers through the floor-to-ceiling windows in front of us, just like my view at my dad's.

"Did you ask them? Really? Or are you just saying that?" I meet her eyes and I know. "You didn't ask. You just presumed it would be OK. Bonnie, come on."

"Beg for forgiveness, am I right?" Bonnie starts the climb to her bedroom, which is actually a suite of rooms commanding one-half of the upstairs of the home. Her parents share the other half. Everything is soaring ceilings, dark wood beams and moldings, sparkling crystal chandeliers, and white: walls, bedding, furniture. It's like a beautiful five-star hotel, only it's not. My dad's house, in comparison, looks a little off, a little showy, a little overdone. My mom did the house like she did her face and body: too much, too often.

At Bonnie's there is plenty of room, thousands of square feet, but it doesn't feel as cavernous as my dad's. Bonnie's parents likely wouldn't even know I was here. But still. "I'd feel better if they said yes officially. I could relax. Go get all my stuff and move in here. You know, feel permanent."

Bonnie shrugs and drops my box onto the couch in what once was her playroom and now serves as her guest bedroom. I know all this because I'm the most frequent guest. The nanny's bedroom is just down the hall. I know that, too. Her nanny has morphed into more of a cleaning lady, errand runner. I wonder if she's here. Maybe she could help pack up my things over at my mom's?

Bonnie says, "I'll talk to Mom. I'm sure it's not going to be a problem. I mean, look. You already have a room here." Bonnie's confidence is infectious, always has been. She's the leader, and I'm the follower. We both like our roles. She's class president, I'm vice president because she talked me into running. We make a great team.

I see Bonnie looking at the framed photo of the two of us from five years ago, back in middle school, our smiles beaming in happiness. That seems like yesterday, and so long ago. So much can change, so much has.

My mom just left my dad.

"Thanks. So much." I barely get the words out because I'm all choked up. I can't make the stupid tears stop.

"Hey, hey, it's going to be all right. Your parents will work things out, don't worry. Nothing has changed. You'll stay here, go to school with me. Nobody needs to be talking shit about you or your family. Got it?" Bonnie can't stand seeing people cry. She really hates it when I do.

"Got it," I manage to say with some enthusiasm.

"You get yourself together, and I'll go talk to Mom for real. OK? Be right back. No more tears." Bonnie hurries out of the room to avoid any of my weakness spilling over onto her.

She pulls the door closed in her wake, and I drop onto the bed. It's going to be fine, I tell myself. You will have a great senior year. You will go away to college and have a blast. Your parents will do whatever it is they do. Reunite. Fight. Get divorced. It doesn't matter.

You be you, Jess. You're going to college in the fall. It's super exciting!

But it all matters. To the other kids at school, to the perfect illusion I've created of my perfect life. Thing is, I thought it was all real. Thank goodness I'm out of here soon. I can start fresh.

The door swings open and Bonnie bursts through. "My mom says you can stay for as long as you like. She also said she'd heard the rumors and was sorry about your family. Gross. I hope people don't do that to you all night at the party."

"Thank god I can stay. Thank you." I smile at Bonnie as some of the tension I've been holding recedes. I have a home, a place to stay, where I belong. I remember her concern about our friends. My parents' divorce is a hot topic for sure. "They will ask me about the divorce, but that's why we're getting fucked up tonight, so I won't care."

"Cheers to that." Bonnie's eyes twinkle with mischief. "Let's go get the party set up. We can do a little pregaming. Sound good? I can see if some of the guys can come a little early."

I look at my perfect friend and I'm filled with gratitude and relief. "Sounds great. But I may have someone I'm hooking up with later. Turns out there's a cute boy living in the house behind my mom's. Maybe he can come over later?" I can't believe I just mentioned Tom to Bonnie. It spilled out because, well, I'm thinking about him.

"Oh really? Do tell," Bonnie says, and I feel my face flush.

"He's cute, and well, not from around here. He's older."

"Have him come over. He sounds scrumptious," Bonnie says.

And with that, my mood lifts, and I imagine Tom showing up at the party. I wonder what he'd think of my world, what it would feel like skinny dipping in the ocean with him tonight.

Suddenly, my life is looking so much better.

Maybe I'll text Tom now. What harm could there be in a little flirting?

CHAPTER 14

SANDI

When I made it home from Julie's house—I am forcing myself to call it that—my new house was empty. Doug was nowhere to be found, and I must admit it was a great relief. He must have figured out another way to get a loaner car. Now I simply must wait for his return, wondering if he is even angrier or if he's calmed down. It's Friday. Friday nights are for family dinner, that's what my daddy preached and what Doug preaches, too. Sometimes he actually keeps his word.

Traditionally, back at our home church, Doug finished up early and tried not to do any home or hospital visits until Saturday. Only if someone is about to die. That's when he'd go do visitation on a Friday night. He has to get to them fast to save their soul before they cross over. Can't do it without him. Sort of like he's a superhero paving their way to Heaven. At least, that's what I used to believe.

Now I sort of suspect he goes to ask for extra tithes for the church, a donation of sorts for the work he's doing. A megachurch pastor is only as good as the money he brings in, bottom line. So he goes to visit the dying, to wring out more money from their grieving family, to benefit the whole congregation, he tells them. The dying. The helpless. And then, when they give—and who wouldn't give what they have for a promise of eternal life—he blesses them, documents the gifts, and sends the believer on his, or mostly her, way.

That's not where his biggest sins happen, though. No, those things happen with the young divorcées he hosts special group sessions for. It happens with the young believers, the women, who he meets with one-on-one to bless their souls, among other things.

I'm not immune to the gossip. It's been around me since we married all those years ago. I fell in love with Doug and Tom, with all my heart. I promised to be the mom Tom needed, the companion Doug deserved.

I discovered Doug had fallen in love with the idea of a Sunday school teacher as his wife. He liked my pedigree, and my dad liked Doug's in return. I was swept away into a life of righteousness, promised one day that I'd be the first lady of Oceanside Christian. It was what my dad had groomed me to be, a role I would be well suited for if the time came.

I've heard Doug has a way with women, always has. But he always had an excuse, a reason why he had to work late, a reason why some parishioners might think he was coveting another man's wife. Ridiculous, he'd say. The first one was Charlene Melon. I remember her name, her porcelain skin, her shiny brown hair. I remember the way Doug looked at her when she slid into my pew. When I heard she'd moved away, I pushed her out of my mind.

Doug convinced me he loved me, that he would always be faithful, that people were just jealous, telling lies about him. And so I chose to believe. For too long.

The front door bursts open, and my two sons stampede in. They're my heart—my reasons for living. For a while, Doug insisted that we had enough of a family, just the three of us. But I'd always wanted children of my own. I would never love Tom any less. My heart could expand as easily as my belly carrying our child. And it happened, despite my planning, or God forgive me, because of it.

When I became pregnant with Davis all those years ago, Doug came around, got excited even. Not that there was an option. "There will be no baby killing in my home. We will welcome our new child as a blessing," Doug said back then, as I patted my swelling belly and smiled.

When Davis was born, I experienced a love so deep, a feeling of content so wonderful. I had been blessed. Doug was so in love with the baby, he wanted to have another. Said it was good for our brand. The congregation loves a family man, Doug said. Couldn't argue with that logic, and so two years later, Danny joined the family. Truth be told, I could have had another, a baby girl perhaps. But Doug forbade it and, just to be sure, sneaked off and had a vasectomy. I suppose it was for the best, considering where we are now.

Tom was good with his little brothers at first. Helping me feed them a bottle, playing with them as I made dinner. I don't know exactly when he started to be jealous of the two little boys, what triggered his dark anger and feeling of resentment, but I know in my heart I treated him as my own son, loved him with all my heart, from the moment he was mine until this day.

I think the hurt stems from Doug, truth be told. He isn't what he seems to either of us, Tom or me. But for the life of me, I can't get my oldest son to open up anymore.

I won't give up on him, though, not ever. I glance at my watch and realize they're home later than usual. And that means I need to get busy with dinner in case their father does come home.

"Mom, what's for dinner?" Davis asks. He's eight years old and thinks he's a man. His face is red with energy and streaked with sweat. "I'm starving."

"Me too." Danny agrees with everything his big brother says. I wonder if that will change once they're teenagers. Seems to me that everything changes once boys become teenagers, but I only have experience with Tom. An experience I pray will not be repeated. Tom would retreat to his room to play video games as soon as he came home from school and refused to eat family dinner. He started ignoring his younger brothers at best and lashing out in anger with them at the worst. Eventually, he disengaged from all family activities and moved out to the carriage house.

When I tried to make Doug talk to him, he'd shrug. "Leave him alone. He's just pouting. It's ridiculous. He looks like a loser, and acts like one, too. I don't have time for him. He's a disgrace."

I shrug off the memory and look down at my two little boys, eyes shining, smiling faces. Will they lose this joy, too?

"Meatloaf," I answer, patting them both on the head. "It's ready to pop in the oven."

"Ooh gross," Davis says.

"Watch your mouth. I'll make a healthy meal for all of us. You'll love it." I say it with firm control. I need my boys to respect me. I seem to have lost the respect of the other men in my life, Tom and Doug.

"Triggered much?" Davis laughs.

Danny does, too.

I don't care for this tone, and I don't know where he heard that word. I don't like the feeling of them mocking me, but for now, I will ignore my anger. I tuck a strand of hair behind my ear, the same way I've learned to tuck away slights, bury my hurt. "So you two are almost an hour late. Where were you?" I cannot believe I didn't notice how late they were until now, lost as I was in Cherry Hill Lane, our old church, the past. I need to focus on them, on their future.

"Oh, we were just hanging out, shooting the breeze," Danny says. It's as if he is parroting something someone told him to say.

"Did you ride the bus?" I ask. My heart pounds in my chest.

"No, we got a ride. It was cool," Davis says.

"From who?" I ask. I grab hold of the kitchen counter to keep my hands from shaking.

"Guy named Vic. He wanted to take us for ice cream. He's a friend of Tom's. Tom told us he would get us, but he couldn't. Something came up. Vic signed us out at the office, told Mrs. Spencer that he was our brother," Danny says. "He told us to play along. He's real nice."

My heart pounds in my chest. My babies, my God. I grab each of my sons by the wrist. "Never ever do that again without asking my permission, do you understand?"

My anger surprises them and their eyes are wide, glistening. Danny might cry. I'm scaring them. After each boy nods, I let go of them. "Go wash up. Your dad should be here any minute."

Davis stops and says, "Don't tell Dad."

I nod. "Don't let it happen again. Ever."

As the kids run upstairs, I take a deep breath. They could have been kidnapped, but they are fine. My fear turns to anger. I can't believe Tom thought it would be fine to send a random man to pick up his brothers. I look at the clock, realize this is my fault, too. I took my time coming back here, and lost in my self-pity, I didn't know my boys were an hour late coming home from school. I'm tempted to call Tom, but I know it wouldn't do any good.

I need to start dinner before Doug appears. I pull all the ingredients for a salad from the refrigerator and slide the meatloaf I made earlier into the preheated oven. The mashed potatoes are from a box, but the salad will be fresh lettuce. Friday nights are special because we don't have to be on display for the congregation, we don't have to pretend to be perfect. I don't need to worry that the boys are scrubbed and combed, their khakis spotless and their shirts pressed. I don't need to worry about what I wear, and how much or how little makeup I apply. Doug has a certain way he likes to see my face, light blush, light mascara, and that's all.

But on typical Friday nights, I don't wear any makeup, I don't wear a dress. I'm in jeans and a white T-shirt, and the boys are in their outside playclothes, smelling of grass and sweat.

Tonight is the night the boys can be boys, and I can relax. And usually, Doug is in a good mood. Unlike Sundays, when it's showtime and he is tense all day. Unlike Saturdays, when he's preparing his sermon and cannot be disturbed. Unlike the rest of the workweek, when he hurries out the door without so much as a kiss on the cheek. No, Fridays are special.

Usually.

I hear the door open from the garage, and Doug appears. I smooth my jeans, tuck in the front of my white T-shirt, and hurry to greet him with a smile. The kitchen is filled with the loving smells of a home-cooked meal. I always have the highest of hopes for Friday night. Always. In the beginning, these times were so warm, these dinners long. We'd talk for hours, Tom, Doug, and I. After the little boys were born, we'd still manage to have long dinners together. Those times ended with Charlene. And they never came back, not really. And that was years ago now.

"Welcome home. Hope you're hungry," I say and wait for a kiss, even on the cheek. But it doesn't happen.

"Yes, sure, a bit hungry, yes. You know I had to handle getting the loaner car without you. I couldn't wait any longer. I didn't appreciate that. I need to know I can count on you."

"Sorry, traffic was terrible," I lie.

Fortunately, Doug is distracted. He's holding his phone, reading something on the screen. "Whatever. I've got to handle something. I'll be in my office."

My shoulders drop with relief. I add a smile and a dose of artificial cheer. "OK, hurry. I don't want to let the dinner spoil."

"Well, don't let it spoil then," Doug barks, pushing past me. The Doug I thought I married would never treat his wife with disrespect. The man I thought I married is a man of God, kind and warm to all people, but especially his helpmate. The man I thought I married promised to love, honor, and respect me as long as we both shall live. The man I married lies. I take a deep breath.

This Friday evening is not going well. I swallow my disappointment like my preacher dad taught me—"children should be seen and not heard, wives are subservient to their husbands"—and say a quick prayer for patience. I'm not certain whether I should feed the boys without Doug, but I know they're hungry. They played outside for an hour after they changed from school, after their trip to the ice cream parlor with a stranger sent by Tom, and now they're rushing into the kitchen.

"Shhhh!" I warn them. "Your dad's home and has important business in his office."

They freeze and both have worried looks on their handsome little faces. I was too sharp with them just now; again I sounded too much like Doug. I know he's been terse lately because of the change in congregation, because of the shame he feels but doesn't express. If only he would admit his wrongdoing, he could be on the path to forgiveness. It's what he tells everyone else. Until then, we are all just an annoyance, I'm afraid, a family he has disappointed. But instead of apologizing, he has made us victims, too, walking on eggshells around his bad humor, his temper. God, please help us. I turn to my boys.

"Hey, it's OK. You guys know I won't tell your dad what you did this afternoon as long as you promise it will never happen again," I say.

"Promise," they say in unison, and my heart breaks. They are so good. "OK, great. Why don't you sit down and I'll serve you guys dinner. I'll eat with Daddy when he's finished." I smile and watch as they relax, pulling out their assigned seats at the dinner table.

These are new seats, now that our dinner table has only four chairs. When Tom was still living with us at the old house, he'd join us. Sometimes. I made sure there was a chair for him, even though Doug didn't approve. By then Tom and Doug had reached an icy stalemate, each disappointed in the other but unable to express it. Tom had convinced himself that our family didn't include him anymore, that he was an interloper.

I didn't give up on Tom, though. His chair at the table was a little tiny rebellion of sorts, I suppose. But it also was an open invitation to my oldest son.

I think about Tom as I'm serving up the boys' plates. I didn't like the look in his eye today, the way he hit my hands, hard. I didn't like the defiance, the superiority. I don't like the fact that one of his buddies picked my boys up from school. I know he is up to no good, but I don't know what to do about it. I don't like the crowd he's started hanging with, the guys I saw at the bar where he works the one time I stopped by. But I have no one to express my fears to about Tom.

Doug and Tom had a huge fight six months ago. They stood in the backyard, halfway between the carriage house and our home. Doug called Tom a dropout and a loser, told him he'd never been more disappointed in anyone in his life.

"And I take confession from a lot of losers, a lot of sinners, but you're the worst. Get your fucking act together," Doug yelled, poking Tom in the chest with his finger.

Tom had taken a step back and yelled, "You are the world's biggest hypocrite. You act so holy and superior when really, you can't keep your dick in your pants. You can't even keep a job, can you? I mean, they're kicking you out of your own church. And you call me a loser?"

"Get away from me, Tom, before I do something I regret. You're cut off. Effective immediately," Doug said, in a voice still loud enough for me to hear as I listened at the window, tears running down my cheeks.

"I don't need your money. I don't need you for anything. I hate you," Tom said, then turned and walked back to the carriage house.

"Feeling is mutual!" Doug yelled.

Tom opened the door to the carriage house and slammed it closed. They have been seething at each other ever since.

From that day on, Doug forbade me from helping Tom. "No more free meals, no more buying him clothes, nothing. He is a grown man, but he is a failure. No more, Sandi," he said, stomping into the house. "He is cut off, from all of us. You understand?"

No, I don't understand. But it is Doug's rule, and Doug has decided this is how it will be. That's why I can't tell Doug I saw Tom today. He wouldn't like it. He told me to stay away from him. He'd be beyond upset that I'd tried to connect with him. That's also why I won't tell him that Tom sent his friend to pick up our sons. I will keep that little threat to myself. Because I know it is a threat, for me and his dad. He is telling us he can take away everything I care about in a moment. I swallow and take a seat at the table with my boys, pasting a smile on my face.

"Dad!" Davis yells, startling me. I drop the mashed potato spoon, and it splatters on the floor. I watch Doug greet the boys, ignoring me and my mess. A hug for each son.

I don't remember the last time I saw him hug Tom. Was it years ago? Come to think about it, he never hugs me anymore, either. I wonder if the latest Charlene, as I've come to call all his special flock, really is over as Doug assures me.

I drop down to my knees behind the counter and wipe up the mashed potatoes.

"Can I get something to eat over here someday soon?" Doug demands dinner, I guess. "I have to go to the hospital tonight."

"No!" Danny says. "It's family night."

"I know, son," Doug says, slipping into his pastor voice with ease. "But the Lord calls me to do his work. One of our flock is sick. She may go home to Heaven tonight."

"But if she's going to Heaven, why does she need you there?" Davis asks. He's smart, starting to question things.

"That's your daddy's job, Davis. Your grandpa's, too. They help people step across into Heaven. It's the most important job in the world," I say as I stand up, wash my hands, and pull out a new spoon. Doug wouldn't know if I used the spoon that fell on the floor to serve up his dinner. But Jesus would.

"Here you are." I place the plate on the table in front of Doug and hurry back to dish my own meal.

As I join them, Doug smacks his hands on the table and says, "I was so distracted I forgot to say grace. Bow your heads."

We do. I glance side-eyed at Danny. He looks like he's going to cry. I smile at him and mouth "it's OK."

"Lord, thank you for these many blessings. Help my family to appreciate what they have. In your name we pray."

"Amen," the three of us say on cue as I ponder his prayer message. Does he see my restlessness, my pain? Does he care that it's hard for me, starting my life over out here? No, he doesn't. He expects blind devotion and quiet acceptance. He only cares if I'm a good reflection on him. It turns out it's hard to reflect light when you're dying inside.

I'm not sure exactly when he stopped loving me, if it was Charlene two or three. But these days, despite my best efforts to put on a happy face and settle in here, I look in his eyes and see nothing but distaste, contempt. Will the boys learn to see me that way because of him?

"Mom, these mashed potatoes are great." It's Davis, jumping into the tension, cutting through it like a knife in butter. Sweet boy.

"Thank you, honey." I smile. They're from a box, but he doesn't need to know that. He is getting old enough that soon he'll begin to pick up on his dad's duplicities, on the difference between what he delivers in Sunday sermon and how he treats his family. I'll need to teach my boys to be faithful and devoted husbands, ones who would never stray. And, in the meantime, I need to be sure they don't end up admiring Tom, or Tom's friends.

A shiver runs down my spine. In the next moment, Doug says with a big grin, "More meatloaf, please. I worked up quite an appetite today, tending to my new flock."

Oh, I'm sure you did, Doug. Has he already found a new Charlene? Did she drive him to pick up the loaner car? God help me.

"Yes, of course." I force a smile and carry his plate to the kitchen. This time I use the dirty spoon. Sorry, Jesus.

As I drop off his second plate of food, without receiving so much as a thank-you, something in my heart hardens. I can't live like this for the rest of my life.

I can't have my sons see me live like this, tolerate behavior like this. I sit down across the table from my husband and I decide. This is not how it's going to be for us. For me.

For my boys. Because they are learning by his example, every minute they are in his presence. And what they're learning is not holy.

What they are learning is what Tom learned from Doug. Somehow, this supposedly God-fearing, church-leading man has created a monster in his oldest child, has wounded his heart enough that the devil is trying to take hold.

I swallow the sour taste that has filled my mouth and tell myself to calm down. I have a plan, and it is time to execute it. It's beyond time.

"What?" Doug asks, looking directly at me. "Are you sick or something?"

"No, I'm fine. Why?" I manage to hold eye contact.

"You aren't eating. The food is expensive, remember? You're over budget this month, again."

"I know, I'm sorry. It's just with the move, we've had a few more take-out meals than usual. It won't happen again," I say.

"Make sure it doesn't. Pass the salt," Doug says. "The potatoes are bland. You should season more."

I look at my husband and see him clearly. I swallow and pass the salt.

CHAPTER 15

ROGER

Jess isn't picking up her phone, and I don't leave voice mails for anyone: they're a waste of time. If people don't pick up when I call them, it's their loss. I don't have time for messages, and besides, she'll see I called. I know she'll call back soon. She'll be out of money, out of her element on the wrong side of town. It's just a matter of time. I'll do anything to get them back home. And I always win.

That's why, when I read Julie's pathetic letter telling me I didn't care about anything except money, I immediately cut off their cards. If that's what she thinks I care about, I'll show her that she cares about it, too. More than she even knows. She'd already drained her savings accounts, at least the ones I could see, so she has enough to float for a few months. But come on, she's used to this way of living. She'll be crawling back soon enough. And Jess? I can't see her lasting more than a weekend without her American Express. She's my daughter, after all.

I wonder if those stupid rent-a-cops are still outside. I pull up my camera app and view the cameras hidden in the trees, pointed at the street. There they are. Smile, you're on camera, bozos. I wonder what would happen if I called the real cops on them. That could be kind of fun.

Where is that idiotic lawyer? I've got myself all worked up over things, and I really shouldn't be. This is not what a man of my considerable fortune does. We do not get worked up. We get even. Yes, Julie is wife number two. But that's only if you count Rachel, my first wife and my true love. They are very different situations. Rachel died six months into our marriage, aggressive form of leukemia. I almost followed her to the grave. Death by broken heart is a real thing, I'm telling you.

From then on, after Rachel, I knew I couldn't handle love. Not if I was going to be successful. You can't grow an empire with a broken heart. I learned that the hard way. So I pushed Rachel's memory to a special place in my heart and closed it off. I couldn't let anyone in that far, couldn't care that much, not ever again. So I haven't. The next wife would be a convenience, that's what I told myself.

I didn't think I had let her into my heart, but I miss Julie. I do.

And I miss Jess. My only daughter, only child. My heir.

I text her: Hey, I've called twice. Call me back.

Then I add: Love Dad.

Little dots light up my screen. It's Jess: At Bonnie's. She's having a party. Can we talk tomorrow? 🖤

I like that she responded. I like that she sent me a heart. I text back: Come by for breakfast? You're down the street.

Do I sound needy? Lonely? God, I hope not. I add: Or we can just talk tomorrow. Whatever.

Jess texts: Sure! I need to grab my car, too.

Well, that's good. She's still talking to me, and she's coming over tomorrow. I hope it's not just to pick up her BMW. Maybe I should invite Julie, too. We could have a proper brunch. Hell, I'll even spring for Pelican Hill if they'd like that. I pick up a framed photo of the three of us, spring break last year. We're in Hawaii, all sunburned, all smiles.

The girls arrived at our house in Maui a few days before me and when I got there, they were tan and happy. We went to a luau together the first night I was there. I took two days off, and Julie seemed pleased. Was she, though? I wonder now.

I stare at the photo again. Jess does look a lot like me. I wish she looked a little more like every other woman and girl around here. They're like a flock of exotic birds, these ladies. Tiny waists, huge breasts, and some even add padding to their butts. Full lips, full cheeks, long luxurious hair. I mean, Julie's that way.

Not Rachel, though, she didn't believe in any of that. She was sweet and soft, and actually Jess looks like Rachel. I don't know why I never saw that before. I had to find the opposite of Rachel to get past the pain, the reminders, and I did in Julie: my heart couldn't bear to look at a woman each day who reminded me of true love.

My phone rings, and I imagine it's Julie. But it's a blocked number. I answer with caution. I hate those robocalls.

"Roger here."

"Mr. Jones. It's Brad Schneider. I know you heard about Bob's terrible accident," the man says.

I don't know who Bob is or who this Brad is, and I'm about to hang up when he says, "Is there an urgent matter that you need an attorney's help with this weekend?"

Oh, the law firm. "Are you a partner?"

"Yes, sir. Just like poor Bob," Brad says.

I don't think he realizes that I don't care about Bob. "Yes, a shame. I do need an aggressive attorney right away. My wife has left me suddenly, and I want her back. Right away."

"Uh, well, what does she want, Mr. Jones?"

Brad is annoying me. What kind of question is that?

I will talk very slowly. "Unbeknownst to me, Julie drained her savings—the account I created for her—and bought a teardown on the wrong side of town. And then this morning she stole my daughter and moved there. Are you following any of this?"

I don't care if Brad doesn't like my tone. I just want my wife back. Sure, I could replace her right away if I wanted. But I'm too old to play that dating game. I just want things back the way they were.

"Mr. Jones. Why don't I come to your home? We can make a plan. Perhaps mediation, counseling? It sounds like that would be a good idea. My understanding is that there is a prenup, our firm prepared it, and it's airtight."

"Of course I had a prenup—I'm not an idiot. I just want Julie home, and she won't talk to me. But you can. It's your job. Why don't you go talk some sense into her? Can you do that?"

I know. Brad has never met Julie, or me, but he's paid to talk, right? Anybody can see that this house is better than what she bought. Anybody can see that she must have lost her mind. Anybody could talk her into the right thing, even Brad.

I hear him clearing his throat, which is annoying. I hate Brad.

"Look, Mr. Jones. I'm happy to come over to your house, or meet you to discuss this. I'm not comfortable approaching your wife, not given the circumstances. You understand, don't you? Better yet, Bob will be out of the hospital by Monday. That could give you both a cooling-off period."

Is Brad calling me a hothead? Is Brad trying to tell me what to do? I don't need to cool off. I need my wife and daughter here, at my home. "Fuck you, Brad. Get me another one of your partners or I'm changing law firms. You have ten minutes." It's so satisfying, hanging up on someone. In the olden days, back when we had big thick phones, you could slam those into the cradle and—pow!—make an impact. Now I stab at tiny buttons with my thick fingers, but still, he got the point.

How hard is it to get good representation these days? I mean, for $500 an hour, they should jump at the chance to pay Julie a visit.

I need a drink. I make my way to my study and admire the floor-to-ceiling bookshelves, complete with a ladder on wheels, just like the fanciest libraries in the world. I'm a sophisticate, my study says. But it's lying. I wish I read more. Most of these books are for show, a collection, like the wine in my one-thousand-bottle cellar. Give me a scotch and a good movie, that's really all I need. Westerns, those are my favorite. Cowboys have a certain manly appeal to guys like me. We couldn't get the women with our looks, or our horsemanship.

I can't believe Julie thinks she can get away with this.

I pour myself a double, add a huge cube to the center of the glass. I hold my drink up to toast my mom and dad, painted in oil and hanging above the fireplace. They never had clothes like that. They never had an oil painting of themselves when they were alive. I wonder if it would embarrass them, to see their likenesses frozen in time as something they weren't. I don't think my mom would mind. She'd probably like it a lot. I made sure the painter took out the lines on her face, the bags under her eyes, and gave her a smile. That I could do, in oil, after death. I even had a small oil painting done of me as a boy, wearing a cowboy hat and tiny boots with spurs. My dream growing up. I shake my head. My dad never owned a tie, and my mom's idea of fancy was her church clothes.

And their son never was a cowboy.

But I'm a winner. Sure, I've made a lot of enemies, a lot of people hate my guts. What do I care?

The doorbell rings. I carry my drink down the long hall and wonder if it's Amazon with a delivery for Julie. She gets something about every day. If it is, I'll drive it over to her at her new hovel. That will prove to her how great a guy I am. Who needs Brad or Bob or any of them? I'll woo her home.

I open the door. Unfortunately, it's not a delivery guy needing a signature.

It's the two jerks who have been following me.

They're not smiling, which is unsettling. I try to think of what I could possibly have done wrong. If it's not about business, and it's not about my family, that only leaves one possible thing. Crap.

CHAPTER 16

TOM

Vic wants to bang Jess's mom. What exactly am I supposed to do about that? Fortunately, he didn't get a good look at Jess. She must have left before our meeting was over. Thank god.

I drop onto my couch and pull out my phone. I see a couple of texts. I open the one from Jess first.

Want to come to the party tonight? ☺

Is she asking me out? She wants me to come to her party? I cannot believe my heart is thumping. What am I supposed to say? Shit. Of course, on the one night I have "homework" for my mission, Jess asks me to party with her. The girl of my dreams and the group of my dreams.

Everything is coming together on the same day. I don't recognize the feeling I have in my heart. It's a feeling like hope. Crap. I look around the walls of the shed and smile. The brothers loved my place. I see it with new eyes, new fondness now. They all hung around after the meeting and were all like, "How'd you find a place like this?"

"I got lucky," I'd said, acting like it wasn't the back shed of my parents' house.

"It is a nice place," a guy named Bull said. "Oh, bro, Vic asked me to take the ice cream run for him. OK with you?" The man had fist-bumped me when he saw the surprised look on my face. "Yeah, I'm on kid duty."

"Got it. Great to meet you, Bull," I'd said. "I thought Vic was handling the kid run?" I knew I shouldn't worry. If Vic had trusted Bull with my two little brothers, that was fine with me.

"It's all me. One hundred percent, my man, but don't worry—the little guys will think my name is Vic. That's what he told me to say," Bull said. "Better take off. School's out in a couple hours."

"Thanks, man," I said. "Tell the boys hi for me."

"No problem. Kids like me, and well, with ice cream, what can go wrong? You want me to hold them an hour, right?"

A wave of guilt swept through me, but I pushed it away. Doug deserves this. Sandi, too. And the boys need to get used to my new friends. Even if Vic told me he was going to handle it personally. I guess, in a way, he is handling it. "Yes, sounds good," I said.

"Hey, guys, it's time to get moving, some of us have things to do." Vic's distinctive voice had boomed through the crowd. Bull nodded my way and left the carriage house.

Vic was the last to leave, reminding me to get Jess's mom's number.

"I'll come by on Monday, see how you're doing. Meet your lady friends." He patted my shoulder with a smile. It wasn't a request, it was happening. "Let me know if there's any trouble with the ice cream run."

"If you trust Bull, then I do," I said.

"That's the spirit," Vic said, and he was gone.

Despite Vic's focus on the ladies in the main house, I'm stoked about the party in the carriage house. I'm reeling from all the praise. They like me, like my house, the beer, of course. It's nice to have friends. But these guys also know about Julie and Jess now. That part isn't great.

How was I supposed to know the stupid new owners would be hot?

I look out the window toward my room. Jess's room. Our room. It's still dark. Wherever she is, she's staying out late. I'll wait up. I can't go party with a bunch of high school kids. I have work to do.

I text Jess: I can't party tonight, but come home and see me. I'll be up.

I try not to stare at my phone for a response. I won't. I put it down on the coffee table and start cleaning up the beer bottles scattered around the room. I still can't believe I fit everybody in here. When Vic told everybody it was time to go, I was sad. I was having fun.

Speaking of getting kicked out, where the hell am I going to go if I move? Vic told me he will help me find a place to stay, but I don't have any money. What I make at the bar won't cover more than my food. I'm screwed.

I stop cleaning up, sit down on my couch, and pull out my laptop. I open a blank document. Vic told me I should write down why I want to do what I'm going to do. I don't want to write about it, but Vic says it helps to get it out. He says I have more than enough reason to do it from what I've told him. Despite being pumped up by the party, the adrenaline rush I felt when Vic asked me to sit next to him, my energy is fading. It's almost like I could take a nap if I didn't have so much to do.

The blank page on my computer screen is taunting me. But I have time. My plan takes shape on Sunday. And I'm not a big writer anyway. That's another reason I hated school. By the time they all figured out I was dyslexic and had ADHD, I'd already felt the sting of failure and the frustration of trying to sit in those stupid classrooms. All the other kids knew I was a dummy from the beginning. Sandi tried to help me. She was the first to notice I couldn't read in Sunday school. But I just couldn't learn, even when they sent me to the lady at school who works with the "special needs" kids. No, that didn't work. All that did was put a big target on my back for the bullies. And they all told me how stupid I was until I got big enough to mess them up.

I always wonder if my mom left because I was stupid. Maybe so? She didn't even tell me goodbye. Just drove away. I never even knew anything was wrong. Dad told me it had nothing to do with me, that it was her problem, she wasn't a godly woman. He told me we weren't going to discuss her, not ever again. That he'd find a replacement. And he did. Six months later, he found Sandi.

But I'm pretty sure any mom who leaves her kid behind . . . well, there's something wrong with the kid.

I look at the blank computer screen. I'll show everyone just how much I know. I start to type but delete the words as soon as I write them. I sound weak, stupid. Maybe I'll just cut and paste something from someone online. There's a lot of hate out there if you know where to look. And I do.

I stand, walk to the window, and look up at my old bedroom. Jess still isn't home, at least she isn't upstairs, but I do see a shape moving behind the drawn curtains downstairs. That shape used to be my step-mom, jumping and running and serving my dad's every whim. She's so weak, so hopeless. She's like his servant. And that cracks me up because he always talks about how he's a servant of the Lord. My ass. He's only in his line of work because that's all he knows. And he's only barely holding on. It won't be long before his new congregation figures out he's not what he seems.

Just now Julie looks out the back door, the curtain pulled to the side. We make eye contact. I wave. I'm friendly, Julie, see?

Julie frowns, forces herself to give a lame wave back.

I open my door and walk quickly across the backyard. I'm at the back door before she can pretend she's gone. Before she can hide.

I tap on the glass. "Julie, hey, is Jess home yet?"

I check my phone. It's almost eleven at night. Julie should be getting ready for bed. Jess is in high school. Doesn't she have a curfew? A gorgeous girl like her. She should.

I hear Julie unlock the door. She pulls it open, just a crack. "Hi, Tom, I'm about to go to sleep. Jess isn't home."

"Oh, OK, well shouldn't she be? She's in high school." I mean, I haven't been a parent, and probably won't ever get to be one since I'll be alone forever and girls suck, but I do know rules are for the kids' safety. Especially girls. There are a lot of bogeymen out there, for real.

"She's fine. She's at her best friend's house. She'll probably be there all weekend. Good night, Tom." Julie ends our conversation by closing the door. I want to know what friend's house, and what part of town. Should I go by and make sure Jess is OK? You know, in kind of a big-brother way?

I walk back to the shed and text Jess: When will you be back? I'm waiting for you.

I wait a couple of minutes, and she still doesn't answer. I add: It's Tom. At the house. Our house.

My house.

I wait for ten minutes and nothing. Whatever. Her loss. I tell myself she's not a friend, not a potential lover. She's a squatter in my old bedroom, and she and her mom need to be driven away. I can tell her mom is afraid of me already. Those looks she gives me say it all. If I said, "Boo," she'd jump off the roof.

But Jess. She's different. She likes me. I can tell she does. And she has a great smile, and a great ass. And she's so young. I'm torn. I sort of like having her in my room, in my life. But it's not right. I look over at my computer, open and waiting for me to finish my damn letter. It feels like homework. I check my phone again. No answer. Fine. Who needs her? Who needs any women—they just let you down. My friends are antiwoman in general. No girlfriends, just fuck buddies. Vic says women make you weak if you have a relationship. And that they try to get you to share all your secrets so they can betray you. It all started with Eve, Vic says.

I sit down behind my computer. I know I should be writing. But I can't. I check my phone again. No texts. All I can think about is Jess, and that's not a good development, not for anyone.

CHAPTER 17

JULIE

Tom's a creep, his friends are scary, and I should never have agreed to let him stay.

As I climb the stairs to my bedroom, I remind myself that he will be gone on Sunday at noon. It's in the contract. I'll have him forcibly removed if he doesn't get out. And then I'll take a look inside the carriage house for the first time. The Realtor had told me it was appropriate for storage, but maybe it has more potential. I'll sage out there, too, for good measure. Tom and his negative energy will be gone.

It's fine. I made a mistake. But this is my first real estate transaction on my own. It's a learning experience. So now I know not to let wayward sons stay on the property after closing. So there. What else have I learned today? That I'm strong. I am.

I've also learned that a house, like a face, doesn't need to be overdone. When I compare the house I decorated for Roger and me all those years ago to this home, I cringe with embarrassment. Sure, I was only in my twenties when Roger asked me to do it, so I defaulted to what I knew at the time from working in the medi spa: pinks, white leather, lots of crystal, and some faux white fur thrown in for fun. Yes, our oceanfront home, truth be told, looks like Barbie could move right in. And I guess she did: me. The only room spared was Roger's library. He insisted on handling that room himself. Most likely because he knew that was the only room he'd spend any time in.

I walk into my new bedroom and appreciate Sandi's spare style, her clean decorating, the way I feel at ease the moment I walk in. The wall color is a pale blue, the trim a bright white. The lighting is soothing, spare. The fireplace is brick painted white. It's the opposite of everything I came from and exactly what I need.

I walk through the closet—two simple sliding doors on either side revealing a perfect setup—and think about my old closet with shame. I had an entire section, larger than this, for each of my favorite designers and a system like a dry cleaner's moving rack to change out the old for the new.

Not that I kept anything past LY (last year). No, that wouldn't have been acceptable in my group. It's either off the runway or vintage, nothing in between. I shake my head and walk into the bathroom. Simple white countertop and backsplash. The shower is tiled in a black and white.

This is me. This is real. I am so happy I'm home.

I hear a sound, a crunch, outside on the driveway and a spike of fear punches through my illusions. I walk to the bedroom window. There aren't any new cars parked on the street, and from what I can see from here, the driveway is empty. I need to calm down, I need to do something to make this house feel safe. To make it my home.

I search through the box in the corner of my bedroom and my fingers wrap around my mezuzah, a gift from my mom when Roger and I married. It's made of stone and opens to reveal the parchments inside.

Mom instructed: "It's to fulfill the mitzvah. You must put it on your home to write the words of God on your house. No matter what Roger says. You will be protected."

It didn't work out that way, though.

"What exactly is that?" Roger asked after I'd unwrapped the present from my mom.

"It's a way to bless our new home," I had said, holding it up. "I'll just tuck it right here in the doorway. No one will even notice it. Except me. It's for protection, for our home."

"No. I don't like it. It's weird, kind of fringe. And we aren't fringe. We've arrived," Roger said, pushing the box away before walking inside. It took a while for me to train myself not to kiss the doorpost every time I walked into the house because the mezuzah wasn't there.

It's as much my fault as Roger's. If you don't stick up for yourself, traditions that matter, then how do you expect someone else to respect you? That's my mom's saying. I realize now, it's easier said than done. I need to call my mom and apologize to her for not respecting her all these years.

But there is something I can do tonight. This is my home, and it needs a blessing. It needs this. I carry the mezuzah down the stairs, flipping on all the lights I just turned off. I disarm the alarm and step out onto the front porch. A quick check of the street makes me think I'm alone. I reach up to the right side of the doorway, a little more than halfway up, and hold the mezuzah in place while reciting: "Blessed are You, Lord our God, King of the Universe, Who sanctified us with His mitzvot, and commanded us to affix a mezuzah."

My mind flashes to my bat mitzvah, when cousins and aunts and uncles I barely knew celebrated me, my future. I remember my mom and me standing at the front of the synagogue with the rabbi as I recited the haftorah. I remember feeling nervous at being watched but loved and cared for—a part of a tradition bigger than myself, a people who are survivors.

I screw the mezuzah tightly onto the doorway. One last touch to make sure it's secure and I hurry back inside and set the alarm.

I did it. Mom would be pleased. Jess is likely going to be shocked. Back upstairs in my room, I find my pajamas and all my toiletries, and go about setting up my bathroom. There are two sinks. I can use either, or both at the same time. I'm like a kid in her first hotel room.

As I brush my teeth, I remind myself that tomorrow is a new day. That all in all, I accomplished a lot in the past twelve hours. That thought shocks me. It was this morning that I left the only real home I've ever lived in as an adult and moved here. It was just this morning, in the rain, that Jess and I pulled up to this place, our new home.

I wish Jess were here with me, to help me settle in. But I need to do this myself. She'll be away at school starting in the fall, and I'll be forced to make it alone. I suspect I'll be alone forever now. I mean, who wants to date a fortysomething-year-old? I'll focus on my career, that's what I'll do. I'll dust off that UCLA design and media arts degree and get to work. I'll start with business cards, and then I'll wine and dine all the real estate agents I know, starting with mine. So many people are overwhelmed when they move to a new space, and most aren't as lucky as I am to have Sandi's good taste already in place. My new house is perfect. I can do this for others. I can. I'm so excited.

Before I plug my phone in for the night, I decide to check in with Jess. I doubt she'll answer me, but she'll see my note in the morning.

I type: I love you honey. Hope you're having a blast with Bonnie. Can't wait to see you in the morning. I miss you! xo

That might have been a little too syrupy. What can I say? I need to make up for lost time. It seems the older Jess got, the more I couldn't connect with her. I was a great mom for tea parties and trips to the American Girl store. Jess's birthday parties were always over the top, themed and expensive, catered and party planned. But the day-to-day connection, somehow it slipped away. We became roommates, vacation buddies, but not too much more. I suppose it's because my mom tried so hard for deep connection that I stayed on the surface, afraid if I dug too deep, I'd drive Jess away like my mom did to me.

I push the tears from the corners of my eyes. And I focused too much on things that didn't matter. Like lunches and charity work, like tennis and Botox parties. I have been around, but I haven't been present for my daughter. Not until now, which is ironic.

Jess isn't going to come home from Bonnie's. Not tomorrow morning, not before graduation. Not if Bonnie's parents agree. I could try calling the parents, but we aren't close and I doubt it would make any difference to any of them. Jess picked Bonnie over me. Period. But I'm not giving up. I know my daughter wants a deeper connection: every mother and daughter have their struggles. She'll see the changed me, the free me, the real me and want to hang out. I'll win her over. I will.

It's a process, one I've worked on. I met a counselor at yoga class. I made an appointment with her and started working on me. On my dreams. Once Roger asked what the expense was for, Roberts & Associates. I told him they were art consultants helping me spruce up the pool house. He didn't ask anything else, just nodded and headed to his library.

I sometimes wonder what could have happened if he'd taken me in his arms and asked if I was happy. Asked how I was doing, what I wanted out of life. But he didn't. He walked away. I can't blame him for his actions. I've learned, with help, that I can only control mine. And that's when I decided to break free. And I won't go back there, no matter what.

My phone buzzes on my bedside table.

Jess texts: I love you mom. Sleep well.

Well, that's something. Jess loves me. She'll be home in the morning. She's not too mad about the move. As I turn off the bedside light, I hope I'm not just kidding myself. About everything.

When I close my eyes, all I see is the man with the dark, angry eyes from this afternoon, standing on the driveway staring at me, threatening me, licking his lips.

I open my eyes and sit up. A chill runs through me.

I climb out of bed. I need to make sure the alarm is on.

CHAPTER 18

JESS

The music is deafening, so I can't hear what Bonnie is trying to tell me. That, and the room is spinning. I glance down at my phone. It's after midnight, and we've been partying since this afternoon. I need air. I push through the crowd and make it outside to the swimming pool. Clusters of kids dot the backyard, but nobody is here, behind the pool house.

I dump the rest of the red plastic cup of beer on the grass. I've lost count of how many times somebody has refilled it. No wonder I'm so buzzed. My life is so mixed up, so strange. Everything I thought I knew about my mom is wrong. I thought she liked this life, our life, but she hates it, I guess. I don't understand any of it. I just think it sucks.

My phone pings with a text. It's from Tom. Kind of strange we just met this morning and now my stomach does a little flip knowing he's thinking of me. I see his bright blue eyes, his strong arms, his loneliness. I see me in him. He wants to know when I'm coming home. So sweet. Should I text back NEVER? No, that wouldn't be nice. He seems very attached to the house. And sure, I guess it's sort of cute. I get it. It's much more manageable than a place like this, a place like our house. Maybe it's because it's all he knows? I get that. I do. I feel sorry for him.

Another text comes in. It's Mom. She's turning in for the night and hopes to see me tomorrow. Maybe I'll meet her for dinner in town, our favorite café, and break the news that I'm living with Bonnie. Poor Mom. I know she means well, but I'm not suffering across town just because she has decided to. Nope. Not happening.

I text: I love you mom. Sleep well.

That should appease her, at least until the morning.

"There you are. Why are you hiding out here?" Chase Merritt, our class treasurer and the biggest suck-up to parents and teachers and coaches that ever lived, appears like a mirage. As president and vice president, Bonnie and I outrank him and he knows it. I mean, he's cute in that all-American jock way, but different in a way that's hard to explain. Something's off with him, but it's not my problem. Not anymore. We dated freshman year, before I knew any better, before I grew up. He was all about hooking up. And he was a terrible kisser, but I didn't tell him. That would have crushed his ego. He's a volleyball star so he's got that going for him, but emotionally, he's like a toddler. Turns out boys' frontal lobes take longer to fully develop, and here's your perfect proof.

"Just needed a break." I look up into his bright blue eyes and recognize the look. Lust. Beer-fueled lust.

"You look good tonight, Jess." Chase leans in for a kiss.

I turn my head, and his lips land on my cheek. "Stop it. We aren't hooking up anymore, remember?"

"Oh, babe, come on." Now he's wrapped his arms around my waist, pulling me toward him.

This is just another reason I cannot wait to get out of here, even though I'm only going to USC when I wanted to go to a school on the East Coast. My dad was adamant that USC was my future, that its network of alumni would help me like no other school when I graduate. I know it was his dream to go there, that much is obvious. I got into a few of the schools back east, but not any of the Ivies. So I guess in a way, Dad was right. USC was the highest-ranked school that accepted me, so off I go.

It still will be a new start because most of these clowns won't be there. I think only one other guy from our class was accepted, and he is an awkward loner who I never really talk to. I sound mean, but I'm not. The problem is we've all been at school together since kindergarten. It's like we're a big family, brothers and sisters, who hook up and break up and otherwise act like siblings, one-upping each other, competing in class and at sports. It's the same old, same old every year.

I need space. Air. Escape.

"Let's go back inside, OK?" I disentangle from him but grab his hand and pull him toward the party. In just the short time I've been hiding outside, the crowd has thinned. Likely just our core group of seniors, our tightest group of friends, is left now. As for me, I'm ready for bed. It's been a long day. The ground sways as Chase grabs my waist and helps me inside. I reward him with a kiss.

Bonnie is inside the door, a strange look on her face. She sees me and slowly shakes her head. I lead Chase inside and hear his friend Griffin, the men's water polo team captain, say, "There you lovebirds are. Come play. It's a new German-engineered game."

Chase and I make it to the beer pong table just in time for the rest of the kids to raise their arms in some sort of salute. Chase raises his arm, too, laughing. His arm is heavy around my waist. I look at the table and realize the red cups have been pushed into a shape, the shape of the Nazi swastika.

I don't know what's going on, but I do know how to play beer pong. I grab the Ping-Pong ball and toss it, landing a perfect shot.

"Great shot, Jess," Chase says. "You're a natural."

"I've had a lot of practice," I say. Chase looks at me with a combination of awe and lust. I push away from his embrace. I feel sick, and the room tilts.

"Smile!" Ellie says, and we all do as she takes a photo on her phone.

"What's wrong, Bonnie?" I ask as she slides in to stand next to me. I want to ask her more, but the music is so loud and the room sways.

"I don't like what they're doing," she says to me, and then yells, "Party's over!"

"Chill, Bonnie. It's cool. We're having fun," Griffin says. He tosses a ball and chugs.

Another one of the water polo guys, Dane, says, "Smile, everyone," as he takes a photo.

Next to me Bonnie yells, "Stop it. I mean it."

"You helped set up the game, remember? Everyone is playing it. It's everywhere online. Jews versus Nazis. It's fine. It's just fun. Different," Griffin says to Bonnie, pulling her into a hug.

I see the look in her eyes, and I can tell she's over it. I can't believe how mad she's getting. It's just a game.

Beside me Chase is chanting a song I've never heard before. Some of the other guys join in. It's foreign. German maybe?

"It's the ultimate rage cage!" Mark yells. He's the brainiac of our group. Headed to Stanford in the fall. He's wasted, his eyes glassy and his face glistening with sweat.

It seems all the kids around the table are taking photos. Chase is by my side again. He leans in for a kiss, and I let him. More photos, more chants. The room isn't swaying anymore, thank goodness. I just want to go to sleep.

One of the guys yells, "Everybody show me the OK sign—you know, for Oceanside!"

Chase and I do it, we all do, as more photos are taken. This is all getting old. I just want to go to sleep.

"I'm going to get killed if my parents walk down here," Bonnie says to me. She's nervous and slurring. "I'm serious, we need to break this up."

Through my drunken haze I agree. I know I can get Chase to help. I give him another kiss.

"Chase, babe, can you help get everyone to leave?"

"One selfie, babe?" Chase snaps the photo before I can agree or disagree. He turns to his friends around the beer pong table and says, "Let's go, everyone. Bonnie's calling it." And then to me he whispers, "Come home with me. My driver is waiting out front."

"Thanks, but I'm sleeping here," I tell him while fending off another sloppy attempt at a kiss. I tease him with a future by whispering in his ear, "Let's talk tomorrow. Your car is waiting."

My mind flashes to Chase and Tom meeting. Chase would be totally intimidated by a real man like Tom. Tom has no pretense, no designer loafers, and certainly no driver. Chase wouldn't try to kiss me in front of Tom. I know that already. I like that thought.

Chase gives me a wink and leaves when Bonnie turns on all the lights in the party room. The remaining kids blink in the bright light while scrambling to grab jackets and purses and leave in record time.

Bonnie leans against the wall, a stunned look on her face.

I shuffle to her side, blinking and yawning. "What's wrong? I don't get it."

"What's wrong with you? Don't you know what they were doing? The game they were playing? Ugh. I'm so busted."

Bonnie's parents let her drink and have parties all the time. I don't know why tonight is different.

"You're fine. I'll help you. Let's just get all the red cups cleaned up. I swear it will look really good down here. Nobody will know the difference. Just another night of beer pong," I tell her. I know her parents' housekeeping crew will be here in the morning. They work every day, even Sundays, all in white uniforms like a chic hotel.

She's overreacting.

"Look at that table! What do you see?" Bonnie's face is red with anger as she shoves me toward the center of the room. "What if the idiots post about this? Do you see the swastika?"

"Sure. But it's just a game. Nazis versus Jews. Nobody will take it seriously," I say, swallowing. It's just a game like all the other drinking games. "I'll help you clean it up." I hurry to the corner of the party room and find a closet with garbage bags. I pull out two and hand one to Bonnie. We clear the table first, and then start grabbing red cups from tables and the floor. By the time we're finished, my head is almost normal.

Bonnie's stress has pushed my buzz away.

We meet at the door, bags filled with plastic cups. She drops hers on the ground and slumps into a chair.

"Hey, we were all messing around. Don't worry," I say, although I'm beginning to share her dread as my buzz recedes.

Bonnie drops her head. She holds up her phone, open to Snapchat. "It's too late," she says.

I stare at the screen, and it's a blurry picture of red cups. Ellie posted it to her TikTok, too. She's put it everywhere online. This is not fine. "I'm sure she made it private, just to our friends. Let's go to bed."

I flip off the lights to the party room, and we walk the two flights up to Bonnie's suite in silence.

"I shouldn't have gone along with the boys' stupid idea. What was I thinking?" she says when we reach the door to her room. "At least I didn't play. You acted like you loved it. You played with them for real. They probably have a photo of you playing that game."

I can't believe she's trying to blame this on me. "I was outside, hanging out with Chase. I didn't even know what was going on."

Bonnie shakes her head, her forehead lined with worry. "And what were they singing? Some Nazi song? How do they even know a Nazi song?" She looks up at the ceiling and sighs. "I just don't want anything to screw up my acceptance to Harvard. I worked too hard for it to be ruined." Bonnie is still slurring. She needs to sleep it off. She's so gloomy all of a sudden.

"Stop worrying. Didn't your dad go there? There's a building named after your family." I shake my head. "You're fine. Night!"

Bonnie steps into her room and closes the door behind her, still scowling. As for me, I'm not sleepy anymore. I open my phone. Bonnie is right. It doesn't look good. I know the water polo team has a few special songs they sing at private events, but I've never seen them do it in person. It's kind of creepy, seeing it online, hearing it online. But at least it's just shared with our friends. The post will disappear soon, like it never happened.

I hope I'm not kidding myself. I walk to the bathroom and chug two glasses of water, but that doesn't make me feel any better. My heart thumps in my chest as I climb into bed.

To distract myself, I send a text. I wonder if Tom's still awake, thinking about me, too.

SATURDAY

ONE DAY BEFORE

CHAPTER 19

TOM

It's 1:00 a.m. and finally, a text from Jess: Are you up?

I'm bored, sitting in front of my computer, checking my phone every fifteen minutes for a text. So of course, when it comes in, I text back right away, like an infatuated idiot. I haven't felt this way since elementary school. That was the last time a girl liked me that I can remember. Sally Hawk. She was an angel in pigtails. We were best friends, and then she moved away in fifth grade. I was crushed. A lot of people leave me. I guess it's a pattern.

Yes, I'm pathetic. I text: Yes I'm awake! You home?

Oh my god, I used an exclamation point like a frickin' idiot teenage-girl shithead.

She texts: No. At Bonnie's. She's passed out. I'm bored.

I'd be happy to help with that. I text: Come home. Come see me.

I watch for the little dots to appear on my phone like an idiot and hope she'll say she's calling an Uber. Is that too much to hope for?

I stare at my phone.

Nothing.

She's texting someone else. She's just like all the other girls I've known. She's a tease. A flirt. All through high school, whenever I thought a chick was into me, it was "as a friend." She wouldn't want to "lead me on." Jess is the same, I guess. I should have seen it in her from the start. She gets my interest and then she toys with me. She's cute, has money, has it all, so she is just using me. Trying to get on my good side. Maybe she's working with her mom to get rid of me. That's probably it.

I stand up from the couch and kick the wall. I don't care about the mark my steel-toe boots make on the white paint. Not anymore. Sandi isn't here to tell me to clean the marks off the wall, and well, it just doesn't matter anymore. I'm such an idiot. I kick the wall harder this time, pleased with the hole that's starting to form. Take that, stupid women trying to steal my house. If you aren't careful, there'll be nothing left of it by the time I leave. If I leave.

My phone dings. It's her.

She texts: I can't leave Bonnie. And have breakfast with my dad in the a.m. I'm free tomorrow night?

I stare at the phone. Is she serious? Could she be? Am I free tomorrow night? I am always free except when the guys call, but they don't have anything scheduled for Saturday. I can get someone to cover my shift at the bar. Sunday is my day of action, sure, but not Saturday.

I text: I can be free tomorrow night. What do you have in mind?

Ugh. I sound like a letch.

She texts: Let's figure it out tomorrow. Night.

Well, what does that mean? Yes to a date? No? Fuck. I text: Night.

I scroll back through our text exchange, getting more turned on by the minute. Jess is a senior in high school. Old enough to party, old enough to drive, old enough to screw. I don't know what she has in mind, but I know what I'm doing tomorrow night. I'm too excited to sleep, so finally I start to write.

The time I remember becoming a man is easy. Sandi, my stepmom, had sent me to my room for something I did, I can't remember what. But that's what she always did. Wait until your dad comes home. He'll handle things. I heard him coming down the hall, snapping the belt like some big tough guy and there I am, at age nine, and I make a decision. He barges in my room without knocking. Says what have you done this time or something similar, and tells me to drop my pants and bend over.

And then he started swinging the belt. I remember the sting, the pain on the back of my legs, my butt. I remember everything, like always. He was mad this time, though. Because I wouldn't apologize.

He kept yelling, "Apologize!" And then he'd hit me again.

"No!" I yelled back, all sixty pounds of conviction. We kept at it, this standoff, until Sandi opened the door.

"Doug, I think that's enough," she said, her voice shaking as she took in the scene. My welts already bled.

I'll never forget the look in my dad's eyes. He would have kept going, I know he would have. He would have killed me over my defiance.

"You're such a loser, Tom," he spat and walked out of my room.

And even though I had to sleep on my front, and I couldn't sit down for what seemed like days, I'd won that round. We both knew it. That's why he had to escalate the fight, I suppose. But every day, every year, I was growing stronger. And now, I'm ready to win.

My fingers hunt and peck for the right letters. It took forever to write these first few sentences, but now I've finally got my thoughts out even as the memory fires up my hatred. I have a plan, I remind myself. Jess will be proud of me, I think as I finish up. She can never know I'm the one behind it, of course. She'll read about it in the news, and my friends likely will brag about it on the dark web, and she'll look at me with those questioning eyes. She'll be under me, loving me, and I'll nod slightly. And she'll smile.

I'm so turned on I have to take a cold shower. Vic tells us not to jack off. He told us that in the desert. It makes us weak. We must only use girls for that. Without any attachment, of course. If we can't get a girl, we're celibate. We hold our power.

The whole time in the shower all I can think about is Jess. I can't wait for tomorrow night.

CHAPTER 20

SANDI

It's morning, Saturday morning, my favorite time of the day and my favorite day of the week. I like to sit in the kitchen, read the newspaper. It's old-fashioned but comforting. Early morning. Before the boys are awake. There is no mad scramble for school, no schedule to speak of. In the quiet, no one demands anything from me, no one expects me to step into my role: dutiful daughter, perfect mother, doting spouse. This is my time. And today, I will use it to make some decisions. It is time for me to see things clearly.

Doug is not living the word of God, not at all. I know God. I know his expectations for his believers. I need to show my boys the truth and the light, before it's too late.

Typically Doug is not home on a Saturday morning. For some reason this Saturday is different. I suppose it's because he really doesn't have much to do out here with his new flock. It takes a while for a new pastor to settle in with a congregation, some longer than others. Some never do. Some of the old flock actually believe Doug wanted to move out here to the boonies. They pictured themselves joining us out here, Jesus help them. Nice words, but I haven't seen any of them at this new church. I don't blame them. Most of the flock heard the gossip, knew the truth. I held my head high for my boys, while inside the betrayal, the shame, grew like a vine.

It is not my shame. These were not my decisions. I stand and cross the kitchen to turn on the television. I recognize the LA news anchor. She's always dressed as if she's about to hurry off camera to a cocktail party. Day or night. Low-cut dresses, hugging her perfect figure. Today's dress is a neon green. I look down at my white T-shirt and faded jeans. I wonder: If I dressed like a television anchor, would Doug notice me again? I don't know when he lost his desire for me as a woman. Was it after our second baby together? Was it just his quest to conquer whoever he could? I don't really know. I bow my head and pray to Jesus. "Please, give me the strength to see things clearly from now on. Help me guide my sons to the truth and the light, I pray in your name, amen."

I turn my attention back to the television, and I'm surprised to see Tom's high school on the screen. "Let's throw it to Megan, who is standing in front of Oceanside High School. Megan, what's going on down there?" Cocktail Anchor asks with concern and a seductive pout.

"This story is just developing, but it has serious ramifications for this otherwise wealthy and private enclave in Orange County." Megan the reporter looks down at her notes. "Early this morning, at a private home somewhere near the school, a group of teenagers played a drinking game. But it wasn't just any drinking game. This one involved red plastic cups that had been formed into a swastika. The game is called Jews versus Nazis, as the teens' Snapchat stories show. We've blurred the faces, but you can clearly see the beer pong game that turned sinister, complete with Nazi salutes. We'll have more on this developing story at noon. Back to you."

Behind me Doug says, "Holy shit. That's one of the Brennan boys. I'd know him anywhere." I don't know how long he's been in the kitchen, but as I turn to face him, he's shaking his head. "This is bad, Sandi. Real bad for all those kids in the photo. And this is real bad for the Brennans. I mean, it's just a drinking game, but still."

"Of course it's bad. We should pray for them all. They should know better." I don't know what else to say. Teens can be so foolish, but a Nazi drinking game seems more than foolish. It's evil. A chill runs down my spine. Perhaps it's for the best we're away from that town.

"I need to reach out. I'm the Brennans' pastor, no matter what the church officials say. I know them. They'll need me now. I'm still a member of the interfaith hate crime and crisis team, I think." He shakes his head again.

Doug eats a banana in record speed and is out the door without so much as a kiss goodbye. He's amped up. I know that look. It's best to steer clear when he's in that mood. It's almost like he's excited, like this is his moment to shine, like this is all about him.

Maybe he thinks this incident is his entry back into Oceanside, back into the old congregation. I bet he's thinking if he helps smooth this over, just maybe he'll be invited back. He's fooling himself. His fall was swift and deep. When he came home, telling me he'd been replaced and moved to a small congregation, he delivered the news as if it had been his choice.

"Housing is cheaper. We'll get a bigger place. Is dinner ready?"

I stood at the kitchen sink. Stunned. "I love this house. I love my neighborhood. Was it her? Why? You owe me an explanation." I turned in time to see him coming at me, his hand in a fist.

"You will move when I say we're moving. You will sell this home fast, and quietly. Understood? You will be happy in the country," Doug said, spittle forming in the corner of his mouth.

"Yes, I understand," I'd said, turning away from him, tears rolling down my face. It was one of the darkest days of my life. But as always, I carried on.

And so, I've made this place my new home. Besides, I feel shame whenever I'm near our former congregation. The boys are better off here. They have grass and space, their own rooms, and new friends will appear soon. I'll make my way, too. I'm certain I can find common ground out here. If nothing else, maybe I'll find peace here. I need peace—and love. I need God back at the center of my family's life. I hear my dad's voice in my head: *With God, anything is possible.* I have hope.

I toss Doug's banana peel into the trash can as his words echo in my head.

"This is real bad for the Brennans," he'd said.

It's actually bad for all of us. It's not about one family's reputation. But that's all Doug focused on. How bad it was for the wealthy family whose kid did the sieg-heil salute, and how he can use it to work his way back into their favor. Everything Doug does is to benefit Doug. Period.

I wonder who all the other kids in the photo are. I wonder what they were thinking.

But it's hard to explain. It doesn't make sense. That this could happen in Oceanside, in a place where kids have everything. Is this a game they play every weekend? Did Tom play?

I'm going to call him. He knows things; he went to that high school. I hope he'll answer. It's his last day with a roof over his head. Maybe I can figure out a way to help him. It's the Christian thing to do.

His phone rings once and goes to voice mail. "Hey, Tom, just calling to see if you need help packing today. Well, call me. I love you."

I hang up, afraid to leave a message about the drinking game. As usual, I'm afraid to ask what he knows, what he's really up to. I'm afraid of the truth with him, and I always have been. For years, he's been turning darker. It started with the violent video games. And he'd spend hours on the internet, locked away in the carriage house.

One day, when I was weeding the back garden, I looked in Tom's window. I saw a poster of a woman, naked, with a black leash around her neck, hands bound in front of her. I started shaking. How could such depravity adorn his wall?

But then, Tom appeared in the window. He shook his head, and the next thing you know he'd tacked a towel over the window. But I saw what I saw, and I'm assuming there was more.

I should have forced my way inside, ripped down the terrible posters, marched Tom to church with me, had him repent his ways. But these new friends and their beliefs have a pull much stronger than my love for my oldest son.

Tom was a loner in high school, I knew that, but I thought college would be different. Instead he dropped out and returned to his online world. And then, he found them in person, or they found him. His dark, hate-filled new friends found him working at the bar, and now he feels like he belongs somewhere, to a group. It all happened so fast, just before our move.

Forgive me, Lord. I was afraid to confront him then. I chose to look the other way, to focus on the little boys.

And now I'm afraid it is too late.

CHAPTER 21

ROGER

This can't be good. I liked the looks of them a lot better when they were outside, across the street. They looked smaller, too. Now they're in my space. Filling my doorway.

"Mr. Jones. Good evening. I'm Detective Logan, and this is Detective Gonzalez. We're with the FBI. Can we come in?" The muscular guy doing the talking, Logan, seems excited to see me, as if he hasn't been following me all over the damn place. I guess this is his big move. Goody for you, Logan.

I step back and allow them into the foyer. It isn't lost on me that I need an attorney. I can't imagine what all this fuss is about. Smith says all our deals are clean, and Julie wouldn't hire the FBI to tail me. This is harassment then, pure and simple. I'll get rid of them. "We can speak here. What do you want?"

The other guy, Gonzalez—the shorter one with glowering eyes—says, "Sir, we have a warrant for your arrest, and we will be executing this search warrant."

"I need to call my attorney." I take a step back. A search warrant? What the hell? I'll never consent to this. "What the hell do you think I'm hiding here? I worked hard for everything you'll find in my house. This all belongs to me. You will not search my house."

"We can. And we will. You can call an attorney from the station." Logan holds handcuffs. "We'll try to make this discreet, but it seems somebody tipped off the media. So, well, we'll drive away quickly. Turn around, hands behind your back."

The media? "What is the charge? Why are you doing this?" I keep my voice low and menacing, but the fact is I'm scared shitless. Can they do this? Just come to my home like a totalitarian regime and lock me up? I feel my heart racing. I don't have my watch on to monitor it. What if I have a heart attack? Shit. Where are my girls when I need them? I want Julie here to help me.

"Actually, we are arresting you for lewd conduct in a public place, among other things. You know the Gold Club? You like it there, we know. You like the services offered. Well, your buddy who owns it is going down on a full array of federal racketeering charges, including prostitution," Gonzalez says. Logan grabs my left arm.

I chug my drink before Gonzalez takes my glass. I hear the handcuffs click into place behind me. They have got to be kidding. I haven't done anything wrong, not really. Everybody goes there. "This is a big mistake you're making. Do you know who I am? What I'm worth? I don't need to pay to get sex. I'm married."

Both of them chuckle. This isn't funny. I will not have anyone photograph me in this state. "I demand to see an attorney now. I will not leave the premises without my attorney."

The agents each take an arm; even when I try to shake them off, I can't. This is ridiculous. I could give them a lifetime's salary today, but I know I shouldn't say that. It could be used against me. They are enjoying trying to bring me down. Nobody can hurt me, nobody can take what I have. "I demand my attorney. Do you know who I am?"

"You'll call your attorney from the station, Mr. Jones. Come on. You don't want to make a scene in front of them." Logan leads me out my own front door and into what can only be described as a paparazzi circus. There is a downside to living in a fortresslike home. You can't hear anything that is happening outside. There must be twenty or thirty people on my driveway, on my grass, shouting my name, taking my photo. How the hell did they all get in here? I pay a lot of money for privacy. The extremely wealthy do not want to be in the news—we just want to control everything, including the media. This could ruin me. I cannot believe this is happening. The guard at the front gate will be fired. Immediately. I'll see to it.

The agents hurry me to the car, and I slide into the back seat, grateful for the little shelter it provides. I face straight ahead, emotionless on the outside. On the inside, I'm furious. I will make sure none of those photos appear online or in print. I will manage all this.

Someone is going to pay.

These charges are nothing. It's classy as those places go, and discreet. That's the promise. No one will find out you've been there. I'm an adult, she's an adult.

"Wait, I still don't know what I did wrong," I say.

Gonzalez turns and glares at me from the front seat. "Ted, the owner of the Gold Club, kept meticulous records of all your visits, all of your services. He has cameras hidden everywhere. The lady you propositioned last time you were in, offered her a bunch of cash to have sex with her? Well, she was undercover. She has you making the, um, offer. It's all recorded. You think money can buy anything, don't you?"

"It can," I tell him. And then I shut my mouth. Ted squealed. He must have given some of us up to save his own skin. Ted let the cops in. I bet he took a deal. What a scumbag. "You can't touch me. Take Ted down. He owns the place."

"Oh, we are, don't worry," Gonzalez says. "You're all going down."

I swallow and ignore his threats. I can't wait to call my attorney. Well, actually, I'll call Smith and he'll call the right attorney. We need someone to sweep this under the rug. Someone who can call all these so-called "media" folks and kill the story. I can't wipe the sweat from my forehead with my hands cuffed, which is frustrating as hell. This whole thing is beneath me, beneath my family. No one puts Roger Jones in the back of an unmarked cop car. I take a deep breath. I cannot show emotion. It's how I handle a huge real estate deal I'm excited about. Poker face. Never let them see you sweat.

The media throng seems to have pushed closer to the car. There's nothing to see here, folks. Every guy messes around. There's no harm, no foul. I turn my head quickly and give them all a good stare. They all wish they were me. Even now, at this moment. You can see it in their eyes. It's the look of jealousy. I watch as a white van pulls to a stop and a bunch of people jump out and head into my house. I feel like I'm living inside a bad cop reality show. What exactly are they looking for? They better not make a mess. I'll sue them if they toss the place like they do on TV.

Finally, Logan starts the engine.

This is all such a joke. I'll be back home in an hour. Just watch.

I can't help myself. I turn and look out the window and smile.

CHAPTER 22

JULIE

I open my eyes and look around my new bedroom. I'm disoriented, as if I'm in a dream but I'm not. It's real. I'm here. It's strange waking up in my own house. My home. A home I own. By myself—well, with Roger's money, but still, I did this. I'm not the little girl who felt she wasn't pretty enough, who was embarrassed by her mom and her faith. I'm not the trophy wife of an emotionally devoid billionaire. I'm me. Julie Cohen. And tonight my daughter and I will have dinner together to celebrate the start of our new lives.

I smile and push back the covers, glancing at the alarm clock on the nightstand. My heart leaps. I overslept. It's almost 11:00 a.m. I stumble to the bathroom and startle at the sight of my own reflection. Deep lines meander down my face, no doubt from the sheet creases. I remind myself that the filler injected into my cheeks couldn't deflate that fast no matter how drastically my life changed. I rub my left cheek, try to plump it up, trying to massage the lines away.

And then I look again and grin. The reflection in the mirror looks like me. And there's something else there, too—and it looks a lot like happiness. I hurry to brush my teeth and wash my face. I'll be make-up-free today, for the first time I can remember. I pull on my favorite jeans and a well-worn white T-shirt with the word LOVE spelled out in big navy letters. I'm ready for another day of settling into this new life of mine.

First, coffee. As I make my way to the stairs, I notice Jess's empty bed and take a breath. I'm convinced she'll be home today. She wouldn't actually leave me for the entire school year, would she? She needs me. I'm her mom. That's what really matters, not where you live—it's who you live with. In her heart she knows that, too. Bonnie is her best friend, but I'm her mom. That trumps all.

I just hope it doesn't take her as long as it took me to realize it.

I hurry down the stairs and into the kitchen. Sun shines through the windows and bounces off the empty stainless-steel sink. I love this old kitchen. I love the white subway-tile backsplash, the simplicity of the cabinets and countertop, the uncomplicated everything compared to my showy house in Oceanside with Roger. When I think of it now, I see my former house as cotton candy. Everything about it was fake and fluffy but very expensive.

Everything was for show there.

I rummage through the packed box and find my coffee maker and pods. As I fill the water reservoir at the sink, I hear the sound of footsteps on the gravel driveway. I turn off the water and look out the window.

It's Tom. He's on the phone, frowning. He glances up at the kitchen window, and I wave.

"Jess home yet?" he yells.

I want to shush him. What will the neighbors think? Good grief. I am actually embarrassed I felt sympathy for him and let him stay for the weekend. Now, I just want him gone. I see his friend, the one with the leering eyes, and a chill runs down my spine.

"No, she's not." I shake my head while mouthing my response. I hold my finger up to my lips to shush him. He kicks the gravel with his big work boot, black with jarringly white laces, and continues walking toward the carriage house.

I need to make sure he is moving out tomorrow. He needs to honor the contract. Of course he'll honor the contract. I take a deep breath and try to calm my nerves. Tom didn't sign the contract. His parents did.

I decide to have a cup of coffee before going out back to make sure he understands the timeline we've all agreed to here. I'll set expectations. He has until noon on Sunday. That seems fair. Most hotels make you check out by 11:00 a.m., but I'll be more lenient.

All that said, I hope he's packed. I don't think twentysomething-year-old single men have that much stuff. Maybe a bed frame, a mattress, and some clothes. He can likely fit it all into his car. But what if he can't? Has he made arrangements for a friend to come help? One of those scary men who crowded into the carriage house last night could help him carry his stuff out of here, perhaps?

I shake off the feelings from last night. I shouldn't judge those men by the exterior. I mean, we all put on a facade to handle the world. Theirs is black clothing, leather, tattoos, and facial hair. Mine was designer clothes, expensive jewelry, and lots of plastic surgery and fillers. Now, it's going to be a lifestyle of jeans and T-shirts, yoga classes, and growing my own organic vegetables. Oh, and a booming career as an interior designer. I'll use all organic furniture and help clients get LEED certified. It's going to be a whole new lifestyle—one that's authentic.

I walk into the hall and look at my cheek. The sleep lines have lightened up, barely visible even when I lean in close to the mirror. In the natural order of things, my face will be covered with lines like these one day. They will signify strength, individuality, and the wisdom of age. I've been working on this with my counselor, working on seeing the gift of aging. I mean, look at the alternative.

Right now, I'm a reflection of conformity. A product of my environment and my marriage. Much like Tom is a reflection of the company he's keeping. He looks like every one of those men he had over here. Birds of a feather, I suppose.

I head back to the kitchen and start unpacking as I enjoy my cup of coffee. It's not procrastination, not really. I'm being productive while taking my time.

I unwrap my favorite cast-iron pots and pans. Their assorted colors made me smile when I bought them, mostly because Roger hated the nonconventionality.

"For heaven's sake, couldn't you pick one color, Julie? Even the chef is laughing at you, come on." He'd blown through the kitchen on his way to somewhere else, barely pausing except to belittle me. It had become a common occurrence. I realize the stages of our relationship now. First, the infatuation. And then before I knew it, marriage. I'm glad I convinced him to have a child, and I know he is glad, too. When Jess was conceived, that was the last time we made love. Everything since has been a quickie, when Roger wanted it. It was part of the deal. When you've lost yourself in things, it happens. I was such a fool.

But that day in the kitchen, I was starting to make a stand. My counselor had explained it was time to turn back to my passions. Cooking had always been one of them.

"The chef loves the pots and pans as much as I do. They're professional grade, actually. From France."

I could tell he was surprised by that. He seemed to waver, but then said, "Get rid of them. Stainless steel looks the best in here. Otherwise, all black. Your choice. Don't wait up. I'm working late." And then he was gone, off to his library. This was six months ago now. I'd been sleeping alone in our bedroom for what must have been years, with Roger using the guest bedroom. I don't know exactly when it started: when we became nothing more than roommates. I guess it was a slow, sad evolution of hurt and disappointment. The fact was, by the time of the pot-and-pan incident, I didn't really care what he did. That's the sad truth of what our life together had become. Nobody cared.

But for the sake of peace, I'd done what he asked and swapped out the pots and pans, keeping these colorful ones for myself. For someday.

I take a deep breath and smile. My colorful cookware looks perfect in my new home. The white kitchen seems to look even better, even more perfect, with them displayed in some of the glass-front cabinets. I place a lime-green sautéing pan and a bright pink pot and lid on the stove. They are reminders that I'm free.

Almost.

I still need to serve Roger with the divorce papers. And I need to be sure Jess comes home by tomorrow at least so we can get her new school commute down. I'm sure it will take a few days to get into the new routine. I will convince her to give it a try. There are a lot of things still to sort out, but as long as Roger is somewhat reasonable—and he should be since I'm honoring our prenup—we should be finished with each other in just a few months. At least that's what my lawyer predicted. And sure, Jess is unsettled, but it will only take time. I'll transform this place into a home she'll be comfortable in, a place she'll bring her friends home to. I know it.

Even as I give myself this pep talk, there's a feeling of dread in the pit of my stomach, and I can't shake it.

My phone rings, and I jump. It's Cassie, one of my society friends. Cassie and I were doubles partners at tennis before I blew my knee out. She's gorgeous, with long red hair, freckled cheeks, and a big smile. She's gilded, like I was. Her husband is even older than Roger. I wonder if she knows I've left. Could the news have spread this quickly? And then I realize, I really don't care what anyone thinks. I only care about Jess, and well, finally, myself. The school PTA gossip engine can't hurt me now.

"Cassie, hi, how are you?" I smile into the phone. She's been as good a friend as she knows how to be. I'll miss her casual friendship.

"Girl, I'm good. What time do you want me to pick you up?" Cassie is out of breath. She always calls me from the gym, making me feel lazy and a little jealous. Usually. But not today. Not in my new life.

"Pick me up? Have I forgotten something?"

"Um, it's the second Saturday in November. Duh." Cassie pants through the phone.

Oh no. It's the social event of the season. The Glass Guild luncheon and fashion show benefiting the children's hospital. How could I forget that? Roger had been so pleased I'd been asked to be a member of the guild: the pinnacle of social success in his book. I must admit, I was into it for a time. I even bought a $3,000 navy sequined designer gown just for this event months ago. It's hanging inside one of the many garment boxes waiting to be unpacked.

I imagine trying to find it. Trying to psych myself up into getting decked out and being the socialite I have been. That I was.

"I can't go."

Cassie gasps. "Of course you can. You must. We are at the head table this year, finally. Oh my god. We will have front-row runway access, and we get to bid on the silent auction before anyone else. Remember the fur coat you snapped up last year? Come on. It's all for the kids. I'll pick you up at two."

All for the kids. That's what we say. And we do raise a ton of money for the hospital. We do. But we also spend so much on ourselves.

I take a deep breath. "I left Roger. I'm starting over. I won't be able to afford the Glass Guild anymore. And the truth is, I'm focusing on other things."

"Hold on." The background noise changes, and I imagine Cassie has hopped off whatever machine she was riding or jogging on and is headed outside. "OK, I am not surprised you left him. He's terrible, same as my Freddy. But he has a ton of money. Isn't that why you went for it in the first place? I mean, let's be real."

"I've changed, Cassie. I've been in counseling. I've found myself again, and I'm starting over," I say, even though I know I'm shocking her. "That's why I'm making a change."

"Wow, OK. Well you'll have plenty of cash. You get half of whatever, so you'll be fine. Unless you signed a prenup. You didn't do that, did you?" I imagine her well-done exercise face: perfect makeup, fake eyelashes, hair lush with extensions, with a white gym towel draped around her neck. She's in skintight black leggings and a sports bra that barely contains her silicone breasts. In a nutshell, she's every man's dream. Just like me.

"I signed a prenup. But it's fine. I'll be fine. I don't need much. Just a fresh start." I've been through all this with my counselor. I have enough to get me through for a year. By then, my business will be up and running. Roger will cover Jess's expenses, as a minor and then once she's in college. I know he will. It's a matter of pride and control for him. I walk to the entry hall of my house and look out the front door. Tom's gray Toyota is parked out front; otherwise the street is empty of cars. None of his friends are here, at least not yet. I exhale.

"Girl, let's think this through. Do you have money? I'm worried. Where are you right now?" Like the old me, Cassie couldn't function without her over-the-top allowance from her husband. It works for them. Unlike Roger, though, Cassie's old man seems to worship the ground she walks on and treats her like a precious gem, in awe that he is a facet of her life. They have dinner out together every night, and he's always by her side at fundraisers. She's lucky, in that respect.

Maybe I would have stayed with Roger if he had made an emotional investment in our relationship. But he didn't.

"I have everything I need. I bought a home on Cherry Hill Lane. It's just on the other side of the tracks, you know, literally still in Oceanside. You'll have to come over sometime. I love it. It's gorgeous. I'm busy unpacking. Jess loves it here, too. We're starting over, and we're glad." I smile so my voice sounds lighter, more confident. "Look, I've got to go. I'm so sorry about the event this afternoon. Tell everyone the news for me, please."

"Are you sure about all of this? I can't imagine Jess and you living all the way over there. Is it safe?"

I roll my eyes. I can't help it. "It's the same suburb. We're still Oceanside. Of course it's safe. I'm twenty minutes from you, thirty at most. Jess is still in the school district."

"It's another world to me. I've never even been over there." Cassie is back on the workout machine. "OK, I'll tell everyone what happened. The ladies will love this scoop."

"I know. Might as well get it over with. I'll be the talk of the luncheon, and then, hopefully, you guys can move on to something or someone else. Like who has the largest and newest cocktail ring at the event." I cannot believe I used to care about that, too.

Cassie laughs. "OK, I'll serve you up for lunch. You'll be old news by the end of the fashion show. Take care. Call me if you need anything."

And with that, she's gone. I wonder if we'll ever see each other again. The thought brings an unexpected wave of sadness. There was a lot in my old life to like. It wasn't all terrible, not at all. But it's time to move on. I glance down the hall to the back door, pushing away a feeling of dread.

Something tells me that of all the things I need to do to start my life over, the first step is dealing with Tom. Something also tells me the talk with Tom isn't going to go as smoothly as I'd like.

But this is the new me. Independent Julie. She says what she thinks and stands up for herself. A chill rolls down my spine, but I force myself to walk toward the back door. It's time to go pay my unwanted guest a visit.

CHAPTER 23

TOM

For a minute I think it's Jess on my doorstep, knocking on my door. I rush to check the peephole before opening it, my heart swelling in my chest.

Shit. It's her mom.

"Tom," she yells through the door. "It's me. Julie. Can we talk for a moment?"

Oh, that's right. Act all nice and polite, why don't you? I know who you are, and I know what you want. My home. And me out of it. I'm tempted to tell her to go away, but I can't make her mad. Then she'd stop Jess from visiting me.

I really want to see Jess. Jess is my future. She is the possibility of love. My last shot.

"Give me a minute, Mrs. Jones. I'll be right out," I yell back. I watch her turn and walk down the steps into the backyard. She pulls a weed from the grass. Her back is to me, so I open my door and step onto my porch, pulling the door shut behind me. She doesn't know I'm standing here. I bet she's busy in her mind, making plans about how she's going to change around my backyard. She'll add a pool, or a fountain, or something else that rich people do.

She spins around. Her boobs are too big for her body, and her face is shiny, like the skin is stretched too tight. Jess is cuter, more natural. Julie's going to be one of those freaky old people who have scary stretched faces that look sort of young, but then she'll have wrinkly, old hands. At least Sandi didn't do all that to herself. I guess she didn't have the money. I googled Julie Jones; her husband has all the money in the world. She'll be rich, even after the divorce.

She can find a better house than this. She really doesn't have a choice. This one is taken.

"Hey," I say. I'm nice. I smile.

"So I just came over to make sure you're all set for your move tomorrow." Julie's hand flies to her face to shield her eyes from the bright sun. Likely her eyelids are stretched too tight, so she can't blink.

She should have worn sunglasses like I am. It's harder to read people who wear sunglasses.

"Yeah, sure. All set," I say. "I mean, are you in a hurry to gut this place, too?"

She bites her lip. "I'm not sure what I'm going to do with the carriage house. I've never been inside. Your parents wanted to respect your privacy, so I only saw photos of the place. I was OK with that."

I smile. "They're so great. And so are you."

"Your mom is really nice," she says.

I wish she would quit with the stupid suburban small-talk shit. "Sandi's my stepmom, Mrs. Jones."

"Right. OK, well I was thinking if you could be checked out, so to speak, by about noon tomorrow, that would be great." She used air quotes around the words "checked out."

"I'm not sure I'll be ready by then, Mrs. Jones." I am not lying. I'm just not going to be ready yet. I have a big day on Sunday.

"I need you to be ready by then. It's in the contract. Just honor that. And my name is Cohen. Ms. Cohen, not Mrs. Jones." She takes a step back. I don't even know if she knows she did that.

I walk down off the porch so we're standing in the grass together. I'm much taller than she is, much bigger. I'm XL, as the guys call me. I can smell the flowery shampoo in her hair. And I can sense her fear. She's afraid of me, no matter what her name is.

"Like I said, I'll try to check out tomorrow, sometime. It may be Monday, Tuesday. Who knows?" I use air quotes around "who knows," just so she'll know we are on the same page.

"That's not acceptable." Julie's hands are on her hips. Her eyes flash at me in anger.

I wonder, vaguely, if she's good in bed. Her boobs push against her tight T-shirt, stretching the LOVE stamped in big blue letters on the front.

"OK. Good talk. I've got stuff to do, Mrs. Jones. Packing, you know." I smile and turn away from her, heading back to my house.

"It's in the contract, Tom. You're not welcome here after noon tomorrow."

I want to say I wasn't welcome here a long time before that, Julie. But look, here I am. I don't say a word, though. I chuckle, open the door to the carriage house, and slam it behind me. I look through the peephole and watch as she walks back to the main house. She's suddenly in a big hurry.

I hope I didn't scare her too much. I need to keep her on friendly terms, or at the very least, wary terms. I want her to just stay over there on her part of the property, and I'll stay on mine. At least until I can figure everything out. I need time to think. I need to finish my letter. This is my home, too, no matter what she thinks the contract says. I didn't sign anything.

I need Jess to come over for a visit so we can talk. Maybe Julie is losing it, maybe she's already lost it. I don't like the judgment I see in her eyes. Jess will need my protection from her mom.

Maybe Jess and I could run away together. Maybe that would solve everything. I hate to admit it, but the closer it gets to Sunday, the more

I'm feeling uneasy. I mean, I believe in my plan, and the guys' support, but what if I mess up and get caught? I have finally met someone I could have a future with. I can't mess that up. I don't think Vic will let me back out of my plan, though. I can't tell him Jess seems really into me.

Maybe there is a way. Vic is into Mrs. Jones. He can have her, as far as I'm concerned. Maybe I tell Vic she's interested in him, too. Julie looks like one of those unreal women. You can't figure out how all the parts work together, how they were engineered like that. It's like a painting or something. You know it isn't a real person.

I'd take her more seriously if she didn't look like that. I think. Although Sandi just looks like herself, and I don't take her seriously, either. Vic says women are just a necessary evil. They're helpful in a way—to make out with—but not trustworthy.

He's right.

Except for Jess. Jess is different. I can tell at the cellular level. We know each other, we see each other. So what we can do is run away. I'll tell Vic I'm still doing the deed but just pushing it off a few months, and then we run for it. I'll tell Vic he can have Julie in the meantime.

That's my plan. Jess will love it. I know she has school and all, but she can get her GED. I'll help her. She'll help me. We'll go to Canada. It's really open there. We can find space, our own place. I like my new plan.

I hope Vic agrees.

I pull out my phone. Jess hasn't texted me since last night. I really want to text her, but I don't want to seem desperate.

I sit behind my computer. I can lose hours on here, days even. This is where I connect with all my friends from around the world, the guys who can't hang out at the bar with us and the ones who do. This is where I'm at home. I slide into my favorite chat room and recognize at least three of the guys from the meeting in here.

Hey, I type.

XL. Dude. Are you getting psyched? JJ types.

He's not supposed to refer to anything real on here. I don't know what he's doing.

Offline, JJ. Now. It's Vic. He's giving JJ a smackdown.

I hover in the chat room, waiting to see if anyone else connects with me.

You're the man, XL! I don't know BadBoy2, but I smile.

It's nice to belong. To have guys respect you, want to talk to you, be your friend. That didn't happen for me in school. I wasn't good at sports—heck, I wasn't good at anything. And then, like a freak, I had to go to church all the time and be part of the perfect God-fearing family. It was exhausting. I was lost, but now I'm found. Ha.

People don't know it, but there are so many of us out there—lost boys, so to speak. We're not all part of an official group or anything. But we're all searching for something.

Go write me something nice, XL. Vic is back. Now. D-day is tomorrow.

I guess that was a smackdown of sorts. But as I log off, I wonder: Is he using me? Am I being a fool? No, of course not. He wants me to make amends, to do the one thing I must, no matter how terrified I am. I'm fine. They wouldn't send me on a fool's errand. I'm XL now. I'm strong and invincible. I'm going to make him so proud. I'll execute my plan, and then Jess and I will head to Canada. Everyone will be happy then.

Well, except for one person, but he deserves everything I have planned for him.

CHAPTER 24

JESS

My head feels like a thousand tiny pickaxes are attacking my scalp. I open my eyes, realizing I didn't pull the heavy curtains over the floor-to-ceiling windows. As such, my bed is lit by a giant spotlight from the sun.

My tongue is stuck, thick and heavy in my mouth. I haven't partied like that in a long time, not since last spring. All summer I was mellow, had to study for the ACT and SAT. And it was worth it. Now that I'm going to USC, Dad's first choice for me, I can relax. And I did last night. I guess the move got to me—oh, and the fact that my parents are splitting. Yeah, I have enough reasons for a hangover.

I tap my phone and blink at the screen—12:47 p.m. What?

I can't believe how late I slept. I hoist myself out of bed, careful to sit before standing. The room sways, then holds firm. I wonder if Bonnie's awake.

I brush my teeth and splash water on my face. I pull on sweatpants and a sweatshirt and open my bedroom door. Bonnie's door is still closed. I debate about whether to wake her up or not. It's after noon. She should wake up. We need her parents to think we are responsible and all. Selfishly, I need them to like me so I can live here for the rest of the school year.

I open the door. I hear sobbing. The room is pitch black besides the light from the hall spilling in behind me.

"Bonnie?" I whisper. "What's wrong?"

"Everything."

I step into her bedroom and close the door. I cross the room blind, hoping not to trip over anything. I make it to her bed and sit down. "Talk to me."

She doesn't. Instead, she hands me her phone.

The screen is open to a photo. A photo of all of us, at the party last night.

"Who took this?" I ask. Bonnie is in it, standing beside me. The beer pong table is behind us, as are most of the other kids. Some of the kids are doing a salute. I forgot we did this last night. I must have blacked it out. A chill spreads down my spine. I don't really want this to get around, I realize.

"I don't know." She sniffs. "But it's everywhere."

My stomach turns. I feel like I'm going to throw up. "What do you mean 'everywhere'?"

My phone lights up with a text. It's one of the girls from the party last night. Don't post anything from last night! OMG! We're ruined!

I text: What's happening?

She answers with a link to Twitter.

I click on the link. It's to someone named @ShinetheLight. He's written: Help identify these neo-Nazi teens. Let's ruin their lives. And their parents' lives too.

That stupid drinking game has gone viral. The Snapchat posts. I'm shaking.

"What do we do?" I ask Bonnie, who sobs in response. "Somebody, a girl at another school, she took screenshots of all the private posts. We're in these photos."

"What do you think I've been trying to tell you? We *are* ruined. This was at *my house!*" Bonnie yells.

163

I check Twitter again. It's awful what they're saying about us. All of us. "We didn't do anything wrong."

I refresh Twitter again and see a list of names beginning to form. Other kids from school are ratting us out. Strangers on Twitter are posting that we will get what we deserve. That they're going to hunt us down.

Username @person_outing posts: Look at this charming couple.

It's a short video meme. It's me and Chase. You can hear his voice saying, "Great shot, Jess! You're a Nazi!" The video meme flashes the text: *We've identified these two lovers as Jess Jones and Chase Merritt. Go get 'em, Twitter.*

"Chase didn't say that. Someone doctored it. Oh my god, what are they doing to us?" I realize I'm crying, too. They've dubbed over our voices, made memes about us. We look like we are actually white supremacists or something. "What do we do?"

I sit on the bed next to Bonnie. I'm stunned and scared. And ashamed. How could I be a part of something like this? It's terrible. The people on Twitter are right. We should never have done this. I check my phone. This is spiraling out of control on social media. We're doomed.

The bedroom door opens, and Bonnie's parents appear. The light turns on.

Bonnie's dad stands in front of us. "You will say nothing to the media, do you understand?"

Bonnie shudders and manages, "Yes."

"You too?" He points at me and I nod. "Our attorney believes this will go away. The school is having an emergency crisis-management meeting right now to discuss the situation. You will do community service, you will go to a Jewish museum, you will do whatever I say. I've never been more disappointed in you," her dad says before turning and walking back to the door. "Jess, you need to go home. You will not be staying here. Leave now."

I sit beside Bonnie in shock. Her parents hate me now. The looks on their faces, the disbelief. I'll never be able to meet their eyes. Oh my god, my life is falling apart again.

My phone lights up. It's Jack Brennan. The game was probably his idea. He texts: Do not talk to anyone. This was all a joke. We didn't do anything wrong.

He's created a group text with all of us who were in the photo.

One of the girls, Kelsey, who raised her hand and is front and center above the red cups, texts: I don't see what the big deal is.

Beside me Bonnie says, "You need to leave. You can't be here anymore."

"But we're best friends. We stick together, no matter what. Right?" I reach for her hand, but she stands up and walks to her window, her back to me.

"Just go."

Tears roll down my cheeks as I stand up and walk back to the guest bedroom. I don't belong anywhere, not anymore.

I'm packing up my stuff when my phone rings. It's my mom. I need my mom.

"Mom, help me," I manage.

"Where are you?" she asks.

"Mom." I am crying too hard to speak.

"Everything's going to be OK. I'll come get you. Are you still at Bonnie's?"

"Yes."

"OK, stay inside until I pull up. Then run to the car. You don't know who is watching us right now." Mom seems calm and in control. Not mad like Bonnie's parents. She's coming to get me. She isn't icing me out. I feel a tiny bit of relief, enough to get myself under control.

"OK," I say. "Mom, it was just a photo. I didn't know what they were doing." I shove my nightshirt into the box holding all my belongings.

"What are you talking about?" Mom asks.

"The photo from the party," I answer. I'm so relieved that Mom is being so chill, my tears are subsiding. Maybe it really will be OK, just like I told Bonnie.

"What photo? Did someone drug you? Were you assaulted? My gosh, what happened?" Mom asks.

She doesn't know about the drinking game. "It'll be fine. We played a stupid drinking game last night, with a swastika in the center of the table. It got out on social media."

"No, you wouldn't have."

The sound of my mom's voice makes me hate myself. It's dripping with disappointment, with sadness. But then I realize . . . if she wasn't calling about the photos, what was she calling about? "Mom, why are you calling me? Why are you telling me to hide until you get here? What happened?"

There is a pause so long I'm about to speak again. Finally, my mom says, "You haven't heard about your father? His arrest?"

Something happens and my knees drop out from under me. I land hard on the floor. "Dad was arrested?"

My mom is talking again. "Just stay there. I'm in the car now. I'll be there soon. I'll try to explain."

She hangs up the phone and I stay on the ground, pulling my knees to my chest. I wonder what my dad did wrong. I know what I did, but what did he do, on the same night?

My poor mom. She wanted a fresh start, and now my dad and I have messed it up. We've made the Jones family a disgrace. Correction: I've made the Jones family a disgrace. I don't even know what my dad did.

With shaking hands, I type my dad's name into the search bar on my phone. He's trending.

The first result:

OC real estate developer Roger Jones arrested in prostitution scandal

I can't read the story. I already know how this is going to end. I scroll down the results until I find my name. Bonnie is right. We'll forever be linked to last night.

All in the family: Jess Jones part of Nazi drinking party, dad Roger Jones part of strip club scandal.

I throw my phone hard, and it smacks into Bonnie's guest room's thick plaster wall. I watch as it falls to the hardwood floor.

I sit in silence, hugging my knees.

My life is over.

CHAPTER 25

SANDI

When Julie calls me, asking about Tom and his plans, I have to admit he had slipped my mind. And it was nice. I'd left him a message, and he never returned the call. Instead, in my spare time, I've been painting again. I went into the basement and dug out my easel and my brushes. I set up in the family room, where I can watch the boys playing in the backyard through the windows. I'm rusty, but I still see the "natural talent" the woman at church told me I had all those years ago. She'd leaned forward during my dad's service—I must have been twelve—and whispered, "I saw your painting hanging up. You have real natural talent. Don't stop painting. Hear me?"

I'd turned and smiled at the woman, her wrinkly, old hand still on my shoulder. She'd said, "Promise me." And I had.

But for too many years I'd pushed that passion aside. With the boys and Doug and church and running our lives, that dream had been on hold.

P   not any longer. Ever since we moved out here, the space

ny family and Doug's son has given me room to breathe. I

how on edge I had felt around Tom. I am already on edge

It's hard to have an angrier, directionless version of my

around in the shadows.

I was painting when Julie called. A sunny landscape with flowers and butterflies. My favorite nature themes. I plan to begin a portrait of the boys next. At least, the two younger boys.

"I just don't think he has any intention of moving out tomorrow," Julie says once we've exchanged pleasantries.

"What makes you so sure? We told him exactly what we've all agreed on," I answer, dread beginning to seep into my words like a slow leak, a dripping faucet.

"Could you call him? Or maybe come over here and help make sure he's packed up? I just don't see any indication that he's moving out tomorrow. He told me as much himself," Julie says.

And this is the problem. Because he won't listen to me, not anymore. My power over him, my respect from him, is gone. I still love him, but he's turned cold as ice. And dark—dark as the devil. But I need to help Julie. It's the right thing to do.

"His father, Doug, is heading into town today to meet with the Oceanside school officials and some parents. How about I ask him to swing by and talk to Tom?" I offer. Of course, I have no idea whether Doug will agree.

"That would be great. Thank you," Julie says. And then she gasps, "Oh my god."

I try to imagine what's happening. Has Tom frightened her? "What's wrong? Are you OK?"

"Yes. It's just the news. My husband. He's in handcuffs on the news. I've got to go." She sounds like she is in shock as she hangs up the phone. Understandable. I know I would be in shock if my husband was in shackles for everyone to see. I flip on our television, catch the end of the story. It's the same serious reporter who brought me news about the other big story happening in Oceanside.

"Roger Jones, a prominent member of the Oceanside community—a pillar of the community, some would say—was led away in handcuffs last night. According to sources, he's being charged with lewd conduct, soliciting prostitution, receipt of sexual services for payment. We'll update you with more when we have information, along with anything we find out regarding the Nazi drinking game scandal. There is a lot of breaking news in this Southern California town. Stay tuned." Both anchors' faces fill the screen as I turn off the television.

Poor Julie. I wonder how long it will take the media to find out the two of them are separated. I wonder how long it will take for them to find Julie, hiding out in our home.

I mean, our former home.

I don't want my old house on the news, not associated with something awful like what Roger has done. I think about their daughter, how this will affect her. I say a quick prayer for them, and then one for me. I need help talking Doug into getting Tom out of the house.

He's not going to like it. Doug enjoys the role as savior, not the role where he's reminded that he's kicking his own son out on the street with no money, no job, and nowhere to go.

No, that's not the role he sees for himself. But it's the one he created. I take a deep breath and call him.

"Look, I'm at the school district headquarters, about to go into an emergency meeting. Can I call you back?" Doug sounds excited. He's feeling important again. After losing all his clout in the congregation, after the deacons decided he should go, he has been lost. This scandal has him fired up and ready to do something. His former sheep need help, and Doug's just the kind of guy to make excuses for them. Turns out he's a practiced liar.

"Doug, listen, I only need a minute. Tomorrow is the day Tom is to move out of the carriage house." I'm struggling to be concise, not boring. I need him to help, but I can't beg. I've learned my place. I paint the petals of a pink daisy to keep myself calm.

"So?" he answers. "Good riddance."

"Julie, the new owner, called me just now. She says he hasn't packed, and as far as she can tell he's not planning on leaving." I don't add that we are both worried. I think that is obvious.

"What's her last name again?" he asks.

"Who? Julie? Julie Jones. She is married to Roger Jones. But I don't know what that—"

"Oh my. So her husband has been arrested, did you know that?" he asks.

"Yes, I just saw it on the news. Terrible. But that doesn't have anything to do with the Tom problem," I say.

"It gets worse for the Jones family, I'm afraid. Their daughter is in that photo. I have all the names." He says this in an excited tone, because he's in the know, because he's feeling superior. "Can you believe that? Two members of the same family, embarrassed to the core. They'll never be able to live here. They'll have to move. Several of the families involved are thinking about boarding school and a move to the East Coast."

What? I don't think Julie knew about her daughter's involvement in this when we spoke. I'm sure of it. She wouldn't have had the emotional energy to call me.

"Are you advising the Brennans to leave town? Really?" I ask. "Wouldn't it be healthier to apologize to the Jewish community? To all of us?"

"Be right there!" Doug says to someone who calls his name. Pastor Doug, they say.

"No. Not if they didn't do anything wrong. And I don't think they did. Stupid drunk teenagers, that's all. I have to go." Doug hangs up on me without committing to a visit to his son. He also hangs up without condemning what those kids did last night. Instead he made excuses. That is not what Jesus would do. My husband is a fraud and a phony. He loves the power of the office and what it gives him. He loves the access to these rich people he ministers to, who he makes feel better for all their excess, for all their ignorance.

I hang up the phone and say a prayer. I know the right thing to do. If Doug won't pay a visit to his son—our son—then I must. He's our responsibility. It's not fair to saddle Julie with our issue, especially when she has enough to handle. I'll go over tomorrow morning and help him pack up if he needs it. Tom's very secretive, protective of his stuff. He's never let me inside the carriage house, not since he moved out there when he turned eighteen years old. I shake my head at my mistake. I should have gone inside the carriage house. I should have forced a confrontation.

In my dreams I still live on Cherry Hill Lane. In the beautiful white house, with the mature trees, and the big purple hydrangeas flanking the front door. I hear the click of a hummingbird demanding that I fill his feeder. I'm cleaning the diamond glass in the front door with Windex. The ammonia floats through the air. Everything is clean and in order. It's perfect.

In my dreams I walk across the backyard to the carriage house, and it has been transformed from whatever Tom did to it into my artist's studio. It's where I finally have the nerve to paint, to try it again. Bright canvases line the walls, all original art by me, Sandi Wallace Dean. In my dreams, elegant, art-loving customers ring the carriage house bell and step inside, eager to purchase an original.

I wipe my hands on my jeans and stand up. Enough dreaming. At this moment, I remind myself, I should be happy my boys aren't going to go to a high school that breeds this sort of nonsense. They will know better than this; they will be better than this.

As I wait for them to appear for lunch, I do an online search for news about Roger Jones. So many articles appear. The media works fast these days, stories spread like wildfire. Some of the articles mention his wife, Julie. Some mention his daughter by name, some don't.

Some of the comments are so ugly, so vicious that I close out of the story. On other media outlets, the comments are encouraging, calling Roger a hero, calling his daughter a prime example of white supremacy. These comments are by anonymous people who like Jess's blonde hair, blue eyes. They like that she's one of them. Who are these people? Are there more of them than I realize?

These people with their anonymous comments cheer Jess on in her hate, or ignorance, or whatever it is that's in between. Is there anything in between? God help them.

I try to pick up my paintbrush, to return to the happy scene in my painting, but I can't. I reach for my Bible and begin to read. I haven't made it through more than a verse when the boys run through the back door, yelling at the top of their lungs.

"Mom!" Davis says. "There's a dead rabbit in our tree fort."

"It's really gross," Danny says. His eyes are shiny with terror.

I don't understand. How could a rabbit get up into their tree fort? It's four feet off the ground, up a tree.

I swallow and pull them into my arms. "Let me handle this. It's going to be all right."

I leave the boys inside and hurry across the grass. I climb the four steps to their fort and look inside.

A rabbit has been decapitated, both parts left bleeding inside the boys' happy place. I don't know who is doing this to us, but I do know it is on purpose. I back down the steps and jog across the lawn.

When I reach the back door, I hurry inside, then close and lock the door.

CHAPTER 26

ROGER

I've just read Smith the riot act. If he doesn't get me out of here in the next twenty minutes, he can find a new COO job.

I don't have a watch on. They took everything away, so I can't be sure if it is under twenty minutes when the dick-face police idiot comes and tells me I'm out on bail. I'll give Smith the benefit of the doubt one last time because at least I'm getting out of here. They have me in some sort of holding pen with a bunch of guys who smell like shit and look like hell. One of them is shoeless. Another has so many tattoos covering his body I can't tell what color his skin is. One of them walks up to me, tries to start a conversation, says I'll need protection in the slammer.

"Get the fuck away from me," I say, although I have to admit I am terrified, my heart racing. The guy is six four and three hundred pounds. He has the number *88* tattooed on his left forearm. I don't know what that means, and I couldn't care less.

"You're gonna need me, you'll see. I'll be watching. And now it'll cost you double."

"Get away from me!" I roar. I hope I sound tough. Shit, I know I sound like a scared idiot. I need to focus on lining up the best legal defense team money can buy. I'll do it. I'll beat these made-up, fake charges. They've messed with the wrong guy. I mean, everyone does it, goes to strip clubs and the like. Why are they picking on me?

Some guy finally arrives. He looks a bit familiar. He tells me he's my attorney and escorts me out of the police station. I would follow anyone out of this hellhole. We don't talk. Smith greets me as I step outside. I'm grinning at the media, and despite my hours-long stay in a holding cell, I know I look better than any of them ever could. I have the finest clothes money can buy. They hold up under pressure.

"Sorry it took so long to get you out of here. You OK?" Smith asks as we drive away from the media circus.

"I was considering my options for a new COO," I say just to goad him.

His face goes pale. "Sir, I really did my best. It was under half an hour."

I chuckle and pick up my phone. "Is that attorney out of the hospital yet? Do we have a plan?"

Smith lets out his breath. "Yes, he was released earlier than expected, and he's part of the team. And so is this guy. Horace, meet Roger."

"It's an honor, sir," the man in the back seat says. I don't answer.

Smith continues, "The attorneys are all assembled at your house waiting for us. Ready to get a game plan together."

"My wife? My daughter? Have you spoken to them? They need to avoid the media. No comment."

"No, she didn't answer. Neither did Jess."

"Shit. OK. Well, they'll be mad, but it will all work out." I rub my chin, feel the stubble. I need a shower and a shave. I'll take control of everything. They'll all fall in line. "Keep trying Julie. She can get to Jess. Explain that none of this means anything. I only love them. You know, blah, blah, blah."

Smith keeps his eyes on the road. "Anything else?"

"Tell Julie everything will go away soon. Tell her to come back home. I need her, for support. I hate to be alone, Smith. You know that. I need my family. Just get them home, Smith. Understand?"

Smith swallows. "Understood, sir."

I can tell from the look on his face that he thinks I'm asking the impossible. Screw him. Nothing is impossible. We pull into my drive-way, and my shoulders relax. Home sweet megahome.

"Sir, one other thing before we go inside."

"What? I mean, why so grave? What else could possibly matter right now?"

"It's about Jess. She's, um, in trouble," Smith says. "She was at a drinking party last night."

We pull to a stop at my front door. I'm opening the car door. "So what? Everybody drinks in high school. It's the thing."

"It's not about the drinking. It's about the drinking game. They were playing a Nazi drinking game, sir."

I pull the car door shut again. "What the fuck? What do you mean, a Nazi drinking game? I don't get it."

Smith shrugs. "Neither do I. But there are photos of kids doing the Hitler salute and stuff. Anyway, Jess is in the photos. It's making national news. Bigger news than your arrest."

I push the door open and step outside. I know the media is camped out on the street with their big lenses and their loud questions. I ignore them and walk with confidence into my home. Once Smith is inside, too, I slam the front door.

The attorneys can wait.

"You're telling me my goddamn daughter is a Nazi?"

Smith blanches again. He should wear makeup or something. "No, sir. I'm not. I don't think Jess is a neo-Nazi. I think she was in the wrong place at the wrong time. She's not doing the salute, by the way, so that's good. She can just say she was drunk. They do have a video of Jess and a guy saying 'Jess, you're a natural' that someone dubbed to say 'Jess, you're a Nazi.' It's all over social media."

"She can just say she was drunk." I mimic him. "'I was drunk. That's why I played a Nazi game.' Are you kidding me? What's wrong with her? Let me see the photo."

Smith hands me his phone. I see Jess smiling, standing in front of a swastika made out of red plastic cups. Behind her, boys and girls raise their arms in sieg heil. It's my daughter, front and center. What was she thinking, the poor girl? I touch her face on the screen, wish I could wipe the smile off her face. Wish I could make this into a bad dream. All of it. I wonder if she was targeted, framed like I was, because of who I am.

And just like that, I see her future go up in smoke. Bye-bye, USC. She'll be lucky to get into community college.

"This is bad," I say, handing Smith his phone.

"It's not optimal," he agrees.

"Another reason she needs to come back home. Both of them. I can protect them here. Get them home, Smith." I lead the way down the hall to my library, where I know all the attorneys assembled. We have two issues to address now: mine and Jess's.

"Understood. Welcome to the war room. We'll solve this. It's just that there will be blowback on you for this. So we do need to reach Jess," Smith says before we enter the room.

"I don't care about blowback. I care about fixing all of this." I walk to my chair and take a seat. "Let's get my family home and get a defense mounted, shall we, gentlemen?"

No one speaks.

"Now!" I yell, and they all jump. "Fix this!"

CHAPTER 27

JULIE

Jess isn't answering her phone. Not texts, not calls. I've been sitting in my car in Bonnie's driveway wondering what to do. I suppose I should be thankful for the guards at the gatehouse, for the privacy of this community. The media circus has been held to the entrance, and I drove through without being noticed. I hope Jess is all right. She was so upset about that photo. It was wrong of her to play that game, and she knows it. I'm worried about her.

I need to call Smith back. He's calling on Roger's behalf, probably trying to get me to help rehabilitate his image. Fat chance. I need to focus on Jess. She's going to be devastated by all this.

I want to hug my daughter. I get out of the car and walk up to the massive front door. The scale of Bonnie's house makes me feel like I'm Alice in Wonderland. If it was built to intimidate guests, it's doing a great job. The doorknob itself is the size of my car's tire.

After a time, the door is pulled open. It's not Jess, but a woman in an all-white uniform.

"I'm here to pick up my daughter. Jess?" I say.

"*Sí.* Wait here." The woman closes the door, and I'm left standing outside. Every other time I've been here, I've waited for Jess in the foyer. No doubt Bonnie's parents have heard about Roger's arrest and decided we all should be banned. Poor Jess. I hope they didn't upset her any more than she already is.

The door opens again, and Jess flings herself into my arms. She's sobbing. The woman in the uniform places a moving box at our feet and closes the door.

"Shhhh, honey, everything is going to be OK. Whatever was portrayed in the photo, we'll sort it out. You're a good person, a wonderful girl. You drank too much and didn't think. And as for what your father pulled, this isn't about you. It's about Dad. I promise everything will be OK. Let's go home." I lead her to my car and settle her in the front seat. I hurry to the driver's side, and we're off. Good riddance, once again, to Oceanside's finest street. The air here is choked with entitlement.

I look closely at Jess at the next stop sign.

"Honey, talk to me," I say.

"No. Mom. There is nothing to talk about. My life is ruined." Jess turns away, facing out the passenger window.

A car honks behind me, and I start driving again. "We'll figure out a way through this together. You'll apologize. It's going to be OK."

"That photo has gone viral. People all over the world think I'm a Nazi," Jess manages, her voice faltering. "I'm the worst person in the world."

"Oh, honey, no, it was a mistake. Everyone makes mistakes. You'll apologize."

"Mom. I'm posing in front of a swastika. What can I possibly say to explain that?" Jess sobs as I drive.

My brain starts to process the depth of her problem, the reality of what she's done. It turns to Roger, and I wonder how long he's been visiting prostitutes. I wonder if he worried about me, about diseases? Everything around me has blurred into slow motion. The other cars. The houses along the street sway. I pull through the guard gate and onto the main street. Jess is hiding, slumping in her seat below the window.

I feel like I'm an actor in a bad movie. My vision blurs and comes back into focus. How could Jess do something like this?

"Mom! Stop!" Jess yells at the same time my car sensors alarm and the car automatically slams on the brakes.

I almost rear-ended the people in the car in front of us. Oh my god. The light turns green eventually, and I'm able to somehow drive us home. I pull into the gravel driveway for once, blocking Tom's easy access to the carriage house. My carriage house.

Jess follows me up the steps to the front door.

"Mom, what's that? The thing on the side of the door?" Jess asks.

Even if I weren't Jewish, what my daughter has done is horrible. How could she participate in something like this? Because she doesn't know her heritage, doesn't understand. And that's my fault. I will change this now.

"This is a mezuzah. Jewish people put it on the front door of their homes as a blessing." I unlock the door, and we both walk inside. I lock the door behind me.

"Who put it there?" she asks.

"I did. It's mine. From your grandma. She wanted me to put it on our house when we first moved into Oceanside. Your dad didn't think it would be a good idea. I have to admit, I agreed. But it's here now."

"You're Jewish? We're Jewish?" Jess asks, her eyes wide.

"Yes."

"Dad too?"

"No, he's not, honey. I know this is confusing. And I haven't been practicing. I've just recently been drawn back to my faith, to my roots. You need to know your heritage. I can explain."

She shakes her head before running up the stairs and slamming the door to her room.

I walk into the kitchen, my legs as heavy as lead. The adrenaline of the drive—and near crash—is gone, and I'm overwhelmed. I don't know where to start, how to begin. I am lost as to what to do. But I will help Jess through this.

First, I need to understand what exactly she's done.

Shockingly, when I enter my seventeen-year-old daughter's name into the Google search, she's everywhere. Everywhere you would never want to be.

My eyes are drawn to the photo of Jess and her friends. All attractive, all smiling, all looking so incredibly clueless as to what the symbols could mean to people. This is the fallout from the life I've chosen to lead. My obsession with appearances and money, my lack of deep connections with my husband and my own child caused this. I failed to create a responsible, aware, caring daughter.

I click on a link, and I'm taken to Twitter. I know I signed up to tweet a long time ago, when Jess was in middle school and one of the moms told me we all needed to be on social media to raise money for our school events. I haven't been on here since.

I somehow guess the right password and I'm in. My hands are shaking as I read the death threats against the kids, particularly my daughter. She seems to be the lightning rod, the one people have focused on. I see her name with a call to shame her, to "out" her. To "expel them all"—and worse.

This person, an anonymous Twitter user, has found my daughter's senior photo and posted it next to a photo of Roger. Lock them up, the user tweeted. Scrolling now, I find a tweet that includes a list of addresses of all the kids in the photo. Another user replies: Race War Now. New Order Will Rise. These kids are heroes.

I close out of Twitter and struggle to breathe. I reach the kitchen sink and fill a glass of water. I look down the driveway toward the carriage house but can't see anyone. A chill rolls down my spine as I walk to the back door, make sure it's locked, and then double-check the front door. Fortunately, this was a private transaction completed under my maiden name, Cohen. If anyone is looking for Julie Jones, they won't find her.

But they aren't looking for me, not right now. All the focus is on Jess—and Roger.

Reluctantly, I realize I need to call Roger. I'm sure he's out of prison by now. They can't hold a man like him. He's the only one who can protect us. He'll have a plan, and no matter how dire things may seem, he'll get out unscathed. He always has. He always will.

I call Roger's number.

"Ready to come home, honey?" His voice drips with a forced syrupy sweetness that has never sounded convincing the few times he's used it with me. I can't believe it worked when we met.

"Why did you do it?" I take a deep breath. I need to pretend to be nice, too. In a way it's a relief for the whole world to know why I want a divorce. But I'll focus on that later. Right now, we need to work together to save Jess.

"Because I wanted to get laid, and you won't even touch me." Roger's voice has turned low and mean. "How is Jess? That's my only focus."

"You're right. She's the important one. She's devastated. She needs protection. There are death threats. Can you send security or something over here? Please." I hope he senses my subservience. I've had a lot of practice over the years.

"Of course there are death threats. What was she thinking? Playing Nazi drinking games? Did she miss the entire history lesson on World War II?" Roger yells into the phone. "I know she didn't mean anything by it, but still. Come home, I have security here."

"I need security here. There are death threats—not just because of the stupid drinking game, but also because of what you did. How could you? An undercover cop? You hit on an undercover cop? That was just stupid."

I've gone too far. I know it before the last sentence flows out of my mouth like an angry bird.

My shoulders jump to my ears as I await his reply. Nothing comes. He's hung up on me.

CHAPTER 28

T O M

I saw Jess and her mom pull into the driveway and dash into the house like they were being chased or something. But nobody else showed up. Nobody else is watching them.

Just me.

The thought of Jess being home, right there in my bedroom, makes me hard. I haven't felt this way in a long time. I'd given up on feeling this way. She's going to come see me, I know she will. She feels it, this connection. I'm certain. We could save each other, we could.

I wonder what she's doing. I mean, it's pretty late in the afternoon. She should text me. We have a date, right?

Or I could text her. I don't have anything to do until tomorrow morning. I look over at my computer. I finally finished my "letter" for Vic. It's not that long, but it's enough. He'll know that I'm committed to the plan, that I belong in the group. And he'll know one other thing, too: I may delay my plan. Just for a bit, just to give Jess a chance.

I'm so excited. I feel so alive. But I'm also conflicted. What if I've finally found love?

I text Jess: Hey, I know you're home, want to hang out?

I put my phone down so I'm not an idiot staring at it, begging for a response. I go over my letter one more time, checking for typos. I don't want to look stupid when it's shared. My nickname in the group is XL, the only signature I'll put at the end. I'll be untraceable, I'm told. No one will know who the letter was written by when the guys post it on the dark web. It's what we do. It's like bragging, only online instead of in person. Sharing our dark deeds with others. Earning their respect. Vic's respect.

My phone pings with a text.

Jess texts: Do you know what happened? What I did?

I text: No. What?

Jess texts: I can't believe it. You're like the only one on earth. Google me.

I do. Holy shit. Jess's party last night was a bunch of teenage neo-Nazis. I heard about this when I was in school there, but I was a loser. I never went to these parties. I can't believe she hangs out with these posers. They're stupid jocks. Look at that guy with his arm around Jess. Who does he think he is anyway? Is she dating him? I could take him out in one punch.

I look at the next result. What the fuck? Jess's dad was arrested for paying someone for sex at a rich dude's private strip club. Turns out there was someone working undercover. What the hell? Jess is smart. She didn't need that. I feel sorry for her. And something else: I want to protect her.

I text: Want to come over?

Jess texts: You don't want to be seen with me.

I text: Yes I do.

More now than ever, I don't add. I need to find out who the jerk in the photo is, too. Does she care about him?

Jess texts: My mom will freak out if I leave my room.

I smile. She wants to see me, too. Getting out is not a problem. I did it for years.

I text: Climb out bedroom window to roof. Use trellis on the right to climb down. Easy. I'll be waiting.

Jess texts: Sounds like you're a sneak out pro ☺

I text: Takes one to know one ☺

Jess needs a friend. I'll be here for her. No matter what. We'll get through this together.

I text: Hurry up. I'll be waiting for you with a cold beer

Jess texts: Not sure about the beer. Severe hangover.

I text: Hair of the dog. Come on.

I walk to the kitchenette window of the carriage house and take down the towel I tacked up to keep Sandi from looking at my business. I stare up at my old bedroom window. Will she or won't she?

I bet she does it. What does she have to lose? She's one of us now. A troublemaker. A Nazi sympathizer? Perhaps. Although I bet it was more of a drunk party thing. But maybe she's open to things, to seeing things my way? Once she's over here, I'll show her she's not alone. Together we're not alone. We're strong. I scan my humble abode. I should hide a few things before she arrives. I race around the room, cleaning the place up. I go back to the window, check and see if she's escaping.

And there she is. She's out on the roof. I want to open the door, run over and help her down, but I need to play it cool. If her mom comes out, so far it's just Jess on the roof, getting some air.

Better stay here.

Watching her brings back memories of all the nights I climbed out, nights I'd be wandering the neighborhood, smoking weed, checking for unlocked car doors to steal stuff. Jess reaches the bottom of the trellis and crouches low on the grass. Smart girl. She looks around and then goes for it. She's springing across the yard, and just as she hits my front porch, I open the door and pull her inside, closing the door behind her.

"You did it!" I smile like a proud dad.

"That was awesome actually. Thanks for talking to me, for having me over." Jess's eyes look swollen, probably from crying, and when she pulls out her phone it's cracked, the screen shattered. I don't know how she texted me without cutting her fingers.

"You're here because you need a friend," I say, pivoting her quickly to the kitchenette because I realize I've forgotten to remove the ladies in the bathroom. I'll need to keep her in here, for now. She's so beautiful, so afraid. I'll protect her—from everything. "Come into my tiny kitchen and have a drink with me."

I lead the way into the kitchenette. I have a table for two, a tiny stove, and a refrigerator. I don't have much food, but I do have a lot of beer. That's really what this moment calls for. I open two cold ones and put one on the table in front of her. I watch as she takes a big drink.

"Thanks," she says.

"No biggie. Do you want to talk about it?" I ask. I'm dying to hear her thoughts, but I don't want to push her. Opening up is hard. I found that out last week in the desert. We had practice role-playing sessions. Interrogations, really. Vic told us what to say if you got caught executing a plan: deny any other person's involvement, no matter what. In prison, you'll be protected. Say nothing. That's the rule with the cops. With our friends, though, we had to open up. They put us in pairs, and we had to tell each other about our family life, about why we were here, about what we believed. That part was easy, for me.

Oh no. Jess is crying.

"It was just a joke!" she says. Tears run down her cheeks. "I mean, nobody supports what Hitler did."

"Well, actually, some people do," I say, then take a big drink of my beer. She just needs a little more education. It's not about Hitler, not really. He's dead. Maybe she's testing me? "You all had pretty big smiles on your faces in those photos."

Jess wipes away the tears under her eyes with her T-shirt. I catch a glimpse of her bra, her flat stomach. "We were drunk."

"Sure you were," I say. And then I push a button. "You have to be pissed at the girl who ratted you all out. She says she's Jewish and offended." I'm testing her, seeing if she's for real.

"I know. Unreal. How could she do this? It was a game. This is all her fault. All of us just posted in our own group, but someone must be friends with her and she took a screenshot and started sharing it everywhere. Traitor." Jess takes a big chug. She sighs. "Well, actually, it's not her fault. It's mine. I'm the idiot for playing the game, for being in the photos. Can I have another one?"

"Sure." She passes my test with flying colors as I open the refrigerator and pull out two more cold ones. I pivot and put a beer in front of her. "Seems like the thing with your dad may have a longer shelf life than that little game will," I say. "They arrested like a dozen old rich guys."

She chugs her beer. Puts it on the table and shakes her head. "My life is ruined. Nothing is real. Nothing matters. My parents are disasters. I can't wait to get out of here. I hate it here."

I want to touch her shoulder, give her a hug. But I don't want to move too fast. "You matter, Jess. This will all blow over. And I'm sure there are other colleges who will have you after this has died down, if you decide to go."

She meets my eyes with her red-rimmed ones. "Oh right, they won't let me go to USC. Shit. I need to get out of here. Bonnie's parents are sending her away, to a boarding school back east. There's some sort of meeting going on at the high school. Do you think they'll kick us all out?"

I shake my head. "No way. In Oceanside? Come on. Nobody ever gets in trouble for being right wing here. It's in our roots. It's who we are. Now, if you'd been running around like some liberal hippie chick from Laguna Beach or something, that could get you suspended."

Jess laughs. I love the sound. "It was just a stupid drinking game. The water polo guys play it all the time, I guess. They learned from a video on YouTube. It was just for fun. Something different. Can I have another beer?"

I know for a fact that video's description didn't include the translated lyrics to the SS fight song the water polo guys were gleefully singing. I suspect a few of those guys will find their way to my bar—and to Vic—someday soon, but I won't tell Jess that, not now. I still want to know who the poser was with his arm around Jess.

"I don't want you to get drunk over here. You don't even know me." I stand up and get us both another beer. Despite my lame warning, I'd love to get drunk with this gorgeous girl.

"I know you well enough. And, like I said, nothing matters anymore." She pops the top of her third beer and grins. The smile doesn't reach her blue eyes, though.

"Who was the guy, the one with his arm around you in the meme? The one who said 'great shot' and shit?" I ask. I stare at her until she looks away. "Did he post that video? The one that went viral? Got all of you busted? What an idiot."

"No, that's not his video. But Chase took the selfie where we're smiling like idiots and posted it. He's so gross. Kept trying to kiss me, too. And now, he's one of the reasons I'm the star of this show. I can't even." She shakes her head, pushes the hair off her forehead.

"You're with me now. Forget about him. Cheers." I clink our cans together and our hands touch. Sparks rush through me like a Santa Ana wind-propelled forest fire.

CHAPTER 29

SANDI

I haven't heard from Doug for hours. Despite my worry over the dead rabbit and whatever message it was meant to send to me and our family, I've found solace by painting a whole meadow of wildflowers at the bottom of my canvas while the boys watch their favorite shows. I'm not letting them out of my sight, not until I figure out what is going on. Because something is. Someone is threatening us.

It must have something to do with Doug and all his deceptions. The boys and I haven't harmed anyone. Doug has.

To be clear, I'm not worried about Doug, not at the moment. Right now, I'm sure he's in his element, the center of attention as the pastor with all the answers. Leader of the interfaith council—or he was, until we left.

I know they haven't had time to replace Doug on the council. Likely Pastor Lovett is there, too. I wonder if that's awkward. I know Doug wouldn't care. He feels superior to everyone, and so it's likely Doug is leading the crisis meeting.

What I'm worried about is Tom. I need to know that Doug is going to check on Tom and help him move out.

I call Doug's phone again, and miracle of miracles, he picks up.

"Hey. National media is here, can you believe it? TV reporters like that guy we watch every night. What's his name again? I'm being interviewed by him in a few minutes." Doug is breathless with excitement. This is his big moment. He's back in the spotlight. He sounds like a drug addict who has finally gotten his fix. He even sounds happy to speak to me. I decide the rabbit can wait.

"Do the Brennans want you on national TV? You aren't going to condone this, are you? Does the interfaith council want you to talk as their spokesperson?" I ask the obvious question.

"Oh, no, well, I don't know. I've convinced them to send Jack to a great boarding school in Northern California. Just until this blows over. He'll finish out senior year there, as if nothing happened, and then go on to the Ivy League college he's been accepted to. We made calls. As long as he apologizes and doesn't get caught doing anything else stupid, he'll be fine."

A woman's voice says, "Excuse me, Pastor Doug. It's time for makeup."

Makeup? "Doug, I am not sure this is a good idea. You'll become the face of the community on this. And it's an ugly thing."

"Are you calling me ugly?" he says with a teasing tone. Is he joking with me? I miss this. I miss this man I married. Seeing a glimpse of him now makes things harder, somehow. I can still remember how he made me feel when we first met and married, how special and treasured. He'd surprise me with flowers, pink roses, my favorite. We would hold hands and sometimes sing my favorite hymns together. I don't hear this voice anymore at home. He saves this tone, this disposition for the spotlight, for his sermons, and I imagine for his latest Charlene.

"I'd never call you ugly, you know that," I say. "You were my perfect man."

"Good. Look, let me call you back after this interview. The local newspaper may want to interview me, too," he says, talking fast. It's like he's high on attention.

I swallow. He didn't notice the past tense. "No problem. Please remember to stop by Tom's on the way home. Just to make sure he's packing."

"Sure, right, whatever. Talk to you later." And he hangs up.

This could go one of two ways. I walk over to the television in the family room.

"Boys, why don't you go check your rooms, make sure they're all cleaned up. I need a few minutes of mom time before I start dinner. Sound good?"

The kids moan and grumble, but they do as they're told. As soon as they're out of the room, I change the TV from their cartoons to the national cable news we always watch, then sit down on the couch. For a moment I wonder if I should allow the boys to see their daddy's interview. But I decide not to.

I'm not sure exactly what he's going to say, or how they'll make him look. Makeup? Really?

The familiar music signals the start of the program, and I'm shocked to see the anchor we watch every night on the national news standing in front of the Oceanside High School. Just beyond I get a glimpse of our former church, the immense gold cross on the dome shining in the background.

Then photos of the kids at the drinking party appear on the screen, with their faces blurred out. Doug is sitting in a chair next to the anchorman. On the screen it identifies Doug as the head of the multifaith crisis team. The school district and the parents have declined to comment, the anchorman says. So why is Doug talking? Because he can't help himself: moth to a flame.

"Pastor, I know you are deeply troubled by what happened in your community last evening," Anchorman says.

"I am. We all are. No matter your faith—and I'm a Christian—we all must come together in times like this."

"What does 'come together' look like? I mean, teenagers in your community are drinking around a swastika, laughing, doing the sieg-heil salute." The anchorman shakes his head in disgust. There is an angry edge to his voice.

"Jesus Christ teaches all of us forgiveness. These children made a poor decision, and they took photos. And now they are getting death threats. That's just wrong. These are innocent children who need for-giveness. Like Jesus forgave us all." Doug smiles.

Anchorman is not smiling. "Sir, Pastor, don't you think there should be some sort of punishment for these kids? I've talked off the record to their fellow classmates. One said there are swastikas carved into desks at the school, there are Nazi symbols in the bathrooms. She is Jewish. A fellow student dropped a quarter in front of her and told her to 'pick it up, Jewess.'"

"Christians don't condone that type of behavior. But we do teach a strong sense of faith identity. We believe Jesus is the son of God. Some don't. Some people have hatred in their heart and act out. You see it all over the news. Such hatred." Doug shakes his head, looks to the camera. "These are just children playing a game. A joke. That's all it was. They need and deserve our forgiveness." He smiles again.

I feel like reaching through the television and slapping him. The anchorman has a look similar to mine on his face. How is it possible for Doug to go on television and not condemn this behavior? Sure, forgiveness is important, but so is responsibility. These kids need to take ownership of what they've done. These children and their families float around in a bubble of entitlement and superiority, oblivious to the needs of others. When they're caught doing something offensive, there should be a consequence. They need consequences to learn, that's what my daddy always preached.

I think back to when our neighbors' home was vandalized. Someone spray-painted "baby killer" in red on the front of the house and poi-soned the family's dog. The family was the only African American one in our area, and the dad was a doctor who, among other things, performed abortions. They didn't go to our church, but my daddy took a stand from the pulpit the Sunday after the attack: "What happened to the Miller family is against everything Jesus teaches us. We are to love our neighbors, we are expected to treat others as we expect to be treated. We will pray for the Millers, pray for justice for the Millers. Let's bow our heads."

Someone in the congregation yelled, "But he's a baby killer. Abortion is an abomination, a sin."

Instead of ignoring the outburst, my daddy addressed the man. "Let he who has not sinned throw the first stone. Are you so pure, so good, that you can judge another, Mr. Roy? This is about the perpetrators of the hate crime against our neighbor. This was a hate crime. The parties involved will be found and punished. There is no place in Christianity for this type of behavior. Let us pray."

I was so proud of my daddy in that moment. But Doug is the opposite. I am horrified by his excuses for the kids, by the way he acts all pious but spouts the least Christian answers—on national television.

"What has the community crisis team decided as far as disciplinary actions?" Anchorman asks.

"That is confidential, of course, and between the school and the students. I do know we'll be recommending a visit to a synagogue or maybe a history museum, at the request of my friends at the Jewish center. It's not mandatory, but we hope the kids and their parents will join us. I pray they do—it's important to move on." Doug has that stupid smile on his face still. His eyes glisten in the television light.

A visit to a synagogue? Really? That's all he expects of these kids and their parents? Does Doug really think that will solve a systemic anti-Semitic problem on the school's campus?

"Well, thank you, Pastor. So far, you are the only one willing to go on camera." Anchorman shakes his head.

"It's best to respect the privacy of these fine families. You should see all of the threats and things. I mean, their poor kids. They've been through so much," Doug says.

The anchorman looks at Doug with a look that can only be disbelief, and then faces the camera. "We'll be back after this break to focus on the rise of anti-Semitism in the United States. Stay with us."

I turn off the television, relieved I didn't invite the kids to watch. Doug just made excuses, that's all he did. Made it sound like these kids did nothing wrong. Part of me thinks that's what Doug believes. Part of me thinks Doug is a little proud of them. God help me.

Would Tom play a game like that? Did he? Did Doug when he was growing up in Oceanside? I have chosen to ignore his narrow worldview, his prejudices, his false piety—and now, here we are.

I knew all this, and that is why I need out. Now, the rest of the world can see it, too. I should have taken action sooner to get my kids away from all this. My phone rings. It's Doug. He'll want to know how he did on the news.

"Hi, you looked good," I say. I don't know what else to say.

"Really? You know, that's what the assistant told me. Said I was a natural. Born to be on camera." Doug is so proud, so high on himself. "They may have me back on tomorrow morning, isn't that something? On the *Sunday Morning News* show. And the local stations want to talk to me next."

"Wow," I answer, unable to come up with a way to stop him. But what about the kids? Will they learn anything from this? Will they apologize? Will they change? And what about Tom?

"Don't forget to check on Tom. Please," I say. Tom, our own hate-filled, lost boy.

"Oh, not sure that's going to happen. Gotta go. Call you later."

Well, if he won't confront Tom, I will. It's time to stop avoiding the conflict and step in, do what's right. It's what Jesus would do.

I'm pretty sure Jesus wouldn't be as scared as I am of Tom.

CHAPTER 30

ROGER

I know. I know. I shouldn't have hung up on Julie, but she pissed me off. I behaved badly, though. I texted her an apology, but she hasn't answered me yet. Maybe she's still driving, maybe she's just never coming home. For real.

Smith gives me a questioning look, like he wants to say something to me, ask me a question or something, but he's afraid to do it. Weenie.

"What, Smith?" He and I are sitting in the two overstuffed leather chairs by the window. From here I can command the room. The lawyers sit smashed together on my couch and on folding chairs someone must have brought in from the guest cottage. They look like a haphazardly assembled old guys' fraternity.

"Sir, did you just hang up on Julie?" Smith whispers.

"Yep. I did. She pissed me off." I turn away so he doesn't see that I'm upset.

"But the plan was, I believe, to ask her to come home, with your daughter. Reunited front and all that, for optics." Smith still whispers, but all conversation has ended in the room.

Well, it looks like I might have messed that up. I want them home, more than anything in the world. That's the truth. I miss them, but none of these people need to know that.

"Gentlemen, we're gonna need some different optics." I smack both hands on the arms of the leather chair and watch everyone jump. For once, this doesn't make me happy. It makes me sadder. I take a breath. "Ideas, gentlemen? And who is the beat-up guy in the wheelchair? What are you doing here?"

"Ah, sir, it's Bob. Your lead attorney," Smith says.

This is just embarrassing. It's like a scene out of a bad movie. I ignore Bob for now. "Do any of you have an idea of how to get me out of this? My wife will not be returning home, not today at least."

Someone stands up. I don't know who he is. Don't care.

"Sir. I'm Jeff. I believe we can make that charge disappear with a quick guilty plea. No jail time, small fine. That would be my recommendation. I've talked to my friends at the US district office. They want someone to go first."

Smith's eyes are bulging. He knows I'm not liking this answer. Not one bit.

"So my attorney thinks I'm guilty, is that what you're saying, Jeff? Everyone goes to strip clubs." I stand up. "I'm no different than any of you."

"Sir, with all due respect, the indictment is very clear. They have you on video trying to pay an undercover officer for sex. That's illegal, sir."

OK, yes, yes, they do have me. I don't suppose I could have been discussing much else. "Well, we didn't do anything. She said she had to go home to her kid, so nothing happened. I left," I say. I don't add that I messed up. Big time. I never thought this would come to light. So what if I pay for sex? Everyone does it. I just picked the wrong girl, the wrong club. Damn it.

Jeff drops his head. "But they have you on camera with other women at the club, sir, doing much more than enjoying the show. It's a big sting. And well, propositioning the officer, that wasn't good, sir." He meets my eyes with a steady gaze. "They know what you've done, and they have the proof. This plea deal, it won't last. And the offer of no jail time will be for the first man who pleads guilty. And then, well, it's a crapshoot. They have about a dozen guys they arrested at the same time across Southern California. Someone will take the deal."

Beside me Smith whispers, "I'd take it, sir."

I hate to admit I'm wrong about anything. But I do like to win, and I do like being first. "OK, fine. Let's be first. I'll admit I was wrong to get my name out of the spotlight as quickly as possible, to protect my daughter," I say. This thing will blow over, and so will that drinking-game stunt.

"Sir, I'll go call the district attorney's office now and tell them we are taking the plea deal. Thank you." Jeff scurries from the office like he has won the lottery, or like he thinks I might change my mind. Which I might. In fact, what kind of half-rate attorney talks his client into pleading guilty?

I look at Smith. "So now that we have a plan for the ridiculous entrapment, I need to get my wife and daughter back home. I'll plead guilty. Jess will go into hiding or something until this all blows over." I just want my family home. More than I can even express. My heart actually hurts. It does.

Smith says, "It would be wise to call Julie back, sir. Maybe apologize for hanging up on her?"

Fuck you, Smith. "She pissed me off. Just call her, would you? I mean, you can sweet-talk her. She likes you. Let's give her some money—a return-home bonus payment, we can call it. Always worked before."

Smith drops his voice to a whisper and leans toward me. The room is silent. They can all hear what he says. "I don't think this is like before, boss. She bought a house. She plans to file for a divorce. I heard it through the grapevine she hired a killer divorce attorney."

I lean back in my chair. I can't believe she is actually going through with a divorce. I'm stunned, speechless. After a few moments, and because they're all staring at me like idiots, I say, "Anybody else want to try to talk some sense into my wife? Anybody? Huge bonus to you if you get her back home."

"Sir, that won't be necessary. I'm calling her now." Smith jumps up and starts to hurry out of the room.

Amazing what a little competition will do. "Get her home, Smith, or I'll turn her over to someone who can."

Smith nods and disappears. I've lit a fire under him, that's for sure.

I stand and stretch, and the remaining attorneys get the hint and clear out of the room. I'm alone again. And I hate that. "Come home, Julie," I say to a row of expensive leather books I've never opened. "And please bring Jess with you."

My girls need me—and the protection all the money in the world can provide. It's a dangerous place, the real world. The money I made has insulated them from it. Without it, they're vulnerable. I hope they realize that before it's too late.

CHAPTER 31

JULIE

My phone sits facedown on the kitchen counter, near the coffee maker. It rings again. I grab it and answer. The caller says, "You should be ashamed of yourself. Your daughter and your husband should go to prison. Or better yet, just die."

That caller sounded like a woman. A very angry woman. If she's like the others, they cannot believe my daughter likes Nazis. And, by the way, my husband is terrible.

I've counted five death threats among the twenty calls. I'm not sure why I'm still answering the phone.

But I have to agree with them for the most part. We are an embarrassment. A terrible blemish on society.

One of the callers said she looked at me online. And she was disgusted. She said I look plastic.

"All fake. Everything about you all is a facade. Respectable family, my ass. All those years at PTA and this is who you really are." And then she hung up before I could.

I wonder how people are masking their phone numbers. Most of the calls are from blocked lines, but I suspect I know some of them. I didn't recognize the voice of the last caller, but I'd likely know her if I saw her. I'm sure she was a neighbor, with a child in Jess's class. We probably attended a Botox cocktail party together at some point.

It took me so long to feel like I belonged in Oceanside. I came in from nowhere, literally, and they all knew it. This place is generational, closed. You can be here for two generations and still feel like a newbie. But I'd worked hard, and I'd been accepted, at least at a certain level of status. And what was that all for? Nothing. They turn on us faster, I suspect, than the other kids involved. We aren't from here. Not originally. And in the quest for acceptance, if they think Jess's dad is a sexual predator, well, that's something they'll never forgive. The Nazi drinking game, I suspect, will be forgotten—buried, more like it—soon. Some of the oldest Oceanside families had kids who set up those red cups. They'll stick together. Jess will be left to fend for herself.

Except for me. I will be there for her now, like I should have been all along.

Another caller. A male voice, older, gravelly. I hope he's not a Holocaust survivor. "You are the worst mother ever. How could you raise a daughter like that? Do you know what the Nazis did to us? Go to hell!"

I want to say yes, I do know. I'm Jewish, too, but I don't speak. I take their insults, their anger, in. I don't mind it when they pick on me. I can take it. I made my bed and all.

But when they attack Jess—well, I take that in, too.

As for Roger, he's an adult. He knew exactly what he was doing, and I guess I'm not surprised. We have slept in separate bedrooms for some time. And now he wants me back? He thinks money can buy anything, solve anything, control anything. He must be stunned by this development, by being arrested and all the negative press. But Roger is a man, with all the money to insulate himself from the fallout. He'll be fine.

All I care about is saving Jess.

My phone rings again. The caller ID says Oceanside School Administration.

I answer and put the phone on speaker. It's not so jarring to the ears. Based on recent phone calls, if you put the phone on speaker, the yelling seems to dissipate into the kitchen and soften. When I hold the phone to my ear, their anger heads straight to my heart like an arrow.

"Mrs. Jones? This is Superintendent Cummings. Do you have a moment to talk?" I hear the tenseness in her voice. The stress. Is she calling to expel Jess? Is she aware of Roger's arrest, his sexual perversions?

I swallow. "Sure. Yes."

"As you know there was an incident at a private home last night. Your daughter was in a very unfortunate photo, along with several of our other students. The attention this has been receiving, nationally and now internationally, has given us no other choice than to address the situation, even though it was on private property." She is reading a statement to me, I can tell. There is no emotion, no inflection. This is breaking my heart. How could this have happened? How could Jess not know it was wrong, shut it down, tell Bonnie's parents? But how can I blame her? Peer pressure and alcohol are a powerful combination. I'm a walking example of that, and I'm an adult. Passive compliance. It's so very dangerous. Going along with what you know is wrong makes you just as guilty.

"We are inviting all students involved, and their parents, to a mandatory meeting tomorrow, Sunday, at eight a.m. at the district offices. We will do our best to keep this meeting from being covered by the press and request your help keeping it confidential."

An invitation to a mandatory meeting isn't something you can turn down. "Of course. We'll be there."

"Good. And Mrs. Jones, we'd prefer it if Mr. Jones did not attend. We can't handle that scandal just yet, especially in front of other kids. I'm sure you understand." She sounds like my mother. Mrs. Cummings is beyond disgusted by all three of us.

For good reason; I'm disgusted, too. "I understand. My husband won't be there."

"Good. We'll see you tomorrow."

"Yes, ma'am." I answer like a student in trouble. I hang up like a mom without hope.

I note five voice mails have been left during the time I was speaking to Mrs. Cummings. I'll need a new phone number—now. I walk over to my laptop and type in, *How do I get a new phone number?* The results load quickly. First step, I need to call or text my provider and request a mobile PAC.

My phone rings before I can text. It's Smith, Roger's right-hand man. As much as I don't want to talk to him, I do want to be sure Roger is taking responsibility for his actions. He'd better be.

"Look, Julie, hey, I know this is a bad time, and I'm sorry to bother you," Smith says. He's playing Mr. Nice Guy to Roger's hanging-up-on-his-wife routine.

"Hey, Smith. You do know Roger just hung up on me, right?" I'm pacing across the kitchen, trying to figure out how to get what I want out of this mess.

"Sorry about that. He's in a bit of a pickle. Actually, that's why I'm calling," he says. "Roger needs you and Jess at home, by his side. He will need to rehabilitate his reputation. He has agreed to plead guilty, so that's a start."

"That's funny."

"What's funny?"

"Roger will never change, he'll never be rehabilitated. And I'm never coming back home to Roger. I'm getting a divorce. It will all be public soon. But the thing is, I'll stay away from the media if he does what I say. And he'd better." I take a deep breath. This is hard, playing tough, seeing things through. But this is the new me. I take stands for what is right. I stand up for myself.

"Let's try to be reasonable here. I know you don't want to throw everything away. Your life together has been pretty special. I mean, you have it all. And I'm authorized to offer a returning-home bonus," Smith says.

He thinks he can throw money at me and I'll come home. I realize with shame that it worked before. Oh my god. "Look, tell Roger to stay away from me and Jess. Tell him to make this right, all of it. My attorney will outline my terms for the divorce. I'm not asking for more than I deserve. Have him agree to it. Or I'll go public. And he has enough going on in the press without adding to it."

There is silence on the other end of the line. I know I've shocked him. He didn't think I had it in me.

"He wants you both home. By tomorrow. He misses you, Julie. And he loves you. That's all I know."

"I am home." I hang up feeling strong but alone. It's likely I need my attorney again, even though I hate paying all that money.

My voice mail is now full, thank God. I dial the number for my attorney as I walk to the front door and check the street. There's nothing unusual out there that I can see.

I can't imagine what will happen if the press finds our address. But I know this relative anonymity can't last. It won't take very long for someone to find us.

Roger did.

We probably need to move to a hotel.

I get my attorney's voice mail. "Hello, this is Julie Cohen. Since we last talked, there have been a few developments. I need your help. Can you call me back as soon as possible? Thank you."

My phone buzzes in my hand. This time, I'm not answering. I've heard enough. Slowly, I climb the stairs up to Jess's room. I need to tell her about the meeting at school tomorrow. I need to tell her I'll be by her side every step. We will take responsibility and apologize.

I knock on her closed door.

"Can I come in?"

There's no answer. I turn the knob and walk into an empty room. The bathroom is empty, too.

Goose bumps cover my arms.

My daughter is gone.

CHAPTER 32

JESS

I like this, drinking in the middle of the afternoon with a guy I barely know.

It's almost like I can forget I'm the most hated person in town—one of them, at least. I'm so embarrassed. I was such an idiot. I am not that kind of person. I was so stupid. I will do better. I'm part Jewish. That makes what I did doubly horrible. All I feel right now is shame.

"You doing OK?" Tom seems to read my mind.

"Uh-huh. Sure." I'm suffocating here in this town, where everyone knows I'm a joke. I'll never be able to show my face at school again. There's nowhere for me here. I feel sick. I've got to go. "Do you want to run away with me?"

I watch Tom's face turn bright red. I don't know if that's a good sign or not. Maybe he just thinks I'm a kid?

"Well, sure, that could be good. I just have some stuff to do in the morning, tomorrow, but after that I can go anywhere. I like that idea, actually." Tom smiles.

I think he's serious. I know I am. How can I ever show my face around here again? My mom's expression when she saw me for the first time after learning what I did is burned into my memory. The shock and crushing disappointment were written all over her face. Try as she might, she couldn't hide it. I've hurt her to the core.

Everyone else just thinks I'm a dumb Nazi lover. I need out of here. "Where should we go?"

"You're serious?" he asks.

"I am."

"You're drunk. Probably a good idea to think it over. Maybe give it a night?" Tom says.

"I want to leave tonight. Why can't we?" I sound a little whiny, but I need to get out of here. "Please. You have a car. I have a credit card courtesy of my dad. Although he might have cut it off. But I'll call him. I have money, don't worry. You're supposed to move out, right?"

Tom walks out of the kitchen and into the other room, so I follow him. I haven't been in here yet. It's his bedroom, but it has a couch in the corner and a TV. There's a bathroom on the far side of the room. I think I see a gun on the counter. I blink. I must be wrong. I've never seen a gun before. I'm sure I'm wrong.

"Uh, you should stay in there." Tom points to the kitchen. "This is kind of my office. And you know, my private stuff."

He pulls the bathroom door closed, but it's too late. I try to hide my shock. I can't let him see my thoughts. I paste a smile on my face. Oh my god, I realize, I don't know him at all. What am I doing here?

"I said go back into the kitchen." Tom's voice is firm, his hand on my shoulder steering me away.

"Fine," I say, but I need to get out of here. My phone vibrates in my pocket, and I open a text. Another idiot is sending me another photo of me and Chase, and the rest of the idiots from the party last night. As if I want to see any more of these.

Tom is watching over my shoulder, so I can't text for help. "He thinks he's such a tough guy, doesn't he?" He points to Chase in the photo.

"I guess. But he's just a friend," I say.

"Looks like he thinks you two are a lot more than that," Tom says.

I turn to face him. "Well, we're not. I already told you about Chase."

"What are you doing, flashing the OK sign?" His voice is quiet. His eyes are large, shiny.

I meet his stare. "I'm just telling everybody everything's OK in Oceanside."

"That's a white-power symbol. Did you know that?"

"No. Oh my god. That's not what I meant. I meant OK. Do you really think I'm a racist?" I'm horrified, but when I meet Tom's stare, he looks amused, happy even. It's hard to breathe. I tell myself to calm down. I need to play the role until I can run.

"Uh-huh. Sure." He shakes his head. "I'm not sure what to make of you, sweetie."

"OK, well, you know, people are complicated." I take a sip of beer, try to figure out how to get away from him. I'll ask for another beer and make a run for it. "Can I have another beer?"

"Sure, whatever you'd like," Tom says, walking to the minifridge.

I stand up fast and start to go for the door, but his hand is on my shoulder. "Here you go. Drink up!"

I sit down at the table again. I need to keep him calm. I need him to think I'm still on his side. Maybe I can talk him into going outside and then I can scream for my mom. "Let's leave now, want to?"

He shakes his head. "We can't leave until after tomorrow morning."

"What's so important about tomorrow morning?" I ask. Why won't he tell me what he's up to? He is scaring me.

I think about my mom, alone in the house. My hands shake, and I drop them into my lap. All I want to do is run away. I don't think he'll let me leave. I will make him talk, keep him calm. I need to keep him away from my mom.

He sits down across the table from me, staring hard. He pounds the kitchen table with his fist, and I jump. He asks, "Are you for real?"

I'm as real as I'll ever be. "My life is ruined. Let's go, let's get out of here. Let's leave tonight."

"I can't. I told you that. You should listen better," he says. "I'm busy in the morning, but I can leave after."

"Tell me what you're doing tomorrow. What could be so important?"

"I can't say anything. It's a secret."

I stare at Tom, and I see something I didn't see before. Why would a man like him have secrets? Why would a guy like him have anything to do besides run away to a beach with me?

"What is this, second grade? I just told you I'm running away. I asked you to go with me. Anywhere. I have money. I made a bad choice at the party last night, and my dad got busted and everyone knows it, so now my life is over. I'm leaving tonight," I say. "Are you coming?"

"I can't. It's important. I have to do this," Tom says. His brow is full of wrinkles, like he's suddenly an old man, thinking.

I don't understand what could be so important. But if I can get him to tell me, I can use it to my advantage. He'll have to let me go. He'll leave me and my mom alone.

"Fine. If you want me to wait for you, you need to tell me something. It's only right." I take a big gulp of beer, swallow it slowly, and pout. I hope he still thinks I'm into him. I lick my lips and smile. "This better be something more important than you and me heading to Mexico. Tequila shots on the beach. I really can't imagine what it could be." I reach out and touch his hand on the table. "Come on. Tell me."

Tom pulls his hand away from mine as if my touch were a burning flame. He jumps up and begins to pace. "You've gotta understand. I just can't leave until after I'm done."

Dramatic much? "Seriously, finished with what? What do you think I'm going to do? Who would I tell? All of my friends are being sent away to boarding school after last night. I don't have anyone. Except you." I take a drink of my beer to calm my nerves and wink at him. I'm a terrible flirt, but I hope this is working. I've got to keep him into me.

Tom seems to consider my fall from grace. Consider me, the kid who is likely kicked out of school. The lucky person who used to live in one of the biggest mansions in Oceanside and had all the best friends, but now has nobody.

I open my phone and see that Chase texted: Where are your parents sending you? I leave in the morning. Some boarding school. In Virginia. My dad went. Supposed to be the best. Could be worse.

I can't believe his parents are getting him out of here. I need to get out of here, too. I text: Our photo is everywhere. I can't believe you're leaving me to handle it all. Goodbye.

"What are you doing?" Tom says.

"Texting obviously. You can read it. I don't care. I'm saying good-bye. They're all leaving," I say. I hand Tom my phone and he scrolls through.

"Spoiled shits," he says. When he hands my phone back, I'm flooded with relief.

I briefly consider texting Chase that I'm in trouble but decide I can handle Tom. He's into me. He'll let me leave when I want to.

I look at Tom. Still pacing. His phone rings. "Oh god. What does he want?" Tom asks. He's looking at me, but he doesn't see me. His eyes are filled with hate.

I shrug but don't say a word.

Tom answers his phone, "Why would you be calling me?"

I can't hear what the caller is saying, but I can tell Tom doesn't like it. His face is red and hardened.

"You're not in charge of me or my life. Not anymore. We're through, do you hear me? You're about to find out how much I'm over you," Tom says. He kicks the wall, expanding the hole. He begins to laugh. A strange, scary chuckle.

"Oh, is that right? Well you'll see what I'm going to do. I've learned from the best bastard around. I'll be here for as long as I want to be, and there's nothing you can do about it." Tom hangs up and looks at me. The cloud of anger surrounds him like a tangible field.

I need to calm him down. He says he's sticking around for as long as he wants to, not moving out. I wonder what that means for me and my mom. How dangerous is he? I need to find out.

"Who was that on the phone?" I ask.

"Nobody. Nobody at all."

Whoever it was on the phone, Tom hates them, that much is clear. "Hey, take a breath. You have options. Look, I'm leaving tonight. I've got the money." I lean back in the chair and cross my arms. I hope I look serious. I need to flirt, too. "You look cute when you're pacing."

That gets his attention. So does the money. I know he doesn't have any.

"Listen, if I tell you my plan, my friends won't like it. Vic hates women, says you can't be trusted. None of you." Tom kicks the wall. Not hard, not soft. His boot leaves a dent in the wall. Now I notice similar dents around the room. Anger issues, too, great. He is not the guy I thought he was, not at all. Who am I kidding? I just met him. My crush-at-first-sight illusions are all gone. Just another mistake.

"Do you actually believe that? That all women are bad?" I look at Tom. He wants to believe I like him, I know it. I lean forward as he sits down across from me. It takes every ounce of willpower in me to reach across and touch his hand. Touching him used to give me tingles, but now it gives me the creeps. "Tell me what's so important that I should wait for you. I'll wait for you, if I agree it's important."

Tom spins the kitchen chair around and mounts it like a horse. "There's never been anything more important in my life."

I swallow. His stare is making me uncomfortable. "OK." I flash him the sign, and he laughs. It's a dark laugh.

"I have a plan. I need revenge. It's the only answer. It's what I must do."

A chill runs down my spine. I'm almost certain I should run out the door, climb back into my room, and tell my mom about this. But I don't know what he has planned. I can't help anyone if I can't find out. I take a deep breath.

"Tell me," I say.

CHAPTER 33

SANDI

I need to save Tom.

Or, more likely, save Julie from Tom. But right now, I'm home with the boys, trying to act like everything is normal. When nothing is. But I can't take the boys to confront Tom, and I can't leave them alone, not at night, not with vandals and rabbit killers and worse stalking us. There are a number of male church members from Oceanside who would like to get even with Doug, of that I'm certain.

If Doug would stop this ridiculous showmanship and do his job as a father, none of this would be happening. We were supposed to sneak away to the country, live a quiet life, and pray the parishioners in Oceanside would forgive him. Now he's on national television.

I don't have a good feeling about any of this. Not at all.

I call Doug's mobile, and it rolls to voice mail. "Please remember that we agreed to leave Oceanside quietly. And we did. You aren't a pastor there anymore. Nothing good can come from this attention, especially since you were banished from that church. You are needed at Tom's. You need to evict your son from our former home."

I take a deep breath and change my tone. Flattery may still work on his big ego. I reprise my submissive role. "But I know you know what you're doing, honey, because you're so much smarter than me.

You know we signed a legal, binding contract with the new owner of the house. Tom must be gone by tomorrow morning. Please. You're the only one he'll listen to. You are his father. Go to him."

I toss in the sentiment to soften his heart. I need to honor my word to Julie. I think of her and her daughter, all the trouble that has come their way. The last thing they need is Tom lurking in the backyard.

The news comes on, and I brace myself against the kitchen counter. I hope nothing else terrible is revealed about our former hometown. I hope Doug doesn't speak again.

They start with the same reporter who has been covering the story since it broke. The bottom of the screen identifies her as Megan Green. She's alone, standing in front of the high school. She says, "It's been a very hard day for students, faculty, and parents of Oceanside High School. Here is the story as it has unfolded so far."

I watch as the photo of the kids playing that drinking game fills the screen, their young faces blurred out.

"These students thought it would be funny to play a Nazi drinking game. But according to school officials, this behavior is anything but tolerated at Oceanside." This is like a nightmare. For all of us. What must the country think of the behavior in this wealthy enclave? How can this happen here?

The screen flashes to Superintendent Cummings. "We have zero tolerance for hatred. These students will be meeting with the full senior faculty soon, and there will be swift action taken, I assure you."

The reporter asks, "What type of punishment do you anticipate?"

Cummings says, "Disciplinary matters involving minor students are private."

The reporter is back on the screen. "This is a developing story. In a coincidence of fate and timing, one of the students in the photo is also embroiled in another news story. Her father was arrested last night as part of the strip club scandal involving a myriad of celebrities and wealthy businessmen. Roger Jones is out on bail."

The anchors in the studio appear on the left side of the screen. "So are you telling me the daughter was playing that Nazi drinking game while her father was being led away in handcuffs?"

"Seems to be the case." The reporter stares at the screen.

"Oh my," anchor number two says. "Well, thank you for staying on top of this, Megan. Any other community response?"

My heart races.

"Yes, I spoke with a pastor who emphasized forgiveness for the kids. But I also talked to the spokesperson for the Anti-Defamation League. They are pushing for a chance to educate these students. To teach them about the Holocaust. He warns that there has been a rise in hate crimes across the country and that incidents like this should be considered a warning sign."

These words ring in my head as they confirm that my husband as good as sanctioned the hatred on display by these kids, almost tried to sweep it under the rug on national television.

Have I been missing warning signs with Tom?

The first anchor says, "That's terrifying. Seems like the least we can do is educate these kids—all kids."

The second anchor says, "We all learned about World War II and the Holocaust in high school. What were they doing?"

The reporter shrugs. "I don't know, I really don't know. Back to you at the station."

I turn off the television. A bubble of fear is growing in my heart.

Davis bursts into the room and I jump. "Mom, I've been invited for a sleepover at Troy's. Can you believe it?"

I can't help but smile. This, to Davis, is the pinnacle of acceptance in our new hometown. Troy has a nice family. I'd love to get to know Troy's mom. Maybe with Davis as our bridge, I will. He's achieved way more than me, I have to give him that. He'll be able to do it again wherever we end up. Because I've decided we're leaving. But for tonight, one last night, Davis can be happy. And it's a great escape plan for him.

"Of course I can believe it! Let's get you packed up," I say, my heart still pounding in my chest. Can I pull this off? I must. As we climb the stairs to his bedroom, I can't help but think about Tom.

Where will he go? How will he live? What will he do with his hate?

I hope Doug is happy with the situation he's creating here. The desperation I heard in Tom's voice when I spoke with him in our backyard isn't something I'll forget anytime soon.

The hatred isn't something that will diminish anytime soon, either.

My phone rings. It's Doug. My phone shakes in my hand as I answer.

"What a day. What a day!" Doug is still on a high from his sudden fame and purpose.

I put the phone on speaker. "Davis has a sleepover tonight, isn't that great?"

"Dad! I have a sleepover at Troy's. Troy is like, the best." Davis grins from ear to ear.

I want Doug to say something nice. To be happy for his son. I close my eyes.

"Son, that's great. You go have fun. Don't stay up too late, and use your manners."

I open my eyes and grin at Davis.

"Sandi, I need a word with you privately," Doug says.

I take the phone off speaker and hold it to my ear, still smiling at Davis.

"What is it?" I keep my tone light.

"I called that damn son of mine. And he told me I wasn't in charge of him anymore. And he basically told me to screw off." Doug sounds shocked that Tom would talk in this manner, but in all actuality, Doug has spoken to his oldest son like that for years.

"Did he say he's moving out?" That's really all that matters. Once he's out, I can move on knowing I held up my end of the deal. For Julie.

"No, he said he's staying as long as he wants, and that it's not my business." He exhales hard into the phone. "If the new owner wants him out, she's likely going to need the police. He's not right in the head, not right at all. There's something wrong with him."

I want to say I know, that I told you so. I want to say that he should have been helping his own son when he was so involved in helping those divorced women's children in a transparent attempt to get into the women's pants. I want to say, *Tom was watching you.* It's all too much. I cannot take it anymore. I want to tell Doug he is a hypocrite and a sinner, and he has created one in his oldest son. Tom is what you made him into. The other two will not suffer this same fate.

But I don't. I don't say any of that. He won't listen. He'll never change. I have a Go Plan. I just need a little more time. "Will you be home for dinner?"

"Ah, no, they need me here, at the church," he says.

"Which church? Surely you aren't at Oceanside Christian, are you?" I bite my lip.

"I can be wherever I goddamn want to be."

So he is. Back where he was "excused" and "removed from the pulpit" by the church. What must the elders think? What does the new pastor think? I shake my head. This is no longer my problem.

I walk into the hallway, out of earshot of Davis. "So you'll be home tomorrow?"

Doug's answer comes back fast and mean. "Maybe, I just—I'm needed here. Can you understand that? Get that through your tiny brain? Jesus Christ! Some of us have important things to do. God's work. Got it?"

He hangs up on me. Tears spring into my eyes as I wonder again why I've stayed so long.

"Mommy, come help me?" Davis asks.

I look at my innocent boy and find the answer. "Of course I'll help you. I'll always be there for you, honey."

I've made up my mind.

We will disappear.

CHAPTER 34

ROGER

I didn't think this house was too big, not before. I mean, I know it's grand. I like it that way. I like gleaming marble, shining surfaces. Intimidating entry halls and sweeping staircases.

I dial my daughter's mobile again, and again get her voice mail. I'm about to leave a message. I will tell her that I'm sorry, that I know she didn't mean to play that drinking game. I'll tell her I want to help her. I'll tell her I miss her at home. I will tell her I'm sorry about the strip club.

A mechanical voice answers, "The voice mail is full. Goodbye."

I fight the urge to hurl my phone at the wall. I text my daughter: Call me honey. Let me help you. I'm sorry. I love you.

I walk out on my balcony. The waves pound onto the shore on the sand below me. It's a foggy evening, a thicker and darker marine layer than normal. Someone knocks on the sliding glass door, and I turn around. Smith doesn't look like the confident COO I need. He looks exhausted. We've spent hours since he talked to Julie trying to figure out a way to lure her back to me. Back to this life. She never returned my text.

"Let me guess, when she told you it's over, you really believed her," I say as he joins me on the balcony. "You think she's over me."

"Yes, pretty much. I think she's finished, sir," Smith says.

"Finished. How nice for her." I grab the glass railing. "I'm not finished with her. I love her."

"I know." Smith stares out at the ocean.

"I need Julie. I need her by my side."

"You know I told her that earlier on the phone, sir."

We stand on the balcony in silence, waves crashing. Someone laughs in the distance, an irritating sound. One of my neighbors must be having a party. It's Saturday night. I check my watch. It's after 11:00 p.m. Noise restrictions kick in. I pull out my phone and dial security.

"Front gate. How can I help?"

"There is a lot of noise coming from a house just down the street. Go warn them, please."

"Oh yes, it's the Stevenses' fiftieth wedding anniversary. So great. But, of course, if you insist?" the guard says. He's hoping I don't. What a softy.

"I insist," I say and hang up. If I'm miserable, everyone else will be, too. I'll make sure of it. I take a breath. What's making me mad is the fact that these jerks are celebrating a fiftieth wedding anniversary, and here I am alone. I miss my family. I want to celebrate our next anniversary. I want to do it right this time.

And then I decide. I'll go over to Julie's new excuse for a home on the wrong side of town and talk to her in person. I'll tell her we'll spend more time together. I'll work less. And I'll apologize to Jess while I'm there. She needs me, even though I messed up.

"I'm going over and seeing Julie. I need to apologize. I need to figure out how to help Jess. I need them to forgive me," I say to Smith.

"I wouldn't do that if I were you. Not tonight. Maybe tomorrow?" Smith says, acting as if he has any say over me.

"I can't wait until tomorrow." I want Julie home.

"Sir, you need to wait. You've been drinking. It's late. She's likely in bed, asleep." Smith sounds like he is feeling sorry for me.

A man laughs in the distance. Another wedding anniversary attendee, no doubt.

"Shut up!" I bellow at the top of my lungs, at the ocean, at the man at the party, at the universe.

Smith puts his hand on my shoulder. "I think it's time for me to head home and for you to get some rest, sir. Tomorrow's a new day."

"Whatever," I answer but follow him inside. I sit in my favorite chair in my office and turn on the television, which rises like a phoenix from the fancy console that hides it when I'm pretending this room is a serious library. The local news is on. Some guy identified as Pastor Doug is speaking.

"It's a tough time. We need to come together as a community and remember Jesus's love. These are just children. They didn't understand. We can forgive them—we must. We will get through this as a community."

He looks slimy, like he doesn't really believe what he's saying but likes being on television. I hate those guys who cloak themselves in religion. The jerk.

A blonde bimbo starts talking. I'm not paying attention until my face fills the screen.

"This man, Roger Jones, head of a huge real estate empire, is accused of paying an undercover cop for sex at the Gold Club," the overdressed blonde on camera says. "His daughter is a part of the Nazi beer-pong scandal."

I erupt. "Smith, I want to sue all of them for libel. How dare they go after my daughter like this." Sure, I know it's not libel, but I have money. I'll keep them embroiled in a lawsuit for years.

The Anchorman Jerk says, "We'll have to see how this all unfolds, but it's definitely a sad day in Southern California. We expect to hear the names of more locals caught up in the prostitution scandal. Stay tuned."

I turn off the television, watch as it slips into its hiding place.

I hate this. I never want my face on TV. I like being powerful, but behind the curtain. Like a real Wizard of Oz. This is Ted's fault. How dare he betray his best customers like this. Crap. I look up at the ceiling and shake my head. That's when it hits me. This isn't just about me. I bet Jess saw me on TV, too. I bet Jess believes her life is over. I remember being her age. As for Julie, she must hate me right now. This time, for good reason.

"I'm going home now, sir," Smith says. He's at the door of my office. "You OK?"

"Uh-huh. Fine," I say, waving my hand at him.

I sit in the dark in my office, and for once, the reality of what I've done washes over me. Sure, I can move on from this, assuming the prosecutors take my plea deal, but I can't erase the damage the publicity has done.

There likely isn't a way to fix any of this, but I do need to try. I think back to when I was young, when I was Jess's age, before I focused only on work and making money. I love Julie and Jess. I do. I'm not this awful guy they made me out to be on TV. He's not who I really am. He's not. I'm not.

I suppose it's long past time to prove it.

SUNDAY

THE DAY

CHAPTER 35

JULIE

I don't know how long I've been sitting on Jess's bed. In the dark. Waiting. For something. Likely hours. I wipe my face on Jess's duvet cover and try to stop the tears. I look at my phone. It's one in the morning.

I cannot bring myself to believe that Jess won't be coming home tonight. Her stuff is here. Her favorite pillow, her teddy bear from toddlerhood.

Her mom. I'm here. A fresh wave of sorrow sweeps through me. This is not how it is supposed to be.

I know she's humiliated. It's despicable what she was a part of. But we're going to walk into that high school meeting with our heads held high. I need to introduce Jess to my faith. We will go to synagogue together, we will pray, and we will repent. She can do community service, she can heal. It's going to take time.

My heart sinks. I wonder if USC will rescind her acceptance letter. The realization sends a bolt of electricity through my body. This is what we've been working toward, what all those long nights of studying were leading up to. Jess and USC. Or Jess and wherever she wanted to go. There will be a black mark next to her name. Forever.

But we will make good come from this. Together. News cycles are short. This will be forgotten.

I walk to the windows overlooking the backyard. The lights are on in Tom's carriage house. I hope he's packing. I need him to be packing. Tomorrow is a big day. Tomorrow, I will take full control of my new home. For a moment, I wonder if Jess is over at Tom's place. But no, that would be ridiculous. He gives us both the creeps. We both talked about how dark and scary all his friends are.

I wrap my arms around myself, trying to tamp down the worry, the fear—trying to make myself believe that everything is going to be fine. I need to find Jess. Now.

I search for Bonnie's number in my contacts and call her. I know it's late, but teens never sleep on the weekend.

"Hey, Mrs. Jones. How are you?" Bonnie answers but she's slurring her words.

"Fine, thanks. Is Jess with you?" I ask.

"No. My parents kicked her out. She can't live with us anymore, because of the game and, well, the other stuff," Bonnie says.

"Jess wasn't going to be living with you anyway," I say, anger squeezing my throat. But there's something else, too. My heart pounds.

If Jess isn't at Bonnie's, where is she?

"Cool, whatever. She's not here. And I'm leaving in the morning. Boarding school," she says.

"What? No. You and your parents need to go to the high school tomorrow. We have a very important meeting. You all need to take responsibility for your actions. All of you kids," I say. I'm furious with Bonnie's parents. How dare they simply sneak her out of town?

"Well, most of us aren't going. Everybody is leaving school. It's for the best," she says. "You should send Jess away. She's got it worse than all of us. She's got the double whammy, you know, with her dad and the strip club."

"That has nothing to do with my daughter." I can't imagine how devastated she is.

I hear mumbling in the background, a man's voice. Whoever it is has heard our entire conversation, or at least Bonnie's side of it.

"Whatever, Mrs. Jones. Um, I guess I'll see you later. Good night."

Bonnie just hung up on me. Jess clearly isn't there.

I have half a mind to call Bonnie's parents. Tell them that sending Bonnie away doesn't solve anything.

But the reality is, I was considering the same thing just moments ago. It's so easy to fall into old patterns, enabling entitlement. We will face this, we will fix this.

I shake my head and walk out of Jess's room. I don't know who she could be hanging out with. I don't know where she'd turn if Bonnie and the rest of the kids have shunned her. I consider calling Roger, but he'll find a way to blame me for this. And if she was there, he would have told me. He would have gloated.

I sit down on my bed and turn on the bedside lamp. A feeling of cold doom spreads through me. It's 1:30 a.m., my bedside clock informs me. It's the middle of the night, and my daughter is missing. Briefly I think about calling the police, but what would I tell them? I have no idea where to look.

I'll reach out to her old boyfriend Chase. He was in the photo, too, standing right next to Jess.

I text: Hi! It's Jess's mom. Do you know where she is? It's late and I'm worried.

I know if Jess is with Chase, I'm making things very awkward, but I don't care.

The bubbles come to life on the screen.

Chase is there. He texts: Hi Mrs. Jones. I don't know where she is. I wanted to say goodbye to her in person, but she was busy I guess. I leave for Virginia in the morning, so please tell her goodbye for me and to keep in touch.

Virginia? Really? They really are all leaving. That will make us—Jess—the face of this. She is the face of this. I need to find her. Would she hurt herself? No, not my daughter, she wouldn't. Could someone have hurt her because of what she's done?

I need to find my daughter.

I text: Please. I need you to help me find Jess. I don't know where she is.

He texts: I don't know, Mrs. Jones. I'm grounded. Sorry I can't help. Good night.

I text Jess one more time: Honey, please check in. I know you're upset but you need to come home. We'll face this together. I love you.

I stare at the screen but no answer comes.

CHAPTER 36

JESS

Tom is watching me. My mom keeps texting, but I don't want him to know that, so I don't answer her. I wish she'd go to sleep, stop worrying about me. I'm not worth it.

"Who's texting you at this time of night?" he asks.

I look up at Tom. I've been over here for so long it's after one in the morning. I'm so tired, but I really need him to tell me what he's up to. I hope he isn't planning to do something to my mom or her crummy new dream home. Because even though I don't like it, my mom does. I can't allow Tom to hurt her.

"Nobody," I lie. "Come on. Please tell me what you're up to." I'm sitting next to him on his couch. He has his laptop on his lap, and he's typing something. I feel drunk and tired. But also on edge. This place, his anger, whatever secrets he's holding—the air is filled with darkness.

"If I tell you, you could try to stop me. Would you do that?" He leans over, and I feel his head on mine. I lean against him, fighting the urge to push him away. I need to seem like a girlfriend, someone he can trust.

"No, I wouldn't. How could I? Please, just tell me," I say quietly. He closes the computer and puts it on the coffee table in front of us.

"Are you going to do something to the house? My mom is a really nice person. It's not her fault that she bought it."

Tom looks at me. "What? No, it's not about the stupid house."

I swallow as relief washes over me. "So you are going to move out?"

"As soon as I do what I've gotta do, we're out of here together," he says and squeezes my thigh.

At least my mom is safe, that's something I can feel good about. My eyes close, and Tom pulls my head into his lap. I force myself to stay awake, stay alert.

"It's what I have to do. I figured it out in the desert," Tom mumbles. "You're so beautiful, Jess."

He touches my hair, and my stomach turns.

"OK, so what is it?" I blink. I see two Toms. I close my eyes.

"You're so pretty. I didn't think I'd ever have a girlfriend," he says.

I can't trust myself to open my eyes. I'm cuddling with a freak. I force myself to say, "This is nice."

"OK, if you promise to keep it a secret, I'll tell you," he says. He brushes a strand of hair from my face and my stomach lurches. He reaches over me and opens his laptop. "This is what I wrote so people would know who my dad really is, and why I have to do what I'm going to do. I'm not supposed to show it to anybody but Vic."

Despite that, I think he wants me to see it. Like he's proud of what he's written. He scrolls through the document fast so I can't read much, but I see the words "He must die." My heart thumps.

"You can tell me, though. I'll keep your secret. Promise," I answer, my head clearing with the importance of this moment. I need to know what he's up to, what he's capable of doing. Who must die? Maybe I can stop him, maybe I can do one good thing before I leave town. "I want you to do whatever it is and then come back here so we can get going," I say.

It's a lie. I will not go anywhere with this guy, now or ever.

"I'm going to a church in the morning," Tom says.

"Why would you do that?" I ask. I tell myself to breathe.

"I'm the son of a pastor, that's what we do." Tom's hands are on my face.

I swallow. "OK, well, that sounds fine. You're saying goodbye to your dad?"

"You could put it that way." He smiles, but his eyes don't.

I sit up and the room spins. I lean back against the couch. This doesn't make sense. He shouldn't be at a church. My brain is signaling a big alarm. Even though I'm afraid of the answer, I manage to ask, "What are you doing going to your dad's church? I didn't think you liked him. You aren't religious from what I can tell."

"That's funny. Of course I'm not. I have other plans than attending service," he says. I watch in horror as he stands, walks to a closet, and pulls out a huge gun.

"What is that?" My head is clearing. I only see one Tom, and one big gun.

"It's an AK-47. It can do some real damage. I finished my training on it in the desert last week. It's a beauty, isn't it?" Tom pats the weapon and then puts it down, leaning it against the couch. He sits down next to me again, and reaches under the couch. "I like this Glock, too."

My mouth is dry. I can hear my heart pounding. I swallow but can't come up with anything to say. That was the gun I saw earlier on the counter. He must have hidden it under the couch when I went back into the kitchen. My brain tries to process this. Tom has two guns and he's so angry, so tense.

"I'm going to take this little beauty and give my dad a little wake-up call." Tom waves the handgun in the air while he stares at me with what can only be considered soulless eyes. "The semiautomatic is to keep people from interfering."

Tom is going to kill his dad at church. Oh my god. The room spins, and I feel faint. I lean back on the couch as I try to stifle a scream. Tom stares at me, waiting for my response, my approval.

"Wow. OK, that's intense," I say. I need him to think I'm on his side. That's the only way I'm going to get out of this. The only way I'll be able to sound the alarm.

"It's what is required to make amends. He's hurt too many people. He must be stopped." Tom looks at me, eyes bulging. He's not seeing me. All he sees is vengeance. "You understand, don't you? The pain he's caused me my whole life. He'll feel it soon."

"Of course," I manage as my heart races and my breath catches in my throat. He's insane.

"I'm so glad you get it. I mean, he has to die. It's the only way," he says. "He's taken everything from me. All I have left is my self-respect. He's not taking that, too. Being a man means fighting back. I'm finally ready."

My stomach turns. I don't know what to do, what to say. I look at Tom and really see him. He's pure evil. Pure hate. I need to warn people what he is, what he's planning. I cannot believe I was so blind, so stupid.

I have to get out of here.

"Thank you so much, for everything. I know you've got to do what you've got to do. I think I should go on to bed. It's so late," I say, stretching my arms to the ceiling to distract him. I feel his stare, his eyes on my body. I can barely stand it.

"Sleep here. Please? I don't want to be alone. Not tonight. Stay here, I'll go do my thing, and then we'll leave town." Tom stands close to me and grabs my hands in his.

"I really shouldn't. We are just getting to know each other." I fight the urge to yank my hands away. I want to scream. But I know things could get much worse if I do. I can't have my mom come out here.

"Look, since you're a good girl, I'll let you have my bed. I'll take the couch. You're right, we don't want to move too fast. Tonight's almost over. We'll save the rest for another evening, a celebration tomorrow night. Yes, that's great," Tom says. He leads me to the side of his bed. "Let me tuck you in." He seems happy, cheerful. It's an eerie juxtaposition between the evil he's planning and his smiling face. But he knows I am trapped: he has a gun pointed at my heart.

I don't have any other choice. I climb under the covers. The sheets smell like sweat and something stale, like rotten cheese. My stomach churns.

"Comfy?" he asks. He kisses my forehead. "You're so beautiful. I can't believe you're here. That you're mine."

"Tom, I just—" I say before I can stop myself. I was going to tell him that this is all wrong. He's wrong. That there must be another way. But I can't. I need to keep him calm. I need him to think I'm still attracted to him. I need to warn the church and his family. My heart pounds in my chest. I think of the lady in the pioneer dress. That woman cared about Tom.

"What, honey?" he says.

"Can you bring me my phone please?" I smile.

"Why don't I charge it up for you? You can have it in the morning. Sweet dreams." He pats me on the head and walks away from the bed. He's whistling a song I don't know. He sits on the couch, points the gun at me. "Bang-bang."

I start to tremble and hope he doesn't notice. Now I've really done it. Tom is going to kill his dad in a few hours, and I'm in his bed. Like an idiot.

Like an accomplice. I must find a way to stop him. I must save his dad.

I start to cry. I can't help it, the tears are pouring out of me. I try to keep it under wraps, but a sob escapes.

"What's wrong, honeybunch?"

I hate his voice. "Nothing."

Tom jumps up, all excited. He talks with his hands, the gun bouncing through the air. "This is going to be the best day ever," he says as he paces the room. Finally, he drops back onto the couch, a smile on his face.

Oh my god. "Tom, look, I know you're angry with your dad, but there are other ways to handle things. You could just leave town." I know I should shut up, but I can't. Part of me knows nothing I say will change his mind. But I must try.

"Nah. Besides, I need to do this. For me. I can't take him anymore." He's pointing the gun toward the bed. At me. His eyes are glassy, spooky. His lip is snarling. He's imitating those guys he had over. He is desperate to become one of those guys, desperate to feel like he belongs in their group of friends. He is one of them. I'm such a fool.

I freeze. I believe he is going to kill me, right now, right here in this filthy bed. I close my eyes and say a prayer. God help me get out of this, help me figure out a way to save his dad. Help me, God.

CHAPTER 37

Tom

The Glock feels good in my hands. I pat the AK-47 leaning against the couch. I'm ready. I'm ready for my mission, and there isn't anything that's going to stop me.

Especially not her.

"You know if you run away with me, you don't have to deal with him. You realize that, right? It would be just you and me, and that's all we need," she says.

I wish. But I think she's a liar. No one in my life is ever what they seem. Why don't I know that by now? I look at Jess and think of her as the enemy. My hostage. Nothing more.

"No, I don't. You're faking it. You just want something. You want me to take you out of town." I know her type. That's why Vic told us to get rid of women, swear them off like we swear off drugs. They're not good for you, not one bit. They fuck you over like she's done.

"That's not it. I think you're cute. I'm here, aren't I? I'm not going anywhere." She acts like she has a choice.

"Uh-huh. Well, at least we agree on that." My eyes are so tired I could sleep right here, sitting up. But I can't. I have to watch the enemy, make sure she doesn't try anything.

What an absolute idiot I was to tell her my plans. She could ruin my life. Everything I've worked for. She could take it all away.

I pull out my laptop. Her phone is on the coffee table. She's in my bed. All is under control for now. I'm going to read my words, just one more time, to get fired up. When it's time, I'll just take her with me. She won't say no. I won't allow it.

From what I've discovered as I did surveillance of Doug the Dick's new church, he rolls in about 8:00 a.m. on Sundays. It is a ten-minute drive from their new house to the church. I know, I've done it several times. When I got the photo of the rabbit from one of the guys, I felt a little bad for my brothers. And Sandi. They really aren't the problem. It's Doug. It's always been him.

I hope Sandi and the boys skip this Sunday's service. Either way, I'll handle things before they get there. I plan to shoot Doug in the parking lot to spare them the memory of witnessing Doug getting shot at their new home. I have already done enough damage there.

But if they show up at church too early or ride along with him for some reason—well, it can't be helped.

I'm not insane. I'm not going to kill a bunch of people at a church. I mean, I don't want to die. I just need Doug out of the way, and then I'll leave. That's all. See, I'm not so bad.

"How many guns do you have here?" Jess finally stops crying and is sitting up in bed.

Why the fuck can't she just go to sleep? It's almost 5:00 a.m. The sun will be up soon. I need to think. To prepare. Why the fuck did I tell her my plan?

"Why? Maybe I like to collect them for self-protection. You play drinking games like a Nazi." I squint at her and she flinches. "We all have our things."

"That was a stupid game," she says. "But this, it's just wrong. You won't get away with this. You shouldn't hurt people like your dad, not because they're mean to you. Just grow up. Move on."

"Oh, is that right? You're such an adult. You know what? I've been planning this for some time. You have no idea what he's done to me my whole life. It's all worked out. And it's none of your business." She's making me mad, she's so dense. And I thought she was different, I thought she was one of us. She should know better, see better.

"Oh, great. So which church are you visiting? Where is it?" she asks.

"What's it to you? I mean, I've told you enough." I think back to casing the parking lot two Sunday mornings ago, one of dear old Dad's first days on the job. I'd parked in the lot, and nobody noticed I was there.

"So you're just going to walk in and what?"

Does she think I'm a joke? Does she? I touch the rifle next to me on the sofa. "No, that's not what I'm going to do."

"What are you going to do to your dad, Tom?" She blinks and rubs one eye. She's exhausted, too.

"You'll just have to wait and find out, won't you?" I say. "I'm tired of talking. I have work to do."

I pay attention to my laptop for a little bit. I get some positive encouragement from the guys. They're all waking up and getting ready for my big day. I need coffee. I look at Jess, and she's finally lying down. Could she actually be asleep?

I'm not sure, but I do need coffee, so I grab my Glock and my AK-47 and walk backward into the kitchen. If she moves, she'll be sorry.

Nothing.

I put a pod into the machine and push the button, still watching the bed. She must've finally dozed off. She doesn't have anything to do today. But I do. A shot of adrenaline rushes through me, and I grab the steaming cup of coffee and walk back to the couch.

I've planned everything down to the minute. I've planned my disguise, my approach, how I'll confront him, and my getaway. I know where the security cameras are and how to avoid being filmed. I'm ready.

I crack my knuckles.

Vic sends a message in the chat room: I read your letter and understand where you're coming from. I'm pulling for you. Be brave.

I type back: I will. Thank you.

I decide to close my eyes, just for a minute. They're burning, and I need them refreshed. I lean my head on the back of the couch, keeping the handgun on my lap, the semiautomatic next to me.

I wake with a start. Not sure where I am. In my dream, I was falling from a cliff. Someone had pushed me from behind, and I was screaming.

I stand and my gun falls to the floor at my feet. I look across the room and the bed is empty.

My head is about to explode as I race through the open door.

CHAPTER 38

SANDI

I barely slept last night and was awake as the sun rose.

I'm so thankful Doug didn't come home, although I've been sneaky, so he wouldn't have noticed anything amiss if he had. Today I'm executing my Go Plan, the escape I created with my domestic violence counselor. I've been working on my exit for more than a year. Right now, this morning, it's almost as if I'm walking through a dream. The only thing that could ruin it is if Doug gets home before we leave. It's time to wake Danny.

A year ago I called the hotline in a panic. The woman who answered the hotline was a lifesaver. I didn't know her name then, or that she would become the best friend I'd never meet. Still haven't. Her name is Anna. That night was the first time Doug threatened to take the boys. He promised the next wife would be a better mother than I could ever be. He slapped me, in front of my boys, before leaving to tend to his flock.

"How can I help?" The voice on the phone sounded calm.

"It's my husband. I need to leave him, but I don't know how," I had admitted.

"You have a right to be safe. Are you safe now?" the woman asked.

"He's at work. Yes. But I'm afraid. I'm afraid he'll take my kids."
I started to cry then, and the woman waited patiently for me to stop.

That first call was the start of my plan, the impetus for today. Anna
is my hotline contact, and we've talked at least once a month since then.
When I called her last night, she walked me through the steps again.
She wished me good luck. She told me I was doing the right thing, for
myself and my boys.

And now, I have the car packed and ready to go. I have our iden-
tification—birth certificates and social security cards—and I have the
deed to our home and the car registration. I have the school and medical records, and our marriage license. I have my burner phone, all my
jewelry, and my emergency stash of cash. All the boys' favorite clothes
and toys are in the car. They are so new here, to this place, they haven't
noticed the subtle shift. Of course, neither has Doug, thankfully.

Anna isn't my on-the-run contact. Someone named Judy will meet
us at the designated location—a McDonald's of all places—and escort
us to the shelter. There will be lots of other kids for the boys to play
with. There will be counseling. There will be healing. We will be safe.
We will start over.

I paste a smile on my face.

"Time to wake up, sleepyhead." I kiss Danny's head, smell his sweet
sleep scent. "I'll see you downstairs in five minutes, OK?"

"OK, Mommy," he says, rubbing his eyes.

All is going according to plan. Danny and I eat a quick breakfast.
I have the television on but muted. I don't want my baby boy to hear
all the terrible things people can do to each other. He's got plenty of
time to find out. I also won't disparage his father in front of him. He's
too young to be saddled with my sorrow. The fact is, it's all my fault
for picking a man who loves only himself. A man who appears to love
everyone in his flock, who knows how to say the right things, to use
God and Jesus to get what he wants.

A man who is a fraud, incapable of loving others. Especially his wife.

"Finish eating, honey," I say, distracting him so I can grab his phone. I slide his phone into my back pocket. It's time for me to make a stand to protect my boys. And I will. Beginning right now.

I think back to that first hotline call, how worried I was that God would think I was a sinner if I left Doug.

Anna had said, "Sometimes, the only option is to get out of a marriage."

"I can't. I don't believe in divorce. I worry about my boys. He says he'll keep them if I try anything. That he'll toss me out on the street like the sinner I am. God says marriage is for life, at least that's what Doug tells me. Even though he divorced his first wife." I took a breath, trying to gain control of my emotions. "He's very powerful. He's a pastor of a big church."

"You're more powerful than you think you are. We can help you, when you're ready." Her voice had every ounce of confidence I lacked. Her voice was what I wished to become. "Do you have a job?"

"No. Doug forbids it."

"That's OK. You do the shopping, right? Start hiding money. Skim a little off of each transaction. Put it in a bank account known only to you. When you call back next time, we'll go over step two. If you can't get control of this situation, you will need to leave the marriage. You need all the assets you can manage to hide away." She seemed so confident in me, that I could just do this and be ready for the next step.

"How much do I need?" I had asked.

"As much as you can get," she answered. "And good luck to you."

It is time. It's past time to speak to my sons. It is time to tell the truth and to heal.

"Mommy, I'm done. Let's go get Davis!" Danny says, pulling me into the present. I look at his beautiful innocence and my heart hurts.

How could I allow them to grow up with a man so filled with hate? We need to get going.

"OK, let's go!"

"I want to have a real sleepover," he says.

"Oh, honey, you'll have a sleepover soon, I just know it." I smile at him. Over his shoulder I see the television. The screen reads: BREAKING NEWS.

A chill runs down my spine. I hope Doug isn't a part of whatever this is. But I suppose it doesn't matter anymore.

I look at my little boy. "It's supposed to be gorgeous outside. I have a special adventure planned."

"Don't we have church today?" Danny asks.

"No, honey, not today," I say. "Go get dressed in playclothes."

"Yippee!" Danny throws his arms around me and gives me a big squeeze before running out of the room.

Doug tells me I'm worthless. But he's the one who will poison his sons. My only hope is to show them the light, the good path. All I want in life is to raise good sons, own my own home, tend to the hydrangeas, paint, and be a good servant to Christ. That matters to me.

I hurry to the television and turn up the sound. I guess I hope Doug is interviewed. At least I'd know where he was.

"Danny, hurry!" I call up the stairs. What if Doug is on his way home? I pray he will head straight to the church. He has a change of clothes and a shower in his pastor's suite of offices.

"Coming, Mom!" Danny says. I hear his feet pounding down the stairs.

I take one last look around the kitchen.

I wipe a tear away and turn to face Danny. "How does McDonald's sound for lunch?"

"Awesome!" Danny says as he runs out the door.

A chill runs through me as we hurry to the car. This is the most dangerous part of the plan. If my husband catches me leaving him, I don't know what he'll do to me. I can't think about that. I turn on my burner phone and turn off my mobile. I still have Danny's phone, and I've turned it off, too.

"Hey, honey. I charged up this new iPad for you. Thought you'd enjoy playing with it." I hand him the device. I know it's safe. It's brand new. And I've disabled Wi-Fi.

"Awesome," Danny says without looking up. He's fully engrossed in a preloaded game.

I push the garage door button, and it opens swiftly. I look in the rearview mirror. Sweat trickles down the back of my neck as I back the minivan out of the driveway.

I pray as I drive to Davis's sleepover spot that Doug stays busy in Oceanside. Perhaps he's asked the assistant pastor to cover for him today at the new church. I pray for strength. I pray that my words and actions will be a light to my sons. A light that they are drawn to instead of the darkness of hate.

At the stop sign, I turn right. I keep my speed below the limit, careful not to draw attention in any way. In the distance I see a red car driving toward us. Doug's loaner car is red. Doug is headed home.

I turn right, into a cul-de-sac. If he spotted us, I'm trapped. I pull to the curb and wait, sliding low in the driver's seat.

It seems like forever, but it is only a minute until I watch Doug's car drive through the intersection.

Once he's home he'll find the note I left him, explaining I've taken the kids to the zoo, that we'll see him this evening. The note explains that I needed a break from the church this morning. I hope he believes it.

I hope it gives us enough time.

I must hurry. I drive back to the main road, in the opposite direction of my husband. My hands clutch the steering wheel like a life raft. Davis, please be ready.

CHAPTER 39

ROGER

I had a terrible night's sleep. The worst one ever. My house is eerily quiet. I hate it. I'm sitting in my library, alone, as usual. But it feels different. I can't walk to the kitchen and find Julie there.

I answer the phone. It's Smith. "Good morning, sir. Do you want me to go over to her new house and talk to her, sir?"

I take a deep breath. The fact is, I wish this were something I could assign to Smith. I wish it were that simple. Go fetch my family. Make them come home. Make them forgive me. Make us happy again.

I drop my sunglasses over my eyes, look out at the sparkling blue ocean, and decide. "Thanks anyway. But this is my family. My mess. I need to talk to Julie and explain that I was an idiot. An old man taken in by a sting. That's all. Maybe she'll understand. And I need to apologize to Jess. I know she's humiliated by me, my mug shot all over the news. And then there are those photos of her. Maybe I'll send her away?"

Smith says, "I've heard some of the other parents have taken that step."

"What? Really?"

"Yeah, I read a couple of the ones in the photo with Jess are leaving this week. They're headed to exclusive boarding schools. I'm not sure that's the right call, though, sir," Smith adds. "It almost seems like they're condoning the behavior, rewarding it in a way."

"I like the idea. Why not? Get her out of here, out of the spotlight. Give her one more year in high school somewhere else and then she can reapply to college. Maybe use her mom's maiden name or something so they don't associate her with the scandal. Or with what I did. With what she did. I like it, Smith." I do. I can see this working out great. I need to tell Jess the new plan.

I'll get her out of here. Maybe we'll go to Switzerland. Julie and I can start over, have a Swiss chalet. I'll learn to ski.

"OK, thanks. This is a great plan." I'm smiling, but I know Smith is worried.

"Sir, don't be upset if they don't like the idea," he says.

I grab my keys and walk to the garage, giddy with the future and its possibilities. "It's brilliant. They'll love it. Julie loves travel. Switzerland is so refined. Do me a favor. Find an English-speaking boarding school, or two, over there. Send me some options." I slide into my car.

"OK, sure, sir. Will do," Smith says.

"I'll call you later!" I drive off with a big grin. I love a plan. And I have one. Now all I need to do is find my family and tell them.

Jess probably slept in. She's a teenager, and it's Sunday. Julie's there at her new house, doing whatever you do when you move in someplace without a team. I guess she's working? Manual labor. So below her. I'll save them both.

I will admit: at the moment, I do realize it might be me who needs saving.

CHAPTER 40

JULIE

This whole meeting is supposed to be for Jess. About Jess and the other kids.

I look around the conference table. I see a total of five kids, and triple that number in parents. Where are the other children?

The bigger question: How do I explain Jess's absence? I still have no idea where she is.

Superintendent Cummings stands at the head of the table, a whiteboard behind her. She looks tired, and her face is stuck in a pursed frown. She looks at me. "Well, Mrs. Jones, where is your daughter?"

I feel my face flush as I'm about to admit to yet another parenting fail. "I don't know. She ran away last night. She's missing. I can't find her."

The room fills with a buzz.

"Wonderful. And the rest of you? Did all of them run away, too?" She points at a parent I don't know.

"He's gone away. Boarding school. We are handling this situation privately. It's a family matter," he says and crosses his arms. "We are only here as a courtesy to you. And to pick up Griffin's transcripts."

Mrs. Cummings bites her bottom lip, shakes her head. "The five of you students who managed to appear today will not face suspension.

Thank you for being here, along with your parents. Our school community needs to come together at times like this. Together, we will set a better example. There will be no eye for an eye, if you will. Expulsion never solved anything like this. Education is the key here, despite what the news media is trying to force me to do."

Next to me I see a girl lean back in her seat, relief on her face as her mom wraps a protective arm around her shoulders. They're in the clear, it appears.

"There will be work to do. You will be invited to attend an education seminar, with your parents, to teach you all about the Holocaust. Our partners at the Interfaith Council and the Anti-Defamation League have a robust program planned. It is not optional." She begins handing out pieces of paper to the five kids and their parents, skipping the rest of us.

"Mrs. Cummings, please, I'll find Jess. She'll attend the program. I assure you." I hold my hand out for the paper, but she doesn't offer me one. I've never felt this way before. My daughter is missing, I'm trying to do the right thing, but no one will help me. I've never felt so alone. I push a tear away. I need to stay strong—for Jess.

"Mrs. Jones, as you know, Jess has more than the underage drinking and beer-pong issue," Mrs. Cummings says.

I thought we weren't going to discuss this. "Her father's scandal has nothing to do with my daughter." I'm surprised at how angry I feel. "Let's focus on helping my daughter."

"That would be easier to do if she would show up, take responsibility," Mrs. Cummings says.

My phone vibrates with a text. I look at my phone.

And finally, it's Jess: Mom, I need you. Where are you?

I stand. "Jess and I will meet with you as soon as possible. Right now, my daughter needs help. Excuse me!"

I rush out the door as I call Jess. Please answer me. Please.

"Mom, I have made such a mess of things." Jess is crying.

"No, darling, you're fine. We will straighten all of this out. Where are you? Please tell me where you are. Are you hurt?" I'm running out of the school district offices and finally reach the door, pushing it hard as I jog into the parking lot.

"I'm at the park around the corner from our new house. I don't know what it's called. I didn't know where else to go. And Mom, Tom's dangerous. He is going to go kill his dad."

"What? What are you talking about?" I slide into the car and start driving. My phone switches to Bluetooth. "What? Tell me what you're talking about." My mouth is dry. I can barely speak. Tom. My god.

"He has a gun. It's really big. He's going to find his dad at a church," Jess says. "He's going to shoot him, in the parking lot, I think."

I pull over to the curb. "Are you sure? What church? When?"

"Today. He may be going there now. I don't know what time." Jess sobs into the phone.

"Oh my god, are you safe?"

"Yes. He doesn't know where I am. That's why I didn't go home." Jess's voice is shaking.

"Listen to me. You need to call the police. Tell them everything," I say. "Wait, I'll call 911 and patch you in. We'll do it together." I punch the three numbers into my phone, and it connects immediately.

"What's your emergency?" the operator asks.

"Please hold on. My daughter has the details." I switch over to Jess and merge the calls. "Jess, tell the operator what you told me. Jess?"

"What's the emergency?" the operator asks.

My daughter is gone. Did I cut her off? Did Tom find her? Oh my god.

"What's your emergency, ma'am?"

"A man named Tom Dean is going to kill his father at church today. His father is Doug Dean, he's the pastor, but I don't know what church but it's somewhere in Temecula," I say. I'm going into shock. My words are thick in my mouth.

"Please stay on the line. What's your name?" the operator asks.

I can't get involved in this. "That's not important. Go protect those people. He could be there already! Hurry." I hang up. I've done my part.

I need to get to my daughter. I pull away from the curb and drive faster than I have in my life. I hit a stoplight and dial Jess's number. She doesn't answer.

Has Tom found her? No, he couldn't have, not if he's headed to a church to kill his dad. But how did she know his plans? When did he tell her? Where is the park?

This is my fault. She would never have met him if I didn't buy the Cherry Hill Lane house, if I didn't agree to let that man stay in the carriage house.

I stare at my phone. Roger's name is at the top of my favorites list. I dial his number.

"Thank god. I've missed you, babe." Roger sounds happy. Kind even. "So are you on your way home?"

"This is important. Jess is in danger," I say, my words spilling out. I try to keep the tears from coming. I need to be able to see to drive.

"I know. I'm going to fix it. I promise," Roger says.

"It's not that," I say.

"The drinking thing will blow over. All of it will. I think we should move to Switzerland. I have a few chalets I can show you. Start fresh. Jess can finish—"

"Roger. Listen. There's a guy named Tom Dean in my carriage house. I agreed to let him stay one weekend after closing. I'm an idiot. He's planning to go to a church where his father is the pastor and kill him."

I hear a train whistle. I look up and the gates are descending. No. I honk at the car in front of me as the gates close. We're stuck. I'm stuck. I need to get to Jess. There is no other way through to the other side of town.

"What are you talking about?"

"Jess is in danger. She is the only one he told about his plans to kill his father. She's hiding. At a park a couple of blocks away from my new house. Or by now maybe she's hiding at my new house. I'm stuck, behind a train. Please, find Jess." I can't stop the tears from rolling down my cheeks.

"Babe, take a deep breath. I'll find our daughter. I'll protect her. And you. We'll fix this. Don't worry. I love you. Both of you. I'm going to fix everything. I'm almost at your new place now." Roger is in business mode, fix-it mode. I pray he can find her.

"Thank goodness you're almost there. Call me when you find her. Take her home, to your house. Please." My hands shake as I try to hold the wheel. The train seems to rumble past forever, a never-ending string of containers with no end in sight.

"Our house. I will. Don't worry." I watch the train cars continue to rattle past me and I'm thankful he's made it across town before the train came through.

"Get there fast, Roger, please," I say. "If she's not at the house, go to the park down the street."

"I've got this. Turn around and go home. To our home, honey. I'll see you there. I'll bring Jess with me. I love my girls."

"Get Jess," I manage to say as he hangs up.

I try to keep my mind from imagining the worst.

But it's not working. And I'm not turning around.

CHAPTER 41

JESS

I'm shaking as I hang up the phone. I can't believe I know his evil plans.

I hope my mom tells the police in time to stop him. She disconnected me when she merged the calls. I still get the chills sitting here, hiding under the bushes at the corner of the park.

I thought he was going to kill me. I think he still might. I don't know what to do. My mom told me to go home, but it's not safe there. He could be there. If he's left, he could come back.

I wrap my arms around my knees and rock back and forth. I've lost everything now.

All it took was a weekend. I moved to this awful part of town and lost my best friend, Bonnie. I'm ashamed I played that horrible game, my dad is a pervert, and on top of it all, the boy I had a crush on is a potential murderer.

Tom is going to that church to kill his dad. I read some of his letter he typed on the computer as he scrolled down the page. I could feel the anger he harbors for what his dad did to him when he was a kid, the neglect he felt. But he knows there will be more than just his dad at church. It's Sunday. It's horrible. He's sick and terrifying. And he has a gun.

I'd never been that close to a gun. I was shaking as I pretended to fall asleep in his bed. The sheets smelled like sweat—and pee. It was horrible, but I pretended they smelled good. I had to fake it, fake liking him, until I could escape. And then I heard him snore. I couldn't believe it. Quietly, I slid out of his bed and slid underneath it. I was afraid he would wake up. Terrified he'd wake up and kill me.

He kept snoring.

I scooted out on the other side of the bed and crawled to the door. It wasn't locked. It was barely closed. My phone sat where he'd left it on the coffee table. I grabbed it and then opened the door, silently, and started running. I didn't stop. Not until I got here, to this park. To these bushes.

My phone vibrates, and I look at the screen. I need to conserve energy. I only have 5 percent power.

It's my dad. My eyes fill with tears. I answer.

"Daddy." I know I'm sobbing in his ear.

"Jess, honey, thank god you answered. Are you all right?"

"No, everything is wrong."

"I'm so sorry. It's going to be OK. Everything is. We're going to Switzerland," Dad says. "I'm on my way to get you."

I don't understand what he's talking about. "Dad, listen, the boy who lives in our carriage house is planning on killing his dad at a church. He's probably on his way there now."

"I know. I talked to your mom. She called the police. They're on it. I need you to come home with me," Dad says. "I'm pulling up now. Hurry outside."

Dad hangs up the phone. Where is he?

And then it hits me. He's at my mom's house. I try to call him back, but he doesn't answer. He can't go there. As I try to call my mom, my phone dies.

My heart pounds as I climb out from under the bushes and take off running down Cherry Hill Lane. I need to beat them all home.

CHAPTER 42

T OM

I've been sweating like a maniac since I woke up and discovered she was gone. This is all her fault.

Well, it's my fault I fell asleep instead of guarding my hostage.

I woke up to an empty bed and an open door. I'm lucky no one else walked in because I had a loaded gun on my lap, and I'm afraid I would've used it, by accident or something. You know, like if her mom had come to find her and opened the door. But no, there I was like a drooling baby, alone.

I started to run after her, to run to the main house, but then I stopped myself. I walked back into the shed and closed the door. I knew I needed to find Jess, to set her straight about a few things, but I knew where she lived. I'd deal with her later. I also needed to hurry up. It was almost 10:00 a.m. My go time had been 8:30. I was running late. My dad was already on the pulpit, spewing lies. I'd have to get him after the service. I showered, changed into my ops clothes: all black. Black jeans, black T-shirt. I pulled on my black beanie. I looked in the mirror and thought I looked more like a hipster than a killer, but it is what it is.

I logged in to the chat room, just to get some positive support. And that's when I saw it. A message from Vic. You're busted. Someone found out. Church surrounded by SWAT. V

Shit. I type: Ok. What should I do?

I guess Vic is looking out for me, too. Like Jess was. She wouldn't rat me out. Maybe she wanted to warn the congregation something was coming. That's all it was. She was trying to help me. I need to talk to her. I'm surprised how calm I feel all of a sudden. The plan is off, and now Jess and I can be together. It's perfect.

He isn't answering my question in the chat room, so I pull out my phone. I see a message from Vic there, too.

He texts using a *V* to let me know it's his latest burner: Where have you been? Your plan is blown. V

I text: I know. What do I do now?

He texts: How did this happen? V

I stare at my phone. A girl, that's how. But I can't tell him that.

I text: No idea. Lucky fucking police guess?

He texts: Doesn't make sense. Cops are swarming the church. V

Damn it. I know Jess is the one who tipped off the cops. She wanted me to show up at the fucking church, ready to teach my dad a lesson he'd never forget, and walk into a trap out of a fucking movie. I imagine cops everywhere, complete with one of those huge SWAT cars out of a war zone patrolling the parking lot. And then the helicopter flies over.

I am lucky Vic warned me off.

I'm an idiot. Now I'm certain the news will cover the tip-off phoned in by an idiot girl who I never should have trusted. I thought we had a connection. I thought we were falling in love. I was ready to run away with her. I should have gone, left with her last night. But now I'm alone again, and in more trouble than I've ever been in my life. Did she give them my name? Maybe she didn't give them my name. Maybe she just felt bad for the other people at my dad's church, but she didn't want to ruin my life. Maybe she was saving me from doing something terrible. My dad deserves to die, still, but maybe not today.

That's it. She called the cops to save me. She doesn't think I'm really bad. I'm not really bad. I need to talk to Jess. I need to find Jess and thank her.

I stare at my phone. I don't want my friends to dump me. I need them. They're all I've got.

I text: Hey, man, thanks for the support. See you at the bar.

I watch my phone for a response. I wait.

Vic texts: We've found a new hangout spot. Don't reach out to any of us anymore. V

"No, Vic," I scream at my phone. "Please."

These guys are my only friends. Jess did this. She ruined everything. I'm a failure. A loser. I'm alone. I kick the wall, imagine it's Jess's pretty face.

This isn't the end. I will fix this. I'll do Dad tonight, at home. It will be less dramatic since he won't die in front of his flock, but it'll do. That way Vic will give me another chance. This isn't my fault. I feel the hate rising in me like a hot fire as I grab my gun and run across the grass to the main house. I climb the trellis quickly, from habit. As I do, I realize I'm busted.

If Jess told the cops about my plan, she must have told them about me, too.

She's a bitch. A traitor. All women are the same.

The cops are going to be coming for me, too.

So be it. If they're coming to get me, they'll find me at home. I make it to the roof and slide open the window to my room. Her room. Our room. For a minute, I imagine climbing in bed next to her. I imagine what a real relationship could look like.

Then I remind myself she's a traitor.

I slam the window, and it rattles with the force. Her bed is empty. Our bedroom is empty. Of course, the traitor is in hiding. But she can't stay away forever. She has to come home eventually. And I'll be here. Waiting. I sit down on her bed and put the gun next to me. I pull the purple comforter up to my face. It smells like Jess, like flowers and sunshine.

Why did she ruin everything?

Because women are good for nothing, just like my dad taught me. "Son, women are good for two things: screwing and cooking. That's it. Otherwise, who needs them?"

Dear old Dad. He doesn't know today was his lucky day. He literally dodged a bullet. But I'm not giving up. He still needs to die.

I hear the front door open.

Ah, Jess. Welcome home.

I smile, grab my gun, and head for the stairs.

CHAPTER 43

ROGER

I turn the handle of the front door. It's unlocked.

I glance at the little box tacked onto the doorframe, the Hebrew scribbled on the front, and I touch it, hoping a little blessing will rub off on me.

"Jess! I'm here!" I yell as I walk through the door.

"Welcome home."

I follow the sound of the voice and see a man, dressed all in black, walking slowly down the stairs in front of me. He has a gun in his hand, pointed at me, and he's smiling.

Oh my god. I take a step back. And another. My heart is racing. My stomach lurches. What if he has Jess?

"Stop right there," he says. "Close the door."

I do. I put my hands in the air for good measure.

"Who are you?" he asks. He's at the bottom of the stairs, across the entry hall from me.

My brain tells me to turn and run as fast as I can. But my legs aren't cooperating. And I'm here for Jess. "I'm Jess's dad. Where is she?"

"Funny. I'm waiting for her, too," he says.

He's not laughing. A moment of relief washes over me knowing Jess isn't here. She's safe for now. I need to get him out of here.

"Look, the police will be here any minute. You should get out of here." I reach into my back pocket and hold up my wallet. "I have a lot of money. Take my car. Get out of here."

"Walk to the kitchen. Slowly." He points the gun to the left.

"I've never been here before. That way?" I tilt my head.

"It's my home! You shouldn't be here. None of you should be here," he says.

The guy is a nutjob. I feel his breath on my neck as he follows me into the kitchen. I will talk him into taking the money and my car and running. Why wouldn't he? I will save my daughter from this psycho. I need to talk him down, calm him down, convince him to leave.

"It's a nice place, that's for sure. Good bones, I can tell. How about if I give it to you, son? After things settle, of course. No strings attached. For now, you should take my car, and my money, and get out of town. All I need is for you to tell me where Jess is, that she's OK." I swear if he hurt my daughter, I'll kill him. "Did you hurt my daughter?"

"Sit." He kicks a kitchen chair. "No, your stupid daughter double-crossed me. She's going to pay."

I sit. I watch as the young man begins to pace back and forth, stopping to stare out the kitchen window. He's not stable. He's fidgety, sweating. The black soles of his boots leave scuff marks on the kitchen floor as he paces.

The kid is more agitated than ever as he looks out the window. "Oh great. Just what I need right now." Tom spits into the sink like he's eaten something rotten.

He turns and points the gun at me. "Don't move or I'll kill you—and Jess."

He stomps past me and into the hallway, positioning himself so he is blocking the only exit from the kitchen. He keeps the gun pointed at me, shifting his attention between me and the back door. I hear a knock and a man's voice. "Anybody home? It's Pastor Doug."

"Look what the cat dragged in. Ironic, really," Tom says. "Are you trying to sneak up on me or something?"

"No, son, just parked on the side street, didn't want to scare you away," the man says.

"You can't scare me, not anymore. Why don't you come on in, Dad. Or should I call you Pastor Doug, or just dickhead?" Tom says.

Shit. I don't like the sound of his voice. He's unhinged. There is no escape from this kitchen, and no view to the hall. I realize the Doug guy can't see the gun in Tom's hand, the one pointed at me.

"What are you doing in here, son? We don't live here anymore."

"Yes, I'm aware you sold the house out from under me. You suck." Tom's tone has taken a turn for the worse. "But I am glad you're here. I was hoping to surprise you earlier today."

"Really? Did you see me on TV? I've been helping out in the community. Reporters say I'm a natural," Doug says. "Considering starting my own channel broadcasting live from my new church home."

I cannot for the life of me understand why this man is bragging about being on television when his asshole son has a gun pointed at me.

"What?" Doug asks.

The kid rolls his eyes. "You are something, you know that?" Tom says. "Did you deliver the sermon at your new church today?"

"No, I did a national morning show interview, so I had the associate pastor take over," Doug says. "Why? You never come to my services, although God knows you could use a spiritual awakening. Most of America needs one."

"I planned on coming today, this morning," Tom says. "Figures you wouldn't have shown up."

"Somebody called in a threat, and the whole place got shut down," Doug says. "Did you have something to do with that, son?"

"Stop calling me 'son,'" Tom says.

The tension pulses from him. I can tell he hates this man, his father. I can tell I am in the wrong place. I've got to get out of here.

"Look, Tom, I came here to help you," Doug says. "You need to pack up and get out of here."

"The last thing I need is your help, don't you get it? You are dead to me, Dad." Tom kicks the wall with his boot. If I could make a run for it, I would, but he is standing in the hallway between me and the front door. There is no way out.

"Where are the people who own the house? What have you done?" Doug asks.

"Don't worry, I'll take care of them, too," Tom says.

I need to find a way out. I stand up slowly while Tom's distracted, open a drawer searching for a knife.

"Sit down now or I'll shoot you," Tom yells at me, and I hurry back to the table.

"Are you holding someone hostage? My god." Doug's voice is closer. He has walked down the hall and stands in the doorway, steps away from Tom. He sees me. "Put the gun down, son. Let's pray together. We can fix this." His dad is nervous. His voice cracks.

"No, I will fix this. You're a miserable dad, and a worse pastor. You screw around on your wife and turn your back on your own son." Tom's laugh is the most sinister cackle. "I don't need you anymore, Dad. Nobody does."

"What are you going to do, son, shoot me?" Doug asks.

Tom is going to kill his dad. I jump up and lunge at Tom. I've never heard the sound of gunfire until this moment. I hear a scream, but I don't know if I screamed or if Doug did. I fight with all my might as Tom's dad joins me in the fray. Suddenly, I'm thrown against the wall, dazed. The back of my head hurts where I hit the wall. I touch it, and blood covers my hand. Otherwise I think I'm fine. I'm not shot, not that I can tell. Everything is in slow motion, and it's as if I'm watching a movie. Like I'm not really here. I blink. In front of me, Tom stands over his dad, pointing the gun at his head.

"You've been nothing but trouble since the day you were born," Doug says, and I watch in horror as Tom beats him on the head with the gun. Doug's head is pouring blood as he slumps against the stairs, unconscious. I see a gunshot wound on his thigh. My god.

My survival instincts kick in. I push off the floor and run to the front door, but I'm not fast enough. I feel a gun pressed to my neck, a strong grip on my arm. My heart is racing.

"You aren't going anywhere. Not until Jess gets here," Tom says.

I walk backward with my hands above my head until I reach the kitchen table. My brain isn't processing this situation correctly. I think I'm in shock. Is this shock? My phone vibrates in my pocket. Oh my god. Is it Jess? Julie? Tom hears the sound.

I have to save them.

"Give me your phone." He holds the gun to my temple again. I need to stay alive to save my girls. I have no other choice. I give him my phone. "Unlock it."

He's reading my text messages.

"Text Jess. Get her home." He hands me my phone.

I text our family group: DON'T COME HOME

"Fuck you." He grabs my phone. I know he's texting my daughter. "OK, here's what you're going to do. You're going to drag my dad's sorry dying ass into the kitchen. Go."

I do as I'm told, grabbing the poor man under his arms and pulling him into the kitchen, laying him carefully on the floor under the kitchen table, hoping to give him some shelter from his son. Tom's still distracted, pacing in the entry hall, typing on his phone and mine, trying to lure my daughter here.

I must stop him. I hurry to the drawer. This time I grab a knife and slip it under my sleeve before sitting back down at the table.

On the floor, Tom's dad moans as the pool of blood around him continues to grow. I've never been what you'd consider a strong man, not physically at least. In business, I'm ruthless, but when it comes to this, to this situation I find myself in now, I have bodyguards and security for this.

But I know with cold certainty no one will come to my rescue. No one knows where I am. It is up to me to save my family and myself.

CHAPTER 44

JESS

I run up to the front door and find it unlocked. I take a deep breath and walk inside.

I know my dad is here. His car is out front. But Tom is here, too. I can feel it. My heart pounds in my chest, and my stomach lurches. There's something on the floor at the bottom of the stairs, like somebody spilled ketchup, leaving a trail into the kitchen.

"Welcome home." Tom stands at the doorway of the kitchen, pointing a gun at me. I freeze as he comes close to me. My mind is screaming "run," but I am frozen. "Close the door."

"Where's my dad? My mom?"

He wraps his arm around my neck. He pushes the butt of his gun against my head. Hard. "Welcome home, traitor."

I dig my fingernails into his forearm and try to pull him off me. I kick backward. I'm seeing stars. I can't breathe.

"Calm down or I'll kill you. Don't believe me? Just ask my dad." He drags me into the kitchen. I begin to shake all over. Everything is in slow motion.

"I should kill you now. And him. You betrayed me. Just like him."

My dad sits at the kitchen table, a haunted look on his face. My poor dad. What has Tom done to him? My dad struggles to stand. Then I see the knife in his hand. "Let go of my daughter."

Suddenly my dad is running toward us. Tom shoves me to the floor. The man bleeding on the floor yells, "Tom, you are better than this."

My dad slashes at Tom's face and hands as he yells, "Jess, run!"

Tom points the gun at my dad's head and pulls the trigger. The sound crashes through the kitchen and I'm splattered, covered in thick, warm goo. I watch in horror as my dad falls to the floor. Another gunshot erupts, and the man on the floor goes still.

All I can hear is the sound of my screams. I stand and run at Tom with all my force. His back is to me, so I catch him off guard. He falls to his knees on the kitchen floor. His gun skitters out of reach into the front hall.

"You little bitch," he roars, standing up before he kicks me hard in the stomach.

Somehow I manage to grab his ankle and yank with all my might, and he falls to the ground again.

Beside me, Tom's dad stirs. Just in time, he begins crawling toward us. I hold on to Tom's leg with all the strength I can muster.

"You fucking idiot," Tom's dad yells as he climbs on top of his son. I can tell he's in bad shape, though, bleeding from a gash on his head. Blood gushes from his shoulder, blood drenches his pants.

Tom kicks his leg, and I lose my grip. I watch helplessly as he rolls on top of his dad, pins him down with one hand at his throat, and punches him over and over again in the head.

All I can do is scream.

CHAPTER 45

SANDI

It's not that far out of the way to drive down Cherry Hill Lane.

"Mom, where is McDonald's? We've been driving forever." Danny is whining. Poor kid has been a trooper.

"I need my phone, Mom," Davis says.

"Me too," Danny joins in.

"I'll give you your phones later, at McDonald's. It's phone-free Sunday. A new tradition. Isn't it great?" I look in the rearview mirror and see they don't agree. I am pleased with my improvisation.

"Why are we on our old street? It's like torturing me," Davis says. "I want to move back here."

I meet his eyes in the mirror. "I know. Me too. Maybe we will someday."

"Really?" Davis looks excited. As much as he enjoyed the sleepover, this is home. This street. This community.

I slow down as we approach our house. There's a big fancy car out front. A Rolls-Royce, I think.

Danny says, "Mommy, that's our home!"

"Yes, it is." I smile. I take a deep breath and pull over to the curb. Julie has attached something to the side of the front doorframe.

Otherwise, everything is how I left it two days ago. It's me who has changed.

I will make sure that Tom has packed up his things. It's the right thing to do. I know Doug shirked his responsibilities as usual, showing support for other people's kids so he can be a TV star, instead of helping his lost son. His dad has failed him. I did my best, but I failed him, too. I think somehow we all have. His mom. His dad. Me. He's what happens to a child no one really wants, a kid nobody gave enough love to. I think of the homeless on the streets and hope that's not Tom's future. I'm almost certain it is.

In the rearview mirror, I see the boys busy on their new, untraceable iPads. I pull to a stop two houses past our former home, parking in the shade of a large oak tree.

"Look, guys, I'm going to go to the carriage house to make sure Tom's all packed up. You two stay here. Do not open these doors for anyone, do you understand?"

I glance in the rearview mirror at my boys' still-innocent faces. They're so vulnerable to the dark side of the world right now at their ages, with the internet beckoning.

I'm embarrassed and ashamed to say I almost didn't see the danger. It was almost too late.

"Stay here, I'll be right back." I slide out of the car and use my key fob to lock the boys inside. I say a quick prayer as I jog up the driveway to my old home. Julie must have company over, so I hurry to the backyard to handle Tom.

I hope he'll listen. I am his mom. I do love him despite the fact that I must face who he is, what he has become, once and for all.

CHAPTER 46

JULIE

The train seems to have endless cars, but finally the crossing gates swing open. I can't help but honk.

The driver of the car in front of me, some sort of SUV, sticks his finger out the window and flips me off before proceeding to drive at a snail's pace over the tracks, paying me back for my rude urgency. The last of the traffic coming the other way zips by, and I pull into the oncoming lane, floor it, and pass the guy in the SUV before he even realizes it.

No one is coming between me and my daughter. I speed through town, try to stop at stop signs, and finally reach Cherry Hill Lane. The park at the end of the street seems deserted, but I get out of the car and yell for Jess. A woman pushing a toddler in a stroller stares at me like I'm a threat and hurries away.

"Jess, it's me, come out!" I yell. The park is small. A playground, two picnic benches, and a smattering of bushes and trees. My daughter isn't here anymore, I'm sure of it. I run back to my car and drive down Cherry Hill Lane.

I pull to the curb in front of my house and park.

My heart pounds.

Somebody is in my home.

I don't know what to do.

As I watch from the street, I see activity, movement in the kitchen—only for an instant. The next moment the house is as still as before.

I pull out my phone. Do I call Jess, or the police?

The car parked out front is Roger's, but nothing else makes sense. Something is wrong. I know it.

He's in there.

I must do something. There's no time to wait for the police.

I swallow and push the car door open, stepping quietly onto the empty street.

I knew the truth before I saw the lanky shadow move across the kitchen window.

Somebody's home, and he isn't supposed to be there.

I crouch down as I run up to the front door of my house. I left it unlocked on purpose, in case she came home and didn't have her keys.

I know now that was a big mistake.

All this is my fault.

I clamp my hand over my own mouth to muffle my scream as I turn the handle and step inside.

A woman screams. It's my daughter.

My god.

A gun is lying in my foyer. My brain can't process why it would be there, and despite the fact that I hate guns and don't know how to shoot one, I grab it. There is a pool of blood by the stairs. Nothing is right.

I take a step toward the kitchen and aim the gun at the doorway like I've seen cops do on TV. I will shoot if someone is hurting my daughter.

I take another step forward.

CHAPTER 47

Tom

After I finished with dear old Dad, I decided to take care of Jess. As soon as I smacked her on the head once, she stopped screaming. Thank god. But she won't stop moaning. Between us, her dad's body is bleeding out, a gross mess. I'm shaking all over. I need to get a grip. Jess is making weird noises now, like an animal caught in a trap. I need to get out of here. And I'm taking her with me.

I look toward the hallway, and that's when I see Jess's mom, Julie. Her eyes are wide, and shiny. She has my gun in her shaking hands.

I never heard her walk into the house.

"He killed Dad," Jess screams. She's hugging her dad's body, and she's covered in blood and shit.

"You were supposed to be at the park. I looked for you at the park." Jess's mom is shaking, but she's still pointing the gun at me. I don't know if she knows how to shoot a gun. My dad's knocked out, so I focus on my new enemy.

"Stand up, Tom." Julie points the gun at me. This can't be happening. I'm not having a girl take me down. I roll off my dad. I stand slowly, put my hands in the air.

I smile. "You don't know how to shoot, do you?" I take a step toward her, and she backs up. Good.

"Julie, no!" It's Sandi—she comes running in from the back door. Why is Sandi here? Why are they all here? "Please, he's a confused boy. Please take pity on him. I beg you, in the name of God."

"Give me my gun." I take another step toward Julie, ignoring Sandi. "I'll get out of here. Just give me the gun."

Shit. Cops have pulled up outside, I see the blue lights flashing outside the kitchen window. A bullhorn announces: "Tom Dean, come out with your hands up. We have the house surrounded."

I need a hostage. I'll take Jess. I reach for her, grab her hair, and yank her up to standing. She screams, kicks at me. I squeeze her hair tighter in my fist.

"Let her go. Now," Julie says. She steps closer to me, and the gun is steady.

This is not helpful. She won't shoot and risk hurting Jess. She's bluffing.

"We're leaving. Jess and I. So give me the gun, and get the fuck out of my way," I say, yanking Jess in front of me.

Sandi walks toward me. Who does she think she is? Why is she doing this, coming here, getting in my way? Pretending to care about me.

"Let the girl go, son," Sandi says.

"Stay away," I say. But she keeps moving closer.

She tries to touch my shoulder, but I take a step back. She won't back up. She just keeps coming. She says, "Please. Son. I know you don't want to hurt her."

I don't want to hurt her. I don't. I want her to love me. Why can't she love me? Why won't anyone love me? I untangle Jess's hair from my hand, and she drops back to the floor.

Before I can react, Sandi's arms are around me. She holds me tight, like she loves me, like she really does care, like she's my mom. My head feels like it's going to explode, but her arms around me make me feel safe. She whispers in my ear, "It's going to be OK, son. Everything will be OK. I love you, Tommy. Jesus loves you."

Julie keeps the shaking gun pointed at me as the cops break down the front door.

I think I'm crying.

CHAPTER 48

JULIE

Jess and I walk out of the police station and into the evening lit by an orange-and-purple sunset. We promised to be available for more questioning, but for now, we're both exhausted and need to go home.

To Roger's home.

Tom told the police interrogator that Roger died trying to save Jess—and me. He rushed Tom with a knife and was killed during the struggle. Pastor Doug tried to help, too, and ended up dying of his head injuries. Tom killed two fathers. They both died heroes because they saved Jess. I know I'm still in shock, but I also know something else: Jess is alive. I'm alive.

I'd never felt that much anger in my life, and I hope to never feel it again. If Sandi hadn't appeared and wrapped her arms around her son, I think I would have killed him. I shudder at the memory of that cold gun in my hand.

Mostly, though, the last few hours are all a blur to me. Everything is.

"Mom, we can't go to Cherry Hill Lane," Jess says, bringing me to the present. She's wearing a borrowed sweatshirt and sweatpants. Her own clothes were collected for evidence or something. She was coated in blood—Roger's blood. My stomach turns with the memories. I'm so glad they had her change.

Our attorneys are still worried that they might charge Jess with being an accomplice in the plot to kill Pastor Dean, but Smith assured me they'll see the light. Things are just hot right now. That, and likely the photo of my daughter posing in front of the Nazi drinking game isn't helping clear her good name. Poor Roger. He died embroiled in his own scandal and never had a chance to tell his side of the story or to make amends. Maybe saving the life of his daughter and wife will earn him a degree of public sympathy. I hope so. I hope that for Jess, too. Her dad died a hero.

In my eyes, Jess is a hero, too. If she hadn't convinced Tom to tell her what he was up to, his dad would have died in that church parking lot. And what if he'd missed when he shot at his father and hurt innocent bystanders? A chill sweeps over me.

"Mom, where are we going to go?" Jess again. I guess I didn't answer her.

"We will go to your father's house. For now. It's what he wanted, and we'll be safe there. Smith is sending a car to pick us up."

I check my texts. Smith says they're two minutes away. He insisted on private bodyguards, round-the-clock security. At least until Jess is cleared of any charges, and until her name fades from the scandal.

True to his word, Smith arrives with two huge bodyguards and a black SUV. We drive in silence, through the gates, into the security and serenity I am used to. We pull into the garage, the door closing behind us like a vault.

Inside the house, Jess hurries down the hall to her empty bedroom. All her belongings, and mine, are at the Cherry Hill Lane home. A chill runs down my spine. I turn to Smith and finally speak the dreadful thoughts I've been harboring. "This is all my fault. I moved her into a home with a murderer in the backyard. I did this. Roger's dead because of me."

"No, it's not your fault. You likely saved a lot of innocent people at the church in Temecula today. You did that. Everything's going to be OK," Smith says. He places his hand on my shoulder. "Go take care of Jess. I'll be here if you need anything. OK if I set up camp in the library?"

"Please do." I head to Jess's bedroom with a heavy heart, my legs barely able to carry me down the hall.

I knock on her door and step inside. "Hey, honey, you doing OK?" She sits on the floor of her empty bedroom, knees tucked up to her chin, looking so young, so hopeless. And so incredibly sad.

"Mom, I'm such an idiot. It's my fault Dad died." Jess starts crying again as I rush to comfort her.

It's going to take time to recover from this. To heal. But we will. For now, I join Jess on the floor and wrap her in my arms. There are no words.

ONE MONTH LATER

CHAPTER 49

SANDI

The boys and I are back home where we belong. In Temecula. Starting over.

I'm still grieving for Doug, as are the boys. Even though our life together was over before he died, he was still my husband. There is solace in the fact that in the end he was a hero, trying to save innocent people from Tom, finally taking responsibility for his oldest son.

Doug's death set me free. I didn't need to go into hiding with the boys. I didn't need to run. Not anymore.

And now, slowly, I've been recovering. The boys know Tom killed their dad. They know some of the rest of the story, too. They know Tom and his bad friends killed the rabbit in their tree fort, that they were trying to scare us. I show the boys my newly planted garden, bursting with hydrangeas, and remind them we will be fine, that we are stronger than them. They can stomp all our gardens, but we replant. Regrow. We are not afraid.

I told them that Tom was the one who was behind it all. Tom has since promised to leave us alone. In a letter he wrote to me, he thanked me for saving his life. The boys know why Tom is in prison awaiting trial. I tell them he will be in there for a very long time.

"Mom, prisons make people tougher, meaner, I think," Davis says. "There are a lot of gangs."

"I know, son. We're going to have to hope he stays away from that, but we'll see. We're only in charge of ourselves—how we treat other people, with love and compassion and empathy," I say.

"And hearts as big as the moon," Danny pipes in.

"Yes! My boys will have hearts as big as the moon," I say, repeating my new favorite phrase. "OK, time for school. The bus will be here in three minutes."

"Remember I'm going to Troy's after school," Davis says. As the boys hurry to pack up and scramble to the door, I say a little prayer for their protection.

"Bye, Mom!" Danny yells from the front door.

"Bye, kids! Love you!" *Be safe,* I don't add. We are safe now. The boys and I were never the real targets. We were a means to get to Doug. And now that Doug is dead, it's over, the police assure me.

And I try to believe it. We must move on and heal. It's my number-one job as their mom. But if anything scary happens, if Tom sends one of his friends over here to frighten us, we'll leave and start over. I was ready to go the day Doug died. I can do it again, if I must. But for now, we will settle in.

I take a deep breath and grab the boys' breakfast dishes, carrying them to the sink. I'm excited to return to my painting in progress. I've begun to dabble in portraiture, and apparently, some people think I'm pretty good. I have commissions from three families for portraits of their kids. If I do a good job, this could grow into a business. I say a little prayer: "Thank you, Jesus, for the blessing of my art."

I pick up the paintbrush, add a bit more pink to the little girl's cheek. I am blessed. I have everything I need.

And for now, I feel at home.

JULIE

I answer the door, and after I welcome the detective in, I take a moment to touch the mezuzah screwed onto the doorframe. It's new. I added it to Roger's home as a measure of peace. I hope he'd approve.

I escort the detective into the living room, where Jess waits. The two shake hands, and we all take a seat. For a moment, the only sound in the room comes through the open glass sliding doors, the waves crashing to shore just below us.

The detective flips through his notes. "I'll make this brief today, ladies. As you know we've cleared Jess of any wrongdoing, but I thought you'd appreciate an update on where things stand."

I squeeze my daughter's hand. "Thank you, Detective."

"Through our investigation we've learned that Tom was friends with a group of guys who hung out at dive bars, fantasized about world domination, and generally caused trouble around here. As far as we know, he'd only been to one of their brainwashing trips to the desert, but we're still following up leads. It isn't hard to get a lost and lonely kid to do bad things, especially one who harbored all that rage toward his dad. We've rounded up some of these guys and taken their statements, but there are more. We'll keep an eye on them. We all owe you thanks for stopping him. It could have been a devastating crime scene at the church, what with all the firepower he had and intended to use."

"You are very brave, Jess," I say. Jess sits beside me on the couch, holding my hand. I wasn't going to let go. She still doesn't believe she's a hero, but at least she doesn't believe she's the worst young person in Oceanside anymore.

"We'll continue to have a police presence in front of your home until we round up and talk to all of the guys we've identified. We've got a guy who calls himself Vic in custody. We're charging him with accessory to murder for pushing Tom to kill his dad, for prodding him along, and providing him with operational training. Look familiar?" The detective hands me a photo.

My breath catches as I stare at the familiar dark eyes. I remember how he stared at me through the window, the implied threat on his face. "Yes, he was in our backyard. Tom had him over the weekend we moved into the house on Cherry Hill Lane. There were at least a dozen of them. All dressed in black, all up to no good." I hand him the photo, remembering Tom's friend's leering eyes, his bold confidence. "I'm glad you caught him."

"We are, too. Tom kept a lot of records in his room at the back of your property. Not smart of him, but good for us. He had a small arsenal of weapons out there, too. Had you ever been inside?" The detective flips a page of his notebook.

"This is where it all went wrong. I believed his parents when they told me that Tom would move out on Sunday by noon. They convinced me to honor his privacy, and we never toured the carriage house. Sandi, his mom, showed me photos of the place. I liked the rest of the house so much, I agreed to the deal." I shake my head. I'm such a fool. "I should never have agreed to that."

My mind flashes on Sandi's face. She's such a kind woman. I think of her loss. I hope she will be OK without her husband and Tom. At least she has her two boys. And her church will rally around her. Her husband was the pastor, after all. She wrote me a note, asking for forgiveness for her family. I should thank her, too. If she hadn't wrapped Tom in a hug, I may have shot him.

The detective is talking again. "All I can say is Tom was well armed. It could have been much worse." He closes the notebook and stands. "Cherry Hill Lane has been cleared as a crime scene. You're free to move back in."

Jess turns to me, eyes wide with fear. I wrap my arm around her shoulders. "That's not happening, Detective. Ever."

He nods. "I understand. Again, we are so sorry for your loss."

After the detective leaves, I take a deep breath. I carry so much tension with me these days, as if I'm waiting for something else to happen. But it's all in the past. Roger is gone, Jess is safe, we are home. I cross the room and slide the glass doors closed, making sure they are locked. I smile at my daughter.

"You OK?" Jess asks. She has been so strong, so loving through this. Both of us are overwhelmed by grief for Roger.

"Yes, I am," I answer, joining her on the couch, patting her hand.

I couldn't have imagined all that would happen the weekend I left Roger. I imagined his life going on, his business booming, and all his side depravities happening in the dark, as usual, not splashed across the headlines. And my daughter and I would start over, connect on a deeper level, get grounded. I rushed into my new life and made a bad real estate decision because I was excited to get away from Roger and I loved the house on Cherry Hill Lane. Was I being selfish, as selfish as I thought Roger was in our marriage? May God forgive me. *Salachti.*

In the end, Roger demonstrated selfless love. He fought for us, came for us, and tried to protect us from Tom. Seeing how much he loved us has softened my heart.

So we start over. Jess and I. Here in the home Roger loved. I've replaced the furniture in Jess's bedroom, and she seems to have settled in again. The door to the guest bedroom where Roger slept remains closed, all his belongings as he left them. For now, that's what I need to do. Someday, I'll be able to step inside. Not now. But it is a welcome retreat, this secure home Roger built and I decorated.

For now, this is where I belong.

As for Cherry Hill Lane, I'll hire people to clean it up, to move our things back home. And I'll put it up for sale below market.

Cherry Hill Lane will soon be somebody else's.

I hope they can make it a home.

TOM

I sort of like prison. Is that weird? I have a place to stay, food to eat, and I'm starting to make friends. Just like Vic told me, there are a lot of guys like us in here, and we are powerful, maybe more so than on the outside. They all know by now that I didn't handle things exactly right, but in here, they gave me a chance to explain why.

I told them Jess hacked into my computer. I had to. That was the only way I could still hold my head high. None of these guys would be stupid enough to allow a girl he'd just met to read his plan to kill his dad. Only I am that stupid. The guys in here believe me. They have their own stories about women letting them down, ruining plans.

I feel a little bad about it, lying about Jess. I painted a pretty bad picture of her, truth be told. I hope the guys on the outside don't go after her. Part of me thinks she deserves it. The other part of me is still in love. I am starting to believe Jess is my guardian angel. She saved me from being busted, and maybe from doing something stupid. If I had gone to the church parking lot that Sunday and my dad hadn't shown, what would I have done? Would I have shot at other people?

As it stands, Doug is dead. So, in a sense, my plan worked out just fine.

I think of Jess and wonder where she is. Is she safe? Missing me? Is she watching her back? She'd better. I've found a new group of friends. The guys in here don't like traitors. Neither do I.

Sorry, my love.

JESS

After the detective leaves, I tell my mom for the hundredth time today that I'm fine. I need some air, some space. I know she means well, but this newly engaged and helicoptering Julie is a bit much.

I walk out on the back deck and take a deep breath. The ocean sparkles on the horizon, and there is nobody on the beach. I kick off my shoes and run down the steps, relishing the feeling of my toes in the sand.

I won't be finishing my senior year at Oceanside High, of course. And, as predicted, USC rescinded their admission offer. My future is wide open, no plans. It's hard to remember right now how it was before all this, when I was so sure of myself, my future, my limitless potential.

I was so ignorant, so spoiled. So sheltered that I would flirt with a murderer, play a Nazi drinking game, believe I was too good to live with my mom on the other side of town, take my poor dad for granted until he died—for me.

I reach the ocean and allow the chilly water to wash across my feet. Tears spill over and roll down my cheeks. I turn my face up to the setting sun. "I'm so sorry, Dad. I love you. Please forgive me."

The back of my neck tingles and I turn around, but there's no one else on the beach.

Then I see him, a man, running toward me. The sun is behind him, making him a dark silhouette, and I cannot see his face. It could just be a guy out for a jog, I tell myself, but a shot of adrenaline hits my system and I begin to run on the sand toward home.

I hear his jagged breath as he gets closer. I reach the first step of the deck as he seems to turn toward me up the sand.

I realize I've been expecting Tom's revenge ever since I turned him in. This time it's up to me to save myself. And I will.

I race across the deck, dart around the pool. I yank open the back door, rush inside, and bolt the door closed. My dad's house is a fortress. I know I'm safe. For the moment. The man didn't follow me up to our deck. I'm sure he was simply out for a jog.

I tell myself to calm down, to breathe. But as I peer out at the ocean, I realize I'm right. Tom's hatred hasn't subsided. It's likely intensified and found another target: me.

"Jess, what is it?" My mom appears next to me. She senses my terror.

"A man jogged towards me, on the beach," I say. Mom throws her arms around me. "I'm fine. Just overreacting."

Outside, the sun is still shining, the waves still roll in, as if nothing happened. And it didn't. Not this time.

But everything has changed. I'll never feel relaxed again, I'll never feel completely at home. Not anywhere. Not anymore. Because even though he's in prison, there are others out there, just waiting to strike.

"We'll move. We have to move," Mom says. "This time, we will go very far away. Tom and his friends won't find us. Nobody should have to live in fear like this."

I agree. "You're right, Mom."

"We'll leave today," Mom says.

"Where to?" I ask.

"I have a few ideas," she says. "I've been making a plan. Your grandmother would love for us to live closer."

I smile at my mom as my shoulders relax. Soon we'll be out of Tom's reach. We'll start over somewhere else. We will make a new home.

And this time, I'll be grateful for the change.

ACKNOWLEDGMENTS

To my fabulous team at Thomas & Mercer—including Gracie Doyle, Megha Parekh, Charlotte Herscher, and Ashley Vanicek—thank you! Thanks, too, to my wonderful agents, Meg Ruley and Annelise Robey, for thoughtful guidance and collaboration. I'm lucky to have you on my side. Ann-Marie Nieves and Megan Beatie, you both are publicists extraordinaire.

Many thanks to the book world of authors, reviewers, bloggers, bookstores, and bookstagrammers. What a vibrant, supportive community we share.

As always, thanks to my husband, Harley, and our four wonderful kids. I love you all so much. Special hug to my daughter Avery, who has an amazing ear for dialogue and is a gifted screenwriter and producer. Thank you for all your support and insights, especially with Jess!

Thanks to Ellen Goldsmith-Vein, Tara Timinsky, and the book-to-film team at Gotham Group for believing that can happen.

It's readers like you who make this career possible. Thank you. I hope you enjoyed *Somebody's Home*.

ABOUT THE AUTHOR

Photo © 2018 Kristin Karkoska

Kaira Rouda is a multiple award–winning, *USA Today* bestselling author of contemporary fiction that explores what goes on beneath the surface of seemingly perfect lives. Her novels of domestic suspense include *The Next Wife*, *The Favorite Daughter*, *Best Day Ever*, and *All the Difference*. To date, Kaira's work has been translated into more than ten languages. She lives in Southern California with her family and is working on her next novel. For more information, visit www.kairarouda.com.